C90 123305   D0551376

BULL
MOUNTAIN

Brian Panowich attended Georgia Southern
University before taking a twenty-year detour
to travel the country playing music. He started writing
again in 2009. Two of his stories were nominated for
a Spinetingler award in 2013. He is currently
a firefighter in East Georgia, where he lives
with his wife and four children.

BULL
MOUNTAIN

BRIAN PANOWICH

HEAD
of ZEUS

First published in the USA in 2015 by G. P. Putnam's Sons, New York,
an imprint of Penguin Random House LLC

This edition first published in the UK in 2015 by Head of Zeus Ltd

9 7 5 3 1 2 4 6 8

A catalogue record for this book is available from the British Library.

Book Design by Gretchen Achilles

ISBN (HB) 9781784082659
ISBN (XTPB) 9781784082666
ISBN (E) 9781784082642

Printed and bound in Germany by GGP Media GmbH, Pössneck

Head of Zeus Ltd
Clerkenwell House
45-47 Clerkenwell Green
London EC1R 0HT
WWW.HEADOFZEUS.COM

For Neicy

For Dad

The way of the world is to bloom and to flower and die but in the affairs of men there is no waning and the noon of his expression signals the onset of night. His spirit is exhausted at the peak of its achievement. His meridian is at once his darkening and the evening of his day.

—CORMAC MCCARTHY, *Blood Meridian*

When the swords flash, let no idea of love, piety, or even the face of your fathers move you.

—JULIUS CAESAR

BULL
MOUNTAIN

1

WESTERN RIDGE, JOHNSON'S GAP
BULL MOUNTAIN, GEORGIA
1949

1.

"Family," the old man said to no one.

The word hung in a puff of frozen breath before dissipating into the early-morning fog. Riley Burroughs used that word the same way a master carpenter used a hammer. Sometimes he just gave it a gentle tap to nudge one of his kin toward his way of thinking, but sometimes he used it with all the subtlety of a nine-pound sledge.

The old man sat in a wooden rocker, slowly squeaking it back and forth on the worn and buckled pine slats of the cabin's front porch. The cabin was one of several hunting shelters his family had built all over Bull Mountain throughout the years. Rye's grandfather, Johnson Burroughs, built this one. Rye imagined the elder statesman of the Burroughs clan sitting in this very spot fifty years earlier and wondered if his brow ever got this heavy. He was sure it did.

Rye pulled a pouch of dried tobacco from his coat and rolled a smoke in his lap. Ever since he was a boy, he'd come out here to watch Johnson's Gap come to life. This early, the sky was a purple bruise. The churning chorus of frogs and crickets was beginning to transition into the scurry of vermin and birdsong—a woodland changing of the guard. On frigid mornings like this one, the fog banked low over the veins of kudzu like a cotton blanket, so thick you couldn't see your feet to walk through it. It always made Rye smile to know that the clouds everyone else looked up to see, he looked down on from the other side. He reckoned that must be how God felt.

The sun had already begun to rise behind him, but this gap was always the last place to see it. The shadow cast down from the Western Ridge kept this section of the mountain almost a full ten degrees cooler than the rest of it. It would be well into the afternoon before the sun could dry up all the dew that made the forest shimmer. Only thin beams of light broke through the heavy canopy of oak trees and Scotch pine. As a kid, Rye used to believe those rays of light warming his skin were the fingers of God, reaching down through the trees to bless this place—to look out for his home. But as a man, he'd grown to know better. The children running underfoot and the womenfolk might have some use for that superstitious nonsense, but Riley reckoned if there was some Sunday-school God looking out for the people on this mountain, then the job wouldn't always fall on him.

The old man sat and smoked.

2.

The sound of tires crunching gravel soured the morning. Rye tamped out his smoke and watched his younger brother's old Ford flatbed pull up the drive. Cooper Burroughs climbed out and snatched his rifle from the mount on the back window. Cooper was Riley's half brother, born nearly sixteen years after him, but you wouldn't know it by looking at them side by side. They both had the chiseled features of their shared father, Thomas Burroughs, but carried the weight of life on Bull Mountain heavy in the jowls, making both men appear much older than they were. Cooper pulled his hat down over his shaggy red hair and grabbed a backpack from the front seat. Rye watched as Cooper's nine-year-old son, Gareth, appeared from the passenger side and walked around the truck to join his father. Rye shook his head and breathed out the last of the cold smoke in his lungs.

It's just like Cooper to bring a buffer when there is a chance of tempers getting flared. He knows I wouldn't put an ass-whuppin' on him in front of his boy. Too bad he can't use them smarts when it matters.

Rye stepped off the porch and opened his arms.

"Good morning, brother . . . and nephew."

Cooper didn't answer right away, or bother to hide his disdain. He curled up his lip and spit a slick string of brown tobacco juice at Rye's feet.

"Save it, Rye, we'll get to it soon enough. I got to get some food in me before I can stomach listening to your bullshit."

Cooper wiped the sticky trail of spit from his beard. Rye dug his heels into the gravel and balled his fists. The boy standing there be damned, he was ready to get this thing done. Gareth stepped between the two men in an attempt to ease the tension.

"Hey, Uncle Rye."

Another few more seconds of stink-eye, then Rye broke his brother's stare and squatted down to acknowledge his nephew. "Hey, there, young man." Rye reached out to hug the boy, but Cooper shuffled his son past him and up the front steps of the cabin. Rye stood, dropped his arms, and tucked his hands into his coat. He took another solemn look out at the sawtooth oaks and clusters of maple, and thought again on his grandfather. Picturing him standing there, doing the same thing Rye was doing now. Looking at the same trees. Feeling the same ache in his bones. It was going to be a long morning.

3.

"You got to keep stirrin' those eggs," Cooper said, taking the wooden spoon from his son. He carved off a chunk of butter and dropped it into the bubbling yellow mixture. "You keep stirrin' it 'til it ain't wet no more. Like this. See?"

"Yessir." Gareth took the spoon back and did as he was shown.

Cooper fried some fatback and bacon in a cast-iron skillet and then served it up to his son and brother as if that pissing contest outside hadn't just happened. That's the way brothers do things. Gareth was the first to speak.

"Deddy said you killed a grizzly out by this ridge back in the day."

"He said that, did he?" Rye looked at his brother, who sat shoveling eggs and fried meat into his mouth.

"Well, your deddy ain't right. It wasn't no grizzly. It was a brown bear."

"Deddy said you killed it with one shot. He said nobody else could'a done that."

"Well, I don't reckon that's true. You could'a took it down just the same."

"How come you don't got the head hanging up in here? That would sure be something to see."

Rye waited for Cooper to answer that, but he didn't look up from his food.

"Gareth, listen to me real good. That bear? I didn't want to kill it.

I didn't do it to have *something to see*, or a story to tell. I killed it so we could make it through the winter. If you kill something on this mountain, you better have a damn good reason. We hunt for necessity up here. Fools hunt for sport. That bear kept us warm and fed us for months. I owed it that much. You understand what I mean by 'I owed it'?"

"I think so."

"I mean that I would have dishonored the life it led if I killed it just to have a trophy on that wall. That ain't our way. We used every bit of it."

"Even the head?"

"Even the head."

Cooper piped up. "You hearing what your uncle is telling you, boy?"

Gareth nodded at his pa. "Yessir."

"Good, 'cause that's a lesson worth learnin'. Now, enough talking. Eat your breakfast so we can get on with it."

They finished the rest of the meal in silence. As they ate, Rye studied Gareth's face. It was perfectly round, with cheeks that stayed rosy no matter the weather, peppered with freckles. His eyes were set deep and narrow like his father's. He'd have to open them real wide just for someone to tell the color. They were Cooper's eyes. It was Cooper's face, without the calico beard, or the grit . . . or the anger. Rye remembered when his brother looked like that. It felt like a hundred years ago.

When their bellies were full, the two older men grabbed their rifles and stretched cold-morning muscles. Cooper leaned down and adjusted the wool cap on his son's head to cover the boy's ears.

"You stay warm, and you stay close," he said. "You get sick on me, your mama will have my ass in a sling."

The boy nodded, but his excitement was setting in and his eyes were fixed on the long guns. His father had let him practice with the .22, to get used to the recoil and feel of the scope, but he wanted to carry a man's gun.

"Do I get to carry a rifle, Deddy?" he said, scratching at the wool cap where his father had pulled at it.

"Well, I don't reckon you can shoot anything without one," Cooper said, and lifted a .30-30 rifle down from the stone mantel. The gun wasn't new, but it was heavy and solid. Gareth took the weapon and inspected it like his father had taught him. He made a show of it to prove the lessons had stuck.

"Let's go," he said, and the three of them took to the woods.

4.

Cold dirt. That's what morning smelled like on the mountain. The air was so thick with the smell of wet earth, it clogged Gareth's nose. He tried breathing through his mouth, but within minutes he was licking grit off his teeth.

"Here," Cooper said, and handed his son a blue bandana. "Tie this around your face, and breathe through it."

Gareth took it and did as he was told, and they walked.

"I'm not gonna let you do it, Rye," Cooper said, shifting gears from Gareth to his brother. "And before you start carrying on, don't try to give me your normal line of shit about it being what's best for the family. Mama or some of these young punks around here might buy into that nonsense, but you're not about to convince me what you're wanting to do here is right. It's not. It's the goddamn opposite of right."

Gareth listened but played deaf.

Rye was prepared and well rehearsed; he'd practiced this sparring session all morning to an audience of trees from that squeaky rocking chair.

"Anything that takes the worry out of having to put food on the table is the right thing to do, Coop. It's in our best interest to—"

"Oh, stop that shit, right now," Cooper said. "You best have something better than that. We eat just fine around here. There ain't nobody on this mountain starving. You sure as hell ain't." Cooper motioned to Rye's belly.

Gareth let out a small chuckle and his father gave him a sharp smack to the back of the head. "You mind your business, boy." Gareth went back to acting deaf and Cooper returned his attention to Rye. "The trees on this mountain have done right by our family for fifty years. *Fifty years*, Rye. I would think respecting that—protecting that—is what's in our best interest. The idea that you done lost sight of that pains me deeply. You actually think selling off timber rights to land you were born on, to a bunch of goddamn bankers, is good for us? Well, that breaks my heart, Riley. What the hell happened to you? I don't even recognize you anymore."

"The money is more than we will ever see in a lifetime," Rye said.

"And there it is."

"Damn it, Cooper, listen to me for a minute. Stop being so damn self-righteous and just listen."

Cooper spit.

"It will give our children, and our children's children, something to build on: a future. You don't seriously think we're going to survive for the next fifty years runnin' corn whiskey into the Carolinas?"

"We've done okay so far."

"You're not seeing the big picture, Coop. We should be doing better than *okay*. We should be working smarter, not harder. The stills ain't bringing in what they used to. Drinking ain't illegal no more. We can't survive off the back-door bars and pool halls. The money's drying up. I know you know this. It's not the same business it used to be. The rest of the world is getting smarter, and we're staying the same. The odds are against us. This deal with Puckett is going to be triple what we'd make in ten years of runnin' shine. It's a chance for our children to—"

"Hold up a second. You keep saying 'children' as if you got a dog in this race. The last time I checked, that boy right there was the only child on this mountain named Burroughs. You're telling me you want to have a bunch of machines come in here and rape *his* mountain so *he'll* have a better future?"

"Somebody has to look out for him."

Cooper stopped walking.

"Deddy," Gareth said, and tugged at his father's sleeve. "Deddy, look."

Cooper looked down to where his son was pointing, then bent over to pick up a small clump of black mud. He held it to his nose, and then held it to his son's nose.

"Smell that?"

"Uh-huh."

"It's fresh. We're getting close. Be ready."

They kept walking. After a few minutes, the conversation resumed, but with hushed voices.

"The money will strengthen the family, Coop. We can take the money and invest in legitimate businesses. We can stop living up here like outlaws. You have to see the logic in this. We can't live like this forever."

"I've got other plans."

"What other plans? To plant that ragweed over by the north face?"

If Cooper was surprised that his brother was aware of his intentions, he didn't show it. He just shrugged.

"Yeah," Rye said, "I know all about it. I know everything that happens on this mountain. I have to. I also know that ridiculous idea will have us moving in reverse. Bringing that kind of business up here will only bring more guns, more law, and more strangers—worse than any banker. Is that what you want? Is that what you want for him?" Rye motioned to Gareth. "Besides that, what's the difference between you clearing a few hundred acres to farm that shit or Puckett clearing it—legally?"

"Wake up, Rye. Do you honestly believe they'll stop there? Do you really think we'll ever be rid of them once they get their hooks in this place?"

"Yes, I do. That's what they agreed to."

For a moment all the anger and tension fell from Cooper's face. He looked at his brother and then at his son. "It's what they agreed to do?" he said calmly.

"That's right," Rye said.

"So that means you met with them already. You done hashed out terms."

"Of course I did."

5.

They walked, quiet, for the next quarter mile. They stayed on the overgrown trail, stopping every so often for Cooper to show his son proof of the animal they were tracking: broken twigs, hoofprints in the mud, more crumbled deer shit. They were almost to the mouth of

Bear Creek before Cooper said another word to Rye. He spoke in a whisper.

"You already made the deal, didn't you?"

Rye felt more relieved than ashamed. It was finally out there. "Yes," he said, "it's done. They're sending one of their people down with the papers today. I know you don't see it now, but someday you'll thank me for it. I promise you. You'll see."

Cooper stopped walking again.

"Come on, now, little brother, how long do we—"

"Shhhh," Cooper said, and held a finger to his lips. He was looking past his brother at what Gareth had already spotted. Less than twenty yards to their right stood a massive eight-point buck drinking from the rushing water of Bear Creek. The sound of the small rapids covered up the men's approach. Cooper silently motioned for his brother to move upstream while he set Gareth up for the shot behind a deadfall of rotten pine. Rye obliged. He crept through the woods, keeping his eye on the buck. Cooper dropped down next to his son, who already had his rifle trained on the deer. Cooper put his hand on the boy's shoulder and reminded him to breathe.

"Relax, son. Put the crosshairs on the thick muscle under his neck. Where the fur turns white. Do you see where I mean?"

"Yessir. I see it."

The buck looked up from the creek as if it heard them talking, and looked toward their position. Rye was about thirty feet to the left of Cooper and Gareth's perch. No one took another breath until the deer dropped its head back to the water.

"When you're ready, boy. Take the shot." Cooper held his own rifle across the fallen pine, shoulder to shoulder with his son. Gareth was still and ready. As the boy's finger squeezed the trigger, just like his father showed him, Cooper swung his own rifle to the left. Two shots echoed through the forest. Two shots that sounded like one. The big buck staggered backward from the impact, then bounded forward in an attempt to defy its fate. Its back legs quivered under its weight, and finally the animal fell.

Riley Burroughs didn't stagger at all when Cooper's high-caliber bullet pierced his neck. His body dropped immediately with a hard thud and he bled out into the clay.

6.

Cooper cocked his rifle and chambered another round before cautiously approaching Rye's body. He gave it a hard kick in the gut. It was like kicking a sandbag. Once he was assured Rye was dead, he lowered his gun and looked back at his son. Gareth had already dropped his own rifle to the ground and was trying to process what just happened. There were no tears—not yet—just confusion and adrenaline. Cooper looked down at his brother's graying hollow face and spit a stream of glistening brown tobacco juice across it.

And that was that.

Cooper propped his rifle against a tree and sat in the damp grass beside Gareth. The boy briefly considered running, but knew better. That thought left his mind as fast as it had come. Instead, he sat and watched his father pull the plug of chew from his lip and toss it into the brush.

"Look around you, boy."

Gareth just stared at his father.

"I'm tellin' you to do something, Gareth. You best listen. Now take a look around you. I'm not asking a third time."

Gareth did. He looked at the deer he'd just shot on the bank of the creek, and then turned to the trail they'd come in by. He purposely avoided the direction of his dead uncle. Cooper fiddled with a foil pouch of chewing tobacco.

"What do you see?"

Gareth's mouth was coated with chalk. He cleared his throat twice before he could speak.

"Trees, Deddy. Trees and woods."

"That it?"

Gareth was frightened of saying the wrong thing.

"Yessir."

"Then you ain't seein' the most important thing. The trees and the woods are only a part of it."

The tears were starting to show now in the corners of Gareth's eyes.

"It's home," Cooper said. "Our home. As far as you can see out in every direction belongs to us—to you. Ain't nothing more important than that. Ain't nothing I wouldn't do to keep it so. Even if it means I gotta do a thing that ain't easy doing."

"Ain't it Uncle Rye's home, too?" Gareth squeezed his eyes shut and steeled himself for the backhand, but it didn't come.

"Not no more," Cooper said. He reached over to adjust his son's cap again, then wiped the tears off the boy's rosy chapped face. "I'll give you this one time to cry, but then I won't have no more goin' on about it. You understand?"

Gareth nodded.

"Do you?"

"Yessir."

"Good. Then we got us one more thing to do, before we dress and drag out that deer you shot." Cooper loosened the fisherman's knot on his pack and pulled out an old army-surplus folding shovel.

He handed it to Gareth.

Cooper Burroughs sat and chewed tobacco while he watched his nine-year-old son dig his first grave. There was more lesson in that than in killin' any eight-point buck.

2

CLAYTON BURROUGHS
WAYMORE VALLEY, GEORGIA
2015

1.

Well, isn't that how it always goes down? You spend all week, and damn near most of the weekend, too, either cooped up in an office shuffling paperwork or checking off the honey-do list, all for a few hours alone on a Sunday morning, just to have it shot to shit with a phone call.

I should have let it ring.

Clayton wheeled the Bronco into the parking place marked RE-SERVED FOR MCFALLS COUNTY SHERIFF. He stepped out and stood in the empty space his deputy's car should be in—and wasn't—and dropped his chin to his chest. The sun was nudging up behind the motor inn and post office across the street; not the way he wanted to take in the sunrise this morning. He should be hip deep in the creek right now. He let out a slow, disconcerted whistle of breath, hoisted his sagging gun belt, and walked into the office.

"Good morning, Sheriff."

"Well, that's up for debate, Cricket."

Cricket, Clayton's receptionist, was a tiny little thing in her early twenties, and somewhat of a hidden beauty. If the light hit her just right she might be worth a longer look, but most days, with her mousy brown hair pulled back tight in a librarian's ponytail, she had the chameleonlike ability to become one with the wallpaper. She pushed her thick plastic-rimmed glasses up on her nose and closed out whatever she was doing on the station's computer.

"Sorry to get you in here on a Sunday, sir, but we thought you'd want to deal with this as soon as possible." Cricket stood up from behind her desk and handed Clayton a file folder.

"S'okay, Cricket. It's not your fault," Clayton said, thumbing through the papers in the file. "You got me out of having to go to church with the in-laws, so it's not a total loss. I was hoping to do a little fishing, though."

Cricket was all business, as was her way. "Our guest is in cell one." She motioned down a short hallway leading to the two small lockups, a couple cells barely big enough to house a cot and a stainless-steel commode each.

"And where's Choctaw?"

"He's waiting in your office."

Clayton peered down the hallway and then at the door to his office, contemplating which headache to tackle first. He chose the devil he knew.

2.

"Okay," the sheriff said, and sipped his coffee. "Start at the beginning."

Choctaw sank down in the chair opposite the sheriff's desk and pushed his Stetson back on his brow. The deputy was the kind of skinny that made his skin look shrink-wrapped to his bones, and he squirmed in his seat like a high school student called before the principal.

"All right," he said. "I was out a few nights ago with my buddy Chester. You remember Chester? We served together in Iraq. He come down from Tennessee a few weeks back, after he got home from his last tour. I brought him around the office when he first got here."

The sheriff nodded. "Yeah, I remember the guy."

"Cool. Anyway, we got a way of messin' with each other that goes way back to when we were fixing Humvees in the desert—just clownin', you know? Anyway, last week I bought me one of those blow-up dolls—"

The sheriff put a hand up. "Hold on, like a sex-toy thing?"

"Yeah, exactly. A Fuck and Suck Sally. Them things ain't cheap, by the way."

"Good to know. Where the hell did you find one of those around here?"

"The Internet, boss. I even got me one of those PayPal accounts just for that reason."

"A who-pal-what?"

The deputy looked a bit dumbfounded. "A PayPal account . . . ?"

Static played across the sheriff's gray-green eyes as he sat and stroked his beard.

"Look, it doesn't matter. That's not the point. The point is, I bought this blow-up doll to mess with Chester. I should have bought a bicycle pump, too, because I damn near gave myself an aneurysm blowing the thing up."

"What does any of this have to do with last night?"

"I'm getting to that. Bear with me. A few days after I bought the thing, I set it up all pretty-like in the passenger seat of Chester's ride right before he come out of The Pair O' Jacks—that joint headed up I-75 toward Roswell. You know the place?"

The sheriff nodded again. "Uh-huh."

"Yeah, right, so when he comes out to the car, he's expecting to see me, but instead he gets an eyeful of Fuck and Suck Sally. He totally lost his shit. Straight up busted his ass trying to get back out of the car."

The deputy waited for the sheriff to laugh, but it didn't happen. He just stared at the younger man blankly, as if he were trying to gauge his level of stupid.

"Is this remotely leading to why we're sitting in my office this early on a Sunday morning, when we both would clearly rather be somewhere else?" He pushed his own hat up a few inches, leaned back in the swivel chair, and crossed his arms.

"It was funny," Choctaw insisted. "I guess you had to be there."

"I guess so."

"Anyway, now the ball's in Chester's court to get me back, and that brings us to last night."

"Finally."

Choctaw took off his hat, pushed back his shiny black hair, and reseated it deep on his brow. "So I'm out on patrol, and I'm letting Chester ride along with me." Choctaw put up both his hands palms out to fend off another dirty look. "I know you don't like that sort of thing, so don't bother sayin' so."

The sheriff bit down on his lip and sighed through his nose. He took off his hat as well, freeing a head of bushy, rust-brown hair, and set the hat on his desk. "Go on," he said, scratching at his temples where his hat had been pressing down and where the first hints of gray were beginning to appear.

"Chester is all on my case about stopping at the Texaco on 56 to get some chew and whatnot." The deputy paused and thought on what he'd just said. "You know something, boss? I should have known right then. He normally wants to go way out to Pollard's Corner so he can sneak peeks at Old Man Pollard's daughter working the counter. She just turned eighteen, you know, but I swear she looks a lot older than that. I don't see how Old Man Pollard—"

"Focus, Deputy."

"Right. Anyway, I should have known something was off about that, but I missed it."

"The world's finest detective."

"Whatever. So I pull into the Texaco, and Chester hands me a few bills and asks me to go in, like I'm his do-boy, but whatever, he's lazy, I know that, so I go inside."

"Where was Chester?"

"In the car."

"You left Chester in a county-owned vehicle?"

"I trust the guy, boss." Choctaw was spectacular at missing the point entirely. "So I go in and leave the engine running."

"You left the engine running in your patrol car with a civilian in it?"

"Yeah, boss, like you ain't never done it."

The sheriff pulled at his beard. "Go on."

"Yeah, like I was sayin', I walk in and wouldn't you know it, there's this dumb-shit crackhead with a peashooter .22 holding up the place. I about shit and fell back in it. I knew looking at him he wasn't from around here." He raised an eyebrow at the sheriff to emphasize the perpetrator's darker persuasion. "A brother, probably picking up some quick cash on his way back to Atlanta."

Because all brothers originate from Atlanta. Everybody knows that.

"Talk about terrible luck, though. What an idiot. Anyway, he gets all freaked out seeing a deputy of the law walk in, so he aims that little toy pistol at me. I'm like, 'Dude, what the hell? I'm a cop. Put that thing on the counter and assume the position.' I'm sure he knew how to do it, probably been doing it his whole life."

"You know, Choctaw, for a minority like yourself, you sure are quick to profile."

"I'm only fifty percent American Indian, boss. The rest of me is one hundred percent good ol'-fashioned redneck."

"That makes a hundred and fifty percent."

"Right."

The sheriff sighed again. He doubted there was any American Indian in there at all. Choctaw's skin color was tinted enough to notice only if it was pointed out to you. He could even be Mexican, but whatever.

"Did you draw on him?"

"Had no time. As soon as I tell him to put his gun down he starts getting all jittery and starts popping off rounds into the ceiling. Drop-ceiling panels and dust start raining down all over the place and I couldn't see nothing. I drew my gun then, but I didn't shoot it."

"Then what happened?"

"In the pandemonium, this jackass bolts. Before I know it, he got around me and made it outside. As it turns out, this idiot is on foot, so he hops into the first car he thinks he can haul ass in."

"Your running patrol car?"

"Yup. By the time I get outside after him, he's tear-assin' out of the parking lot."

"Where's your friend?"

"Chester?"

The sheriff spoke into his lap. "Yeah, Chester."

"Chester is totally oblivious to what's going on inside, because he's too busy exacting his revenge for the goddamn blow-up doll." The deputy leaned forward in his chair. "Get this, Chester stashed two big-ass bags of packing peanuts behind the Texaco ice machine earlier that day, and that's why he was so hopped up about stopping there. As soon as I walked inside, he went and dumped 'em all into my patrol car."

Silence filled the sheriff's office like ocean water.

The sheriff narrowed his eyes. "Peanuts?"

"Not real peanuts, *packing* peanuts. You know, that white Styrofoam shit you get from FedEx."

"Right, packing peanuts." His head was starting to hurt.

"Yeah, right. So this retard just jacked a cop car full of packing peanuts. That guy's got to have the worst luck of all time. He got that Crown Vic up to about forty miles an hour before it looked like a fuckin' snow globe."

The sheriff coughed up a sudden laugh against his will. He didn't want to, but he did. Choctaw joined in.

"I kid you not, boss. This asshole can't see a damn thing when the peanuts start flying and, *boom*, straight into a telephone pole across the street. I couldn't make this shit up if I tried. That's why there's a black kid all banged up in cell one and car three is in the shop. That's what happened, boss. Honest truth."

"Where's your friend now?"

"Chester?"

This time the sheriff just waited.

"He's at my place, scared to death you're gonna lock him up for obstructing justice, or something like that. At the very least, make him pay for the damages to the car."

"Well, you can tell him to relax, he doesn't have to worry about the damages."

"Thanks, boss, I knew you'd—"

"Because you're going to pay for them."

Choctaw deflated like an untied balloon animal. He squinted and studied the sheriff's bearded face for a hint of sarcasm. Maybe he was joking. He wasn't.

"Oh, come on, Clayton. It was circumstances beyond my control—"

The deputy was interrupted by a beep on the sheriff's intercom, and both men listened as the timid voice of Cricket from the front desk crackled out of the speaker.

"Sheriff Burroughs, there's a federal agent here to see you."

3.

The sheriff looked at his watch.

"It's eight-thirty."

"I'm aware of that, sir." Cricket's lo-fi voice crackled over the intercom.

"On a Sunday."

"I know that, too, sir. Would you like me to tell him to come back tomorrow?"

The sheriff thought on that and wondered if it was possible. Maybe he could just climb out the window.

"Sir?"

"No. No. Send him in." The sheriff put on his hat and looked at his deputy, who shrugged. A few seconds later the door opened and in walked a handsome man in his mid-forties, maybe younger, with sharp features, dark close-cropped hair, and stormy gray eyes. Cricket, who always wore her hair back, had managed to shake it free and even took off her glasses to smile at the agent before closing the door behind him. Clayton found that amusing. Choctaw shifted uneasily in his chair.

The agent was wearing a dark blue blazer, a matching tie, and a starched white shirt tucked into blue jeans. Wearing a tie with blue jeans spoke volumes about a man, but Clayton gave him points for trying to country it up. Most of these feds never even took their designer sunglasses off when they found their way into Clayton's office.

The agent stuck his hand out and flashed a pearly-white salesman smile at the sheriff. Clayton thought it made him look like a cartoon shark from one of those kids' movies, but he stood up anyway. His deputy did not. Choctaw just eyeballed the agent with an expression similar to that of a man who'd just eaten a spoonful of shit.

"Sheriff Clayton Burroughs?" the agent said.

"Unless I'm wearing someone else's badge, that would be me." The sheriff shook the agent's hand and matched his firm grip. Every fed that ever walked through that door felt it was necessary to conduct a dick-measuring contest with a viselike handshake. This G-man was no different.

"And you are?" Clayton said, pulling back his hand and calling it a draw.

"My name is Special Agent Simon Holly."

"You got ID?"

"Of course." Holly held out his badge, and the sheriff nodded. Choctaw tried to take a peek, but Holly intentionally snubbed him and tucked the ID back into his blazer.

"Thank you for seeing me this early . . . and on a Sunday." He winked at the sheriff in an attempt to let him know he was privy to the sheriff's intercom conversation with Cricket. Of course he was. The building had only two rooms. Clayton thought the wink was an odd thing to do, but he sat back down and motioned for Holly to do the same.

"No problem, Special Agent Simon Holly. I wasn't doing anything important. My deputy here was just on his way out."

Choctaw peeled his eyes off the agent slowly, like removing a Band-Aid, and took the hint. "Right, boss." He made his way to the door, then paused and turned around. "Is this about the black kid I got locked up there in the back?"

Clayton regarded Holly for the answer to that as well.

"No, Deputy Frasier," Holly said. "No, it's not."

All the color drained from the deputy's face. He stood in the doorway, mentally racing through every shady scenario that would have put his name on the fed's radar. Holly broke into his shark's grin. The sheriff watched his lone deputy squirm like a little kid who'd just got caught shoplifting, hoping he would be smart enough to figure it out on his own. Clayton felt the ache building behind his eyes. He took another sip of his coffee. Cold. He pushed the mug across his desk. "It says Deputy Frasier on your name tag," Clayton said to Choctaw, clearly embarrassed to have to point it out. Holly nodded in agreement, pursed his lips, and steepled his fingers in his lap. "Right there on your shirt, Deputy."

"Right," Choctaw said, drawing the word out, not entirely convinced but ready to get gone all the same. He tipped his Stetson to the sheriff and slipped out the door like a shadow.

"The world's finest detective," Clayton said.

"I suppose good help is hard to find way up here."

"He's not as bad as he looks."

Holly looked at the office door, then back to the sheriff. "He looks pretty bad."

"Yeah, well, there's a lot to be said for loyalty. But you're right, the pickin's are slim."

"I'll have to take your word for it, Sheriff."

"You don't have to take anything. I don't care either way. I've known that man since he was a boy. He's like family around here, so I'd appreciate you withholding judgment in my office."

"No disrespect, Sheriff. I'm sure he's a fine deputy."

Clayton waved away the small talk like it was a gnat buzzing in his face, and leaned back in his chair. "Are you here to size up my staff, or do you want to tell me what the FBI wants with my office?"

"I'm with the ATF."

"Okay . . ."

Holly stiffened up a bit and gave Clayton a practiced hardcase stare. The sheriff was unimpressed. "Spare me the intensity, agent. It makes you look a little silly. I know why you're here. I wish it was something else, but it's not. It never is. Just get to it." The throbbing behind Clayton's eyes was on the brink of becoming a full-fledged headache, and he could feel his Sunday morning going straight down the crapper.

"Right to the point. I can appreciate that. In a nutshell, I'm here to take your brother out of the game."

Clayton sipped his coffee again, forgetting it was cold, and spit it back into the mug. "I wish that could have been the zinger you wanted it to be. I mean, here you are, so excited to sit there and say that, you couldn't even wait until Monday."

"I don't think I'm making myself—"

"Let me go ahead and stop you there," Clayton said, and fished an aspirin bottle out of his desk. He popped two chalky white pills into his mouth and chewed them dry while he spoke. "Every few years or so, some young FBI or *ATF* agent, much like yourself, comes poking around my office all beady-eyed and barrel-chested, looking to drop a hammer on one of my brothers. The only difference this time between you and them is, I don't need to ask you which brother you're targeting, since one of your people already shot Buckley to death last year." Clayton let that hang between them and hardened his own stare. "And by the way, how much changed after that?"

"We had nothing to do with that, Sheriff. From what I understand, that was a state-level entanglement. I believe the Georgia Bureau of Investigation was the agency involved."

"Same difference. FBI, GBI, you all look alike to me." Clayton's voice was as callous as the hands of a construction worker.

"I'm terribly sorry for your loss."

"I'm sure you are. But like I said, you people accomplished nothing then, and I can't imagine you'll do much other than get more decent people caught in the crossfire this time, either."

"You keep saying 'you people.'"

"And?"

"You're a sheriff. You swore to uphold the law, same as me. Doesn't that make you one of *us people*, too?"

Clayton got up from his chair and walked over to a small coffee-pot on the counter next to the sink. He dumped his mug and filled it fresh without offering any to his guest, and thought about how nice it would be to add an inch or two of bourbon. It wasn't too long ago that that was his morning routine, and sometimes he could still smell it in his cup. He took a sip, unsatisfied, and returned to his chair. He leaned forward, aware for the first time all morning of how tired he was, and gave Holly the autopilot speech he'd given at least six other agents already.

"Listen, Holly. I'm nothing like you. I'm just a guy born and raised less than fifteen miles from where you're sitting right now. I'm no hotshot lawman looking to save the world from the *evil that men do*." Sarcasm dripped from his voice. "I don't care much about what happens out there in your world, Agent Holly. I'm a hick sheriff in a small town doing my best to keep the people of this valley—the *good* people of this valley—safe from the never-ending river of shit that flows down that mountain, *and* the trigger-happy frat boys that think they can come here and show us hillbillies how badass they are. In my opinion, all of you, cops and robbers alike, pose the same threat to my constituency, and *that* makes you and me the very definition of 'nothing alike.'"

Clayton sat back and blew into his coffee.

"Sheriff, doesn't McFalls County butt up against Parsons County up around Black Rock?"

"It does."

"And isn't your office responsible for policing the entirety of McFalls County?"

"I'm sure you already know it is."

"So that means Bull Mountain is under your jurisdiction, not just Waymore Valley. It also means that what's coming down that mountain is coming directly at you. It would be contrary to everything I believe in if I didn't come here and talk to you about it first. Not as some hillbilly sheriff, but as a fellow law enforcement officer. There are a lot of folks that think you're a puppet for your brothers, a way to control this office, but I'm not one of them. The people of this county voted you in for a reason, despite your family, and that says something. It says they want you here. It says that they trust you, and that's good enough for me. I don't mean to scrape dog shit on your welcome mat."

"I can't help you." It was a line Clayton was tired of having to say.

"I understand that, Sheriff. I'm sorry I sounded like an ass for a minute there. It's automatic. Let me start again."

Aspirin wasn't going to cut it. Clayton fiddled with the childproof plastic bottle, wondering exactly how many he'd have to eat to get rid of the headache sitting in his office. He expected Holly to stand up, shove a finger in his face, and spout off some self-righteous bullshit about how he "owed it to the people" and "the county he loved" to stop the bad men—blah, blah, blah. That was normally the routine with these guys, but Holly stayed seated. He was respectful. Clayton reckoned Holly was at least smart enough to play by the sheriff's rules until he had his say.

"I can't help you," Clayton said again.

"I'm not asking for your help, Sheriff."

"Then what do you want, Agent Holly?"

"Call me Simon."

"Go ahead and make your speech, *Agent Holly*."

"Okay, Sheriff. Like I said, I'm not here for your help, but maybe you can help yourself, and that could work out for both of us."

Clayton said nothing and scratched at his beard.

"Maybe if I start from the beginning, I can paint you a better picture of what I'm talking about."

"Good idea."

"I've been with the ATF for two years. In that time, I've focused on one case."

"I'm guessing Halford Burroughs."

"No, your brother didn't pop up on my radar until recently. No, for two years I've been building a case against an outfit set up in Jacksonville, Florida, which, among other things, has been supplying your brother and his people with guns—lots of guns. And for the past few years, they have also been your brother's pipeline to the raw materials he's using to process methamphetamine."

Clayton felt the pressure in his head release. Not much, but some.

"A gentleman by the name of Wilcombe is at the top of the food chain down there. You heard of him?"

"Nope."

"They use some low-rent bikers who call themselves the Jacksonville Jackals to transport the goods. They're dirtbags, smart and loyal dirtbags, but dirtbags nonetheless. They've been at it a long time. I've got them in business with your family dating back to your father's days of hustling weed in the early seventies. Do you know who I mean?"

"Nope." Clayton wasn't as convincing with that answer.

"Well, you're lucky. These people are bad news. They've got their hands in some heinous shit. Dope, money, guns, you name it. Recently we're getting intel that shows them involved in human trafficking as well, and they're getting bigger and richer for the effort. Your brother Halford knows these people well. He has intimate knowledge of their entire operation and they trust him implicitly."

Everything else Holly was going to say clicked in place before he could say it.

"You want to flip him." Clayton almost laughed. "You want Hal to give up your boys in Florida so you can close your case on this Wilcombe fella."

"Yes," Holly said.

"In exchange for what?"

"Conditional immunity."

"What's the condition?"

"He opts out of the meth trade."

"It won't happen," Clayton said. "Halford isn't your average drug dealer. It's against his warped sense of honor. He'd die before turning over on anyone he considers family. If these bikers have been in bed with my kin for as long as you say, you can bet they fall into that category. He'd never rat them out. Never."

"Well, if his sense of honor is skewed, then we appeal to his other sensibility."

"Which is?"

"His money."

"Halford doesn't care about the money."

"Don't be that naive, Sheriff. The money is paramount. The money is *all* that matters."

Clayton shook his head. "No, it's not, and that's why you people will always lose, Agent Holly. Because you don't understand how it works up here. Money isn't the endgame for my brother. It never was. It's simply a by-product of the lifestyle my father raised him on." Clayton leaned way back in his chair, lifting his arms and interlacing his fingers at the back of his neck. He let himself feel the stretch down his back, and debated what road he wanted to walk down with this federal. Most of the time, it didn't matter to these guys how he tried to explain things. They just sat there behind their dark sunglasses and pretended to listen, while they waited to blurt out whatever they were itching to say next. Clayton brought his arms down, and used an index finger to rub the dust from the edge of a small framed photograph on his desk. It was a picture of him and Kate taken by a stranger on their honeymoon on Tybee Island. It was the first, and only, time either of them had ever been to the beach. He couldn't say he was much of a fun-in-the-sun guy, but that was a good day. He smiled, and decided to take the long road. "Are you married, Agent Holly?"

"I was. It didn't take."

"Girlfriend?"

"For the moment," Holly said, leaning back in his chair as well, settling in to the small talk. "For however long that lasts."

"A girlfriend, good, that's good." Clayton reached over and picked up the picture of him and Kate. "You ever pack her up, or the ex, for that matter, back when you were hitched, and just get out of town for a few days? Get away from the daily grind, and go get lost, find a place off the map to just relax, enjoy each other?" Clayton talked more to the picture of him and Kate than to Holly.

"Not as much as either of them would like, I'm sure, but yeah, I try to get away a few times a year."

"Okay, good. We're tracking. Now imagine the feeling you had the last time you took a few days off and packed the car, your girl, maybe a few beers and a camera, and set off to find a secluded spot in the mountains, or by a still pond or lake somewhere. You with me?"

Holly nodded, waiting for the point.

"This is the break from most people's lives that makes the burdens and pressures that come from all the responsibilities we heap on ourselves the rest of the time worth enduring. Would you agree with that?"

"Sure, Sheriff. Everyone needs a vacation sometimes. What does—"

"Bear with me, Agent Holly. Now imagine that same setting, that pretty picture you got in your head, imagine that as the basis for your everyday. Imagine it's the foundation for work, family, relationships, wisdom, pain, all of it. It's a different mind-set. It's not a break from life for these people. It *is* life, and the urge to protect it, and hold on to it, can be fierce."

Holly began to say something, but Clayton kept on.

"There is a subtle symbiotic relationship between the land up here and the people who call it home that folks like yourself never seem to fully understand, no matter how many files you read, or training scenarios you run. It's not your fault, you're just not from here. It goes way beyond simple pride or honor. Pride is a brand-new red bike or a better-paying job. Up here it's something different. It's something deeper than bone. It's not something that they earned or had to fight to get. They were born into it, and the fight comes on real hard when someone threatens to take it away. It's an integral part of who they are—who we are." Clayton wiped the dust from his finger onto his pants, took his stare off the picture and put it back on Holly.

"The point is, the money absolutely does not matter. And that's not me being naive, that's me telling you how it is. No one gets to tell them what they can and cannot do on their own land. No one's going to take what God gave them. Not on *their* mountain. And believe me, Hal thinks it's *his* mountain. He would burn his money before he would give up his home, or his people. Your plan is flawed. He won't betray his kin."

"Even you?" Holly asked.

Clayton didn't have an answer for that.

"Then let me put it another way," Holly said. "The United States government is putting together a multiagency task force consisting of well over a hundred people ranging from the FBI, ATF, the DEA, all the way down to the state police. Homeland is even involved. They're educated, trained, willing, and able to set the entirety of Bull Mountain on fire. That's not a threat, Sheriff. It's a fact. We know the locations of all sixteen cookhouses and we know the routes heading into Florida, Alabama, both Carolinas, and Tennessee. The finger is on the trigger, they are intentionally leaving you out of the loop, and a lot of people are going to die. It's a brand-new ball game. The post-9/11 rules give us the teeth we need to get it done with close to zero accountability. This operation was already supposed to happen. It's been in development since your brother Buckley was killed and exposed Halford's involvement with Wilcombe. The powers that be want the revenue being generated on that mountain so bad they would rather burn it down than see your brother get over on them one more day."

"So what's stopping them?" Clayton said.

"Me." Holly's shark smile returned. "I am." He let his words dangle between them before setting the hook. "I have a better plan, and that's why I'm here, Sheriff."

"Go on," Clayton said.

4.

"Nothing makes a U.S. federal law enforcement agency drool more than a huge pile of money. Nothing, except of course, a bigger pile. That's what I've got in Florida—a bigger pile. If we can take that down, this place dries up by default."

"Couldn't Hal just find new suppliers?"

"Sure, he could, but would he want to? You said it yourself, he was born into this dance with these boys from Florida. He didn't have to go through the bloodshed and double-crossing most entrepreneur types like your brother have to go through. It takes a long time to build that kind of trust, and your father just handed it to him. Do you think he's up to going through all that at his age? Fifty-three is no time to go back to the drawing board. He has no children that we know about. There are no young up-and-comers ready to take his place as far as we know, and the bloodline ends with him." Holly paused and corrected himself. "Well, other than you, of course."

Clayton nodded and spun one finger in the air like a wheel, signaling for Holly to keep going.

Holly said, "He's practically cut off from civilization up there. Take Wilcombe out of the equation and Halford Burroughs could just retire. Take his winnings and cash out."

Clayton hesitated for several moments before speaking. "And you're telling me that you would leave him be?"

"Yes," Holly said without a bit of hesitation.

"And there's paperwork to back that up?"

"Yes," Holly said. He crossed his arms and let the prosecution rest.

Clayton's eyes slowly became skeptical slits as he studied Simon Holly. There was a lack of pretension about this man that Clayton found himself admiring. This wasn't just a chance to put a commendation in his jacket; at least it didn't feel that way to Clayton. This was a chance to do some real good on the mountain. If it wasn't all bullshit, and normally Clayton could smell bullshit a county over. He got the impression this meeting was more important to Holly's case than he was letting on. The agent was presenting well, but fidgety. His knee bounced slightly, and Clayton could tell he was a touch nervous. *This case must be a career maker,* he thought. "Why do you care?" Clayton said. "If you have all the intel you need to pick him up, then why don't you just go in and take him out? Why do you care what happens to the people up here?"

Holly looked mildly surprised, then genuinely hurt. "Why would I not care? You don't have a monopoly on keeping people safe, Sheriff. You said before that you're nothing like me, but with one fell swoop we could shut down the biggest flow of guns and dope in the history of the East Coast—one that floods over six state lines. I won't lie to you and say it wouldn't be nice to be recognized as one of the men who did it, but if you're the man I think you are, living in the shadow of your family's legacy can only make this all the more important to you. The number of lives we'd save, a lot of whom live in your backyard, is the reason I do this job. I would say we're a lot more alike than you think."

Clayton scratched at a rust-colored patch in his calico beard, hardly noticing his fading headache. "And Hal walks?"

"Anywhere he wants."

"If I can convince him to be a rat."

"Listen, Sheriff, I just told you why I'm invested in this, but for the sake of total disclosure, the truth is, nobody is interested in this place. No offense, but it's just a big rock in the hottest, stickiest state in the union. No one I work with would dream of being stuck in this place if your brother wasn't breaking the law, and breaking it so well. If that stops, we stop. Period."

Clayton opened the bottom drawer of his desk, the place that used to be reserved for the *good stuff* when he was drinking, and took out a can of long-cut snuff tobacco. He pinched out a wad and seated it between his lower lip and gum, then spit into an empty Styrofoam cup.

"Nice speech."

"Thanks. I practiced all the way here."

"So you got all dressed up in your Sunday best to walk in here and give the brother of the big bad wolf all your plans to take him down, and you're calling that a better plan?"

"Yes, Sheriff, that's about the size of it, but in all fairness, my mother would never have let me wear jeans to church on Sunday, and to be honest, I didn't think you'd be here today. I was going to make an appointment for tomorrow."

Clayton smiled.

"Well, Holly, in all fairness, I ran unopposed."

Holly laughed. "I know."

The sheriff stood up, walked over to the coat rack, and pulled on his jacket.

"Come on, you can tell me more over some biscuits and gravy. I'm starving. This early, we can get a seat at Lucky's before the church crowd takes over."

"Sounds good, Sheriff."

"Call me Clayton."

"All right, then, Clayton. Lead the way."

Clayton opened the door to the front office, where Cricket and Choctaw had done everything short of holding a glass to the wall to eavesdrop.

"Cricket, will you call Kate and tell her I'm not going to make it to her mother's this morning?"

"She's not going to be happy."

"I know. That's why I want *you* to call her. Choctaw, call up Darby to come swap out watch over your prisoner back there. If we're all here on a Sunday, he might as well be, too. Then call in to Lucky's for some breakfast for our guest and I'll have it sent over."

"Yessir, boss."

"And while you're at it, order up some grub for you and Cricket, too. Sky's the limit. Eat your backs out."

"Feeling generous this morning, boss?"

"Nope"—Clayton winked at Holly—"but the federal government is."

CLAYTON BURROUGHS

2015

Clayton stared at the ceiling. Thirty-five heavy timber logs made of the same white pine that grew not twenty feet outside his bedroom window. He and his father had built the house together as a wedding gift for Kate before she and Clayton were married. His father was nearly seventy then and still worked like a man in his twenties. That was more than a decade ago and not once did that purlin roof ever let in a single drop of rain—not once. Clayton stayed on the top floor of a fancy hotel in Atlanta once, and took notice of the water spots and discoloration growing from the edges of the popcorn ceiling. He thought about that all the time. Two hundred dollars a night in a tower of steel and glass, and they couldn't do what he and his father had done with a couple of hammers and a few nails. It was a small example, but it echoed through everything he was ever taught, every lesson Gareth Burroughs ever tried to instill.

"You're gonna need a real house, boy," his father had said. "If you're gonna take that woman and give a go at being a real man, then you're gonna need a house to match."

A real man.

Clayton's lip curled at the memory. It was always that way. Every good thing Gareth Burroughs ever did for his youngest son came tainted with what he really thought of him. That he didn't measure up. That he was nothing like his older brothers, Hal and Buck. Gareth never came right out and said it, but he didn't have to. It was in his eyes. They were filled with the gray storm clouds of disappointment.

Kate had always seen this place as the kindest thing her husband's father ever did for them, but she didn't know they'd built it in silence. A father following through on his obligation to shelter his son no matter how big a letdown he turned out to be. Those laughing rafters above his bed, the last thing he saw before he closed his eyes at night, were his penance for turning his back on his family. It was also a way to keep Clayton exactly where Gareth wanted him—rooted to Bull Mountain.

Clayton shifted his attention from the pockmarks made by his father's ax in the ceiling to a much more pleasant view of his wife, Kate, drying herself off in the open cedar archway of the bathroom. She had a routine. She would wrap one towel around her body before pulling back the shower curtain, and another around her head in that turban wrap only women knew how to do. Then she'd sit on the edge of the tub and rub lemongrass oil on her freshly shaved legs. That part would take a little longer if she knew Clayton was watching. Then, like a magician's final act, the two towels would hit the floor, and they'd be replaced by one of her husband's McFalls County Sheriff's Department T-shirts. The motion was so fluid, if Clayton blinked he'd miss the split-second shot of her bare ass before she hit the light and nestled a mound of damp chocolate-brown curls on his chest.

Kate never wore panties to bed. Just the thought of that still did it for Clayton even after eleven years of marriage. She adjusted one leg over her husband and nuzzled her cheek against his chest. This was their tried-and-true sleeping position, and she waited for his hands to start roaming her, but they didn't come. "We missed you at Mom's today," she said.

"Yeah, sorry about that. I swear that boy is going to be the death of me."

"Choctaw?"

"Yeah."

"He's a good kid, just a little misguided is all."

"Misguided." Clayton chewed on the word. "That's one way of saying it."

Kate shifted gears. "You remember my appointment is Tuesday, right?"

"Huh?"

"My appointment," she repeated.

"Oh, right. Of course." Clayton warmed up to her a little in an attempt to stifle his cynicism about the "appointment." It wouldn't be the first time in the past decade they got their hopes up just to be disappointed. Parenthood didn't seem to be in the cards for them, and they were about out of time.

She lifted her head to look at him. "Where are you, Clayton?"

"I'm right here, baby."

"No, you're not. Your body's here, but your head's somewhere else. You've been staring up at those rafters for almost an hour like they're fixing to come crashing down."

"They might be, Kate."

Kate looked up at the rafters, too.

"You want to talk about it?"

"I do, but I'm not sure you're gonna want to hear about it."

"Try me."

Clayton ran his fingers through her damp hair and let his hand rest at her neck. Her skin always felt warm as a fever and softer than spun cotton.

"A federal came to my office today, wanting to talk about Halford. They're going to try to take down the mountain."

"Again?" Her tone was low and cautious. It always was when talk of Clayton's family started up.

"Yeah, again."

"And they want your help?"

"Sort of. This guy, Holly, doesn't want information. They already seem to know everything they need to know. According to this guy, they don't even want Hal."

"So what's the story?"

"They want his connection. Some guy in Jacksonville."

"Florida?"

"Yeah, he runs some kind of biker gang. The feds think if they can shut these guys in Jacksonville down, they stop the flow of meth off the mountain as a bonus."

"So why are they up here talking to you? Shouldn't they be in Florida, making that happen?"

Clayton didn't have time to answer before she figured it out herself.

"They want your brother to flip," she said.

"Yup. They think he can be persuaded to give the guy up. If he does, they leave him be. That simple."

"Do you really think he'd do that?"

"No. No, I don't."

"But they want you to try and convince him anyway?"

"That's the gist of it, yeah."

Kate rolled over onto her back, leaving Clayton's bare chest cold and wet. "We've been down this road before, Clayton. There's no convincing that man of anything. He's crazy. You know that."

"You're right, unless . . ."

"Unless what?"

"Unless he thinks it could benefit him." Clayton sat up and faced her. "Listen, he doesn't need the money. Hell, he never has. He's probably got millions buried in coffee cans all over this mountain. If I told him he could finally stop looking over his shoulder, maybe he'd consider it."

"Wait a minute." Kate sat up, too. "You're not seriously thinking of doing this thing, are you?" Kate backed away from Clayton to study his expression.

"Well, yeah. Maybe. This could be my last chance to save him."

"Please, Clayton, your brother is a murderer and a drug dealer. He doesn't need saving. He's beyond saving."

"It's not his fault."

"Don't start with the it's-the-way-he-was-raised routine. I thought we agreed on this. You were raised by the same man he was, and you don't sell poison to children."

"You asked me to talk about this, remember?"

"Well, I think I changed my mind."

"Listen, Kate. The few times I've seen him since Buck was killed, he looked, I don't know, different. Older. Tired. I think Buck's dying might have changed him somehow."

"He threatened to kill you at Buckley's funeral."

"He was grieving."

"You were grieving. Mike was grieving. Big Val was grieving. He was just drunk and hateful."

"People grieve in different ways. He's alone up there now, running things by himself."

"How do you know that?"

"Because I know my brother. He doesn't trust anybody."

"But you think he'll trust you?"

"I'm his brother."

"And you think he cares about that?"

"I think he knows I'm the only blood kin he's got left, and at the end of the day, I think that's *all* he'll care about. He still carries the weight of Deddy's death on him. Maybe I can convince him to retire. He can just live up there, hunt, drink his shine, and give this outlaw bit a rest. Right now he thinks that can never be an option. If he thinks it can be, he might just set the whole thing down like a sack of bricks. No more looking over his shoulder for the next federal sting. No more worrying about being killed by tweekers looking to rob him."

Kate pulled her hair back into a makeshift ponytail. "Okay, just assume Halford does buy that fairy tale, which he won't, but assume that he does. Doesn't giving up those thugs in Florida put him in a new set of crosshairs? Isn't that how it works? Retaliation after retali-ation, and it never stops."

"Baby, the Burroughses have been able to keep ourselves protected from the bulk of federal law enforcement for more than a century. I think we can hold our own against some geeked-up motorheads."

"We?" Kate said.

"You know what I mean."

"No, I don't think I do, Clayton. What I am clear on, though, is that you're thinking of getting into bed with the same feds that killed one of your brothers already, to try and convince your other brother, the self-proclaimed hillbilly godfather of Bull Mountain, to just drop his lifelong criminal enterprise, and what? Go fishing?"

Clayton sank back into his pillow and rubbed his temples. He thought about the bottle of whiskey in the cupboard above the fridge. He'd been thinking about it a lot today. The idea of a drink always sounded better than the actual act of drinking itself. He'd quit drinking so he could have conversations like this one with his wife without ending up on the couch thinking about how to apologize for being an asshole, but still, it sounded good. Kate leaned in over him like a terrier. "Those bastards will get to go back to wherever the hell it is they came from, and you'll end up cleaning the mess they make of our lives. You know all this already, Clayton. We went through this when Buckley died." Kate was practically shouting now, and she took a minute to calm herself. "I know you want things to change up here. I do, too, especially now, but what makes you think this time is going to turn out any different than the last?"

"The agent I met this morning. This Holly guy. Something about him is different. He's not like one of these high-speed super-cops that come up here thinking he can bulldoze a bunch of rednecks because he got high marks at the academy. He's, I don't know, Kate . . ." Clayton stumbled for the right word. "He's genuine," he finally said.

"Genuine," Kate repeated coldly.

"Yes, I got a gut feeling. He's done his homework on this thing and he's figured out the right way to get it done. I think I trust this guy. I think I want to, anyway. If what he's saying is true, this is a shot at doing some real good. I should at least try, right?"

Silence.

"Besides, they're going to do this with or without me, so it makes sense for me to try, right?" It was the second time he'd asked that question and the second time she didn't answer.

"Kate, right?"

Kate swiveled her legs out from under the quilted comforter and sat on the edge of the bed with her back to her husband. Clayton reached out to touch her, but decided against it.

Kate finally spoke but didn't turn to face him. "I love you, Clayton. You know that. I knew what your family was when I met you and I hated it, but I loved you anyway. I couldn't help it. I didn't want to help it. Every cell in my body screamed at me to pack up and move as far away from this place—away from you—as possible. But I couldn't. My heart wouldn't let me. My mama told me not to marry you because of where you came from. *Who* you came from. I told her she was wrong. I knew it was a gamble, and I'm not ashamed to admit some part of me was even turned on by who you were. What girl doesn't want to be swept away by the outlaw? So I stayed and I married you. You wanted something different for your life. Something honorable. It was the biggest leap of faith I ever made, and it scared me to death, but I did it anyway."

"Baby, I know this."

"Right. You *do* know this. But what you don't know is that it *still* scares me to death. Yes, eleven years later I'm still scared that one night you're going to come home and tell me you've decided to follow in your daddy's footsteps or, worse, you're not going to come home at all. Then I'm going to have to wonder if you're buried in a holler somewhere next to everyone else your family didn't agree with. Men with badges like yours killed Buckley, so I get it. You feel compelled to stop it from happening to Halford, too, but it's not up to you to save anybody."

"Baby . . ."

"Let me finish." She turned to face him. "I'm your wife. I swore to stand by you for better or worse and I don't take that vow lightly, and believe me, anything that puts us in direct contact with your lunatic brother is the very definition of *worse*. That being said, you do what you have to do. But hear me, Clayton Burroughs, I will not let some cop, no matter how *genuine* he is, drag you down a hole you can't climb out of to help a man who doesn't want or deserve your help."

"He's my brother, Kate."

"He's goddamn crazy, is what he is."

"That doesn't make him any less my brother. No less my family."

"*I'm* your family now. *I* come first. That's what you promised me when you put that ring on my finger, and you aren't getting out of it. Ever. Do you hear me, Sheriff?"

"I hear you, woman."

Clayton grabbed a handful of T-shirt and pulled her down on top of him. He loved it when she called him Sheriff. He pushed her down on her back and slid himself on top of her. That way, he wouldn't have to look at the rafters.

CHAPTER

4

KATE BURROUGHS

2015

The digital clock from Clayton's side of the bed showed 2:15. The glow of the numbers washed the room in a soft orange hue and seeped into Kate's restless eyelids. Clayton normally covered the clock with a T-shirt or something to block the light, but tonight he hadn't, and the damn thing always kept Kate awake. She was a light sleeper anyway, not that she would be getting any sleep tonight. Not after the bomb Clayton had just dropped on her. She loved him, of that there was no doubt, but she'd never once claimed to understand him. At what point in your life do you just accept a spade for being a spade and move on? Every time her husband raised a hand to help the people on this mountain he'd had it slapped away, but he always jumped at the chance to try again. It reminded her of the *Peanuts* cartoon where Lucy holds the football for Charlie Brown to kick. Everyone knows she's going to snatch it away at the last minute and poor Charlie is going to land flat on his back; even he knows it, but he does it anyway out of sheer faith in the goodness of the world. She'd heard once that the definition of insanity was doing the same thing over and over but expecting different results. If that was true, then her husband was insane. Hell, maybe she was, too. After all, this whole lawman thing was her idea.

It was one of those moments in time that sneak up on you from nowhere, without warning or provocation, and change your life forever. She and Clayton had been dating for a little more than a year and he was bound and determined to prove to her, to everyone, that he wasn't anything like his father. Even so, he still seemed lost. That might have been what initially attracted her to him in the first place. It was clear to her, by the way he cut short conversations about his childhood or took hard left turns whenever the subject came up, that he'd seen, and maybe done, things he wasn't proud of, and it had changed him, robbed him of the things that make falling in love with a girl across a diner table enjoyable. He always acted like he didn't deserve the good things in life that other people take for granted. He was broken, and she liked fixing broken things. She didn't know that about herself then but she knew it now, and this close to forty, she might as well start admitting it. She also knew Clayton would have done anything for her back then. Anything. And that kind of power over a man, in the hands of a twenty-six-year-old woman, could be dangerous. She liked that, too.

They'd been sitting in Lucky's after church—that was saying something right there. Clayton Burroughs had never stepped foot in a church before her, but there he was, hair combed and shirt tucked in, pretending to be comfortable—the two of them sharing a massive plate of cathead biscuits, peach preserves, and fresh butter. Kate had the figure for that kind of thing back then. That memory made her reach under the covers and pinch at her love handles, then cup the pudge of her belly with both hands.

The gossip in the air that morning at the diner was about Sheriff Flowers's stepping down. Sam Flowers had been the law in McFalls County since she was a little girl, but something about a bad shooting, him being drunk or something, was forcing the old man into retirement, and the gossip hounds were out in full force. Kate remembered as if it were yesterday how she'd casually formed the words that would change both her and Clayton's lives. She originally said it as a joke, but the look on Clayton's face when she said it, as if she'd just solved all the world's problems with a single sentence, was enough to wish she could freeze time and erase it from his memory.

"You should run, Clayton. You'd make a great sheriff," she'd said, and after that there was no stopping him. Come November, they both added shiny new accessories to their nightstands—a modest diamond engagement ring for her and a silver sheriff's badge for him. He ran unopposed and considered that a lucky break, although the whispers that coated the edges of every conversation through the election were that no one dared to run against a Burroughs—even the good one. The next decade was filled with the sleepless nights of a cop's wife. A cop whose primary goal was to buy back the soul of a family that had grown accustomed to being soulless. And it was her fault.

Kate got out of bed, crossed the room, and laid a towel from the floor over the maddening glow of the clock. She walked to the bathroom and quietly lowered the toilet seat with mild annoyance. She sat down, letting her head fall into her hands. *And after that fiasco at Buckley's funeral?* she thought. *Is he out of his mind?* Buckley had been completely psychotic, as far as Kate was concerned. He scared her more than Halford ever did. If Clayton was the good, and Halford was the bad, then Buckley was the ugly in spades. It didn't surprise her or anybody else to hear he was shot to death in a gunfight with the police. Buckley was the shoot-first-think-never type, who most likely deserved everything that happened to him, but he was still Clayton's brother. He was still family, and Clayton had the right to pay his respects, no matter what Halford and the rest of them thought.

Kate was supportive of Clayton's attending the funeral; she even insisted on being there with him, but even she'd tried to change his mind about wearing his dress uniform. She groaned now and ran her hands from her head to the back of her neck, pressing down on the tense knot of muscle. She pictured him standing in front of the bathroom mirror, decked out in starched polyester with military creases and polished brass, wrestling with a tie for maybe the first time in his life. His well-worn hat was traded in for a stiff-brimmed sheriff's hat she didn't even know he owned. Standing in the doorway watching him like that, all she could think about was how this thing—this bad decision—would be the thing that got him killed. He insisted without urging that it was a way to honor his brother and in no way a massive *fuck you* to Halford and his cronies, and maybe, deep down, some of that was true, but she knew better. It was Burroughs piss, spite, and ego. Only, he couldn't see it. None of them ever could. None of them ever thought they were wrong. She could smell the whiskey on him, too, no matter how much mouthwash he swigged to cover it up. She knew if she'd searched the cabinets and drawers, she'd find at least one, if not more, drained half-pint bottles of cheap bourbon. She let it go. She always let it go.

They were the last to arrive at the funeral, if you could even call it that. Outwardly it looked more like a crowd who'd turned out for a cockfight. Just a bunch of unkempt men standing around in a circle in their dingy work coats and boots, holding jars of corn whiskey, smoking, and carrying on. The few women who'd been allowed to come sat silent, bound together by expressions of profound sadness that were in no way inspired by the departed. They all looked much older than they were, tired and bleached out, the color of summer hay bales. Kate felt equal parts compassion and resentment toward them all, but also found herself trying to tug a few extra inches out of her skirt to cover more of her bare legs. No reason to rub it in.

Halford wouldn't allow his brother's body in a church, or a preacher to be present, so the men just stood together out on the banks of Burnt Hickory Pond, telling their stories and pouring whiskey on the ground. Soon they would just dump the body in a hole next to the one his father was buried in.

Clayton's grandfather, Cooper, had been buried in a field near Johnson's Gap, intending it to be the burial site for all the Burroughs to follow, but his son, Gareth, Clayton's father, had wanted to be buried here, at Burnt Hickory Pond. No one knew why. The graves spoiled memories she had of this place when she was a girl. Swinging out on the old tire swing with silly teenage boys, beating their skinny bird-chests, being loud and young. This place used to be a symbol of her childhood, of summer, something dear. Now it was the burial ground of murderers and thieves. She was surprised that the lush grass and bright green moss around the pond wasn't rotting and brown, considering the amount of bad blood in the dirt.

From the moment Clayton pulled the truck up next to the line of primered pickups and ATVs, every set of eyes locked on them. First on her, in her not-so-conservative black dress, then on Clayton, in a uniform that evoked the purest form of disgust and hatred these people could muster. The crowd broke in half as she and Clayton approached, revealing Halford Burroughs hunched over a plain pine box next to a freshly dug hole. The box held a man shot to death by men dressed the way her husband was dressed now. Halford's eyes were red and swollen from crying, and it was maybe the first time since meeting Clayton's family all those years ago that she'd ever seen the big man show any type of emotion that wasn't fueled by spit and vinegar, but his face faded back into the slab of cold granite she was used to seeing when he laid eyes on his little brother. Right then, in that moment, Clayton said something to her under his breath, but she didn't hear it. Maybe it was an admission of this having been a bad idea after all, but she couldn't be sure. She did ask him when it was all over what he had said, but he told her he couldn't remember. It was the first time, to her knowledge, that Clayton had ever lied to her. The crowd either stood silent or whispered and pointed as she and Clayton joined the group, but it was Halford who verbalized the mood with just three words.

"How. Dare. You." He fumbled to draw the gun poking out of his pants, and Kate had thought she might pass out right then and there. She felt the tingle in her fingertips and saw the flashing black starbursts in the corners of her vision. It was the most frightened she'd ever been in her adult life. Thankfully, Halford's men grabbed him and held him back. He roared a string of obscenities at them and fought to get at Clayton, but, thank God, his people were successful at keeping him in check. Clayton never flinched. He never reached for his own sidearm, he simply reached a hand across Kate's abdomen and calmly pushed her back a step behind him. Kate remembered in the middle of all her panic how sexy he'd looked at that moment.

"He was my brother, too," Clayton said, "and I deserve to be here."

Halford spit at them, getting most of the slick brown spittle on the pine coffin. One of the men Kate recognized and knew as a good man at least on the surface, a man Clayton called Scabby Mike, yelled back while struggling to contain Halford's gun arm. "Well, be quick about it, Clayton, or we'll be burying two of y'all today." Kate believed that, and nudged Clayton forward. An eternity could be fit into the time it took her husband to say his piece to that simple closed pine box and rejoin her at the truck. She couldn't remember even taking a breath. But he did eventually come back, and they left, driving slower than she would have liked. She looked back and saw the men gathered around Halford. He'd stumbled and they were helping him up off the ground. She saw that he'd started crying again. Maybe it was proof of a soul in there somewhere, but she didn't want to stick around to find out. She just wanted to go home. She put her hand on Clayton's leg and went to speak, but saw that he was crying, too.

HALFORD AND CLAYTON BURROUGHS

1985

"You ever been stung by a hornet?" Hal said out of the blue. He didn't look at his kid brother when he spoke. It was pitch black out, so he just kept his eyes on the dirt road ahead. He had one hand dangling lazily over the steering wheel, and the other gripped around a can of Stroh's in his lap—his third since they'd left the house.

"Sure I have," Clayton said. "It stings like the dickens."

Hal narrowed his eyes and studied his little brother's face. It was a boy's face. "Well, I don't think you have, then, Clayton, 'cause if you did, you wouldn't say 'It stings like the dickens.' That just don't cover it. Those sum' bitches hurt like nothing else in this world. Pain you ain't never gonna forget. You get stung by one of those suckers and it's enough to bring tears to your eyes. God forbid you get stung by a bunch of 'em . . ." Hal paused to find the right wording. He blew out a long trumpeter's breath of air and shook his head. "You get hit by a bunch of 'em—buddy, you're going down."

"No, really," Clayton insisted, "I did get stung once. It was only one and I killed it when I stepped on it, but I thought my foot was going to swell up like a watermelon."

Hal killed his beer and slung the can onto the floorboard at Clayton's feet. "Did you know that hornets will attack you for no reason? Not like a yellow jacket, or a bumblebee like the one you stepped on."

Clayton didn't argue.

"Bees will mind their own business if you do the same by them, but a fuckin' hornet? You could just be walking by a nest and those ornery bastards will chase you down. Did you know that?"

"Uh-uh," Clayton said, shaking his head. He had no idea why his brother was talking about hornets, but he didn't much care, either. Hal never really talked to Clayton at all, so he was enjoying having a little of his attention. The brothers were born ten years apart, with Buckley born slap between them, so they didn't have that much in common. Besides, Hal was normally too busy with the crops higher up the mountain to be fooling with his kid brother. Clayton understood that. Business first. But ever since Clayton turned twelve and Deddy started letting him help out on runs, Hal didn't really pay Clayton no mind. This conversation was probably the most Hal had ever said to him at one time. Clayton liked to think maybe it meant Hal was starting to see him as a man—a brother. That thought made Clayton sit about a foot taller in his seat.

Hal pulled the Ford pickup onto a pig path anyone who wasn't from around here would have missed. It wasn't so much a road as it was two channels of dirt cut into the dander and weeds by the tires of trucks much like this one. Clayton rolled up his window to keep overgrown brush and tree limbs from whipping him in the face, and Hal cut the truck's headlights down to the orange parking lights. Clayton could barely make out the road in the moonlight, but that didn't slow his brother down a bit. He just hauled ass through the dark like he'd done it a hundred times before.

"You remember Big Merle?" Hal said.

"Sure," Clayton said, gripping the armrest with white knuckles. "He was that fat kid that used to come get schoolin' from Miss Adel before she died."

"Yeah, not that it mattered, no amount of schoolin' would help that fat fuck. He was as dumb as a sack of hammers." Hal grabbed another beer from the six-pack on the seat between them and peeled the pop-top off with his teeth. "Anyway, he may have been a dumb-shit, but he was still a buddy. A *good* buddy. The fella would do just about anything you asked without a bitch or complaint." Hal handed the open beer to Clayton, who beamed and eagerly grabbed it with both hands. Hal let a brief smile escape before he popped open another beer for himself. "Anyways," Hal said, "when we was kids, a few of us were out by the Southern Ridge, shooting at squirrels—me, Buckley, Scabby Mike, and Big Merle. He was a fat shit even then. It was the year Deddy bought me that shitty .22 rifle. I think you got that gun now."

Clayton said he did. He didn't tell him that the gun was his prize possession because it used to be Hal's. Instead he took a sip of warm beer and did his best not to gag. It tasted like swamp water.

"We were having a pretty good time," Hal said, "just dickin' around, and Big Merle says he needs to take a piss, so he bolts into the woods. If it were me, I'da just whipped it out right there, but Merle was pee-shy. Little pecker, I guess. Anyway, a few minutes later he comes barreling out of the woods, trying to yank his pants up, screaming like a banshee. Wailing like I ain't never heard before." Hal paused and took a sip of his own beer. Clayton watched his brother remember back on what sounded like a fond memory.

"Hornets?" Clayton said.

"Yeah, buddy. Hornets. A whole damn swarm of 'em. He only got a few feet out of the woods before he toppled over. There must have been hundreds of 'em on his ass."

"What'd y'all do?"

Hal looked at Clayton like he had just asked the dumbest question ever asked. "We ran like hell, is what we did. I ran so goddamn fast I thought my heart was gonna explode, and I didn't stop 'til I was inside the hunting cabin up near Johnson's Gap."

"Dang," Clayton said, "that's far."

"I know, right?"

"What happened to Merle?"

"He managed to get his big ass off the ground and to his folks' house, but he was all messed up. He had to be holed up at the hospital down in Waymore for damn near two weeks. The poor bastard almost died. We didn't get to see him until way after, but even then he had tubes and shit runnin' out of him to drain the pus, and his eyes were swollen shut. He never did talk right again. We felt bad, 'cause of runnin' and all, but damn, what were we supposed to do?"

"That's messed up," Clayton said.

"Yeah, well, we handled it the next day. Once we found out Merle was in the hospital, we headed back up to the Southern Ridge to clear those suckers out. I mean, that was our spot. We hung out there. A bunch of hornets weren't gonna just build a nest and sting up our friends. We were there first. You understand what I'm saying?" Hal shot a stern look at his little brother to reinforce the question, and awareness spilled over Clayton like a bucket of well water. He nodded. They weren't just talking about hornets.

"We marched our happy asses into the woods, and sure as shit, we found the nest hanging in a hollowed-out pine tree probably right over where Big Merle tried to take a piss. We brought a can of gas to torch the thing, but it was way too high for any of us to reach, so Buckley's crazy ass starts dousing the whole damn tree. We could've burned the whole mountain down—dumb-ass kids—but we didn't know no better. Scabby Mike lit that bitch up, and it took off faster than all get-out."

"The whole tree?"

"The whole tree. We just sat back and watched it burn. When the fire took to the hornet's nest, I swear I could hear 'em screamin'. Whistlin' like fireworks. It felt good to hear them burn like that."

"Then what happened?"

"Deddy saw the smoke from the house and him and Jimbo Cartwright come haulin' ass out there. We cut a break to contain it and managed to get the fire out before it spread."

"Was he mad?" Clayton immediately regretted asking that question.

"Well, goddamn, Clayton, what do you think? Hell, yeah, he was mad. I toted a legendary ass-whuppin' that night. So did Buckley." He paused again, then brought his voice down. "But I gotta tell you, little brother, it was worth it. It was worth it to hear those little bastards screaming."

Clayton forced down the rest of his beer and tossed the can on the floorboard like his brother had done. Hal stopped the truck and cut off the parking lights. He popped open the last beer and downed it in three huge gulps. His belch was hearty, loud, and long. Clayton wished he could burp like that.

"We gotta walk from here," Hal said. He grabbed his shotgun, racked it, and quietly got out of the truck. Clayton followed suit. He thought maybe he'd been here before with Deddy, but couldn't be sure in the dark. This part of the mountain was peppered with stills, but a lot of them were in disrepair. Ever since the focus had shifted to the crops under the northern face, this area was tended to less and less. It wasn't abandoned, just not a priority.

They walked about a quarter mile into the woods before they could see the dim light of a campfire through the trees.

"Hey, Hal," Clayton said. "Whatever happened to Big Merle? I haven't seen him around for a while. Did his family move off the mountain?"

"He's dead," Hal said. "Buckley beat him to death with a piece of stove wood and dropped him in a hole. Fat bastard wasn't happy with his place in the pecking order—got greedy. It happens. Now be quiet, we got a job to do."

Hal crept silently through the trees toward the glow of the fire, and Clayton mimicked his every move. The closer they got, the quieter Hal moved until even Clayton could barely hear him from only a few feet away. When they were close enough, Clayton could see it was one of Deddy's stills, one that was supposed to be decommissioned. It wasn't. They stopped at a cluster of pine trees and watched a blond-haired man with a patchy beard stoke a fire under a massive copper boiler. The heat coming off the barrels felt good on Clayton's face after the long hike through the cold woods. He tugged at Hal's shirt to get his attention, and Hal leaned in close.

"There's only one," Clayton whispered. "That's good, right?"

"It's good, but it ain't the one we want."

"So, what do we do?"

"What do you do when you can't reach a hornet's nest?"

Clayton didn't take long to come up with the answer his brother was looking for. "You set fire to the tree," he said.

"Very good, kiddo." Hal ruffled Clayton's bushy red hair. "I think Deddy's got you all wrong. Now stay here." Hal put a finger to his lips and vanished into the darkness. He reappeared less than a minute later directly behind Blondie, who was now copping a squat by a small campfire, thumbing through a skin mag, his rifle propped up against a tree to his left. Hal drew back and hit the man in the temple with the butt end of his Mossberg. Blondie never knew what hit him. He went down hard, face-first into the dirt. It was the coolest thing Clayton had ever seen. His brother was awesome.

"Clayton," Hal said, snapping the boy back into the moment, "get out here and tie this pig-fucker to that hemlock tree."

Clayton shuffled out of the woods with a quickness. He'd always been good with the knots. He was sure Hal knew that. Hal pulled a length of paracord from his jacket and tossed it to Clayton, who bound the unconscious man in no time. Hal kicked over the huge metal boiler—the heart of the ancient still—and the coals spilled out all over the small clearing. Once some of the underbrush started to ignite from the coals, Hal used the high-octane hooch in the barrels as an accelerant, dousing the entire site. Almost instantly the small patch of woods became a blazing inferno.

"Holy shit, Hal! How we gonna put this out?"

"We're not. They are." He pointed to the man tied to the tree.

Clayton was confused.

Hal explained. "This fire is going to be seen by the fella Deddy sent us here to find, and I promise you he'll be along shortly. When him and his boys are all tuckered out from fightin' a woods fire, we'll pick them off like fish in a barrel. It'll be fun. C'mon, let's go find a place to watch."

"What about him?" Clayton pointed to the blond man, who was starting to come around due to the intense heat.

"Fuck him," Hal said. "Come on."

"But he'll burn alive."

"And?" Hal said, beginning to lose his patience. "Get your ass up that path before I leave you here to burn up with him."

Clayton couldn't move.

The man tied to the tree by Clayton's knots awoke completely when the fire started licking his feet and legs. He swiveled his head back and forth, wide-eyed and frantic, taking in the scope of what was happening to him. He struggled to free himself, drawing his knees up to his chin. He screamed at Clayton to help him. He begged. Clayton just stared at him—horrified. Hal gripped Clayton hard under the arm and nearly ripped it off dragging the boy back out the way they came.

From a safer distance, Clayton watched his brother get comfortable against a tree stump and close his eyes. Hal looked rested and content as the burning man's screams became something else. Something unnatural. Clayton would never forget that sound. He wondered if Hal could even hear it at all, or if all he heard were the hornets.

CHAPTER 6

SIMON HOLLY

2015

1.

Agent Holly shoved his key in the lock and tried to remember the last time, if ever, he'd stayed in a motel room that still issued keys to its patrons. Not those flimsy plastic key cards with the magnetic strip, but real, straight-up cut metal keys. As soon as he opened the door to room six of the Waymore Valley Motor Inn, the smell of powdered dollar-store potpourri and stale cigarette smoke rushed his face. It was strangely comforting. As were the bland mother-of-pearl walls and the dim electric-yellow light. This was the kind of thing he was used to. All the fresh mountain air and wide-open spaces were foreign and intimidating. Being out in the open country made him feel like, at any time, he could lose his footing and spin right off the planet. The tight space felt better. More controlled.

Holly unzipped the black government-issue duffel and took out his cell phone. He'd purposely left it behind before the sit-down with Clayton Burroughs. No distractions. The phone showed multiple missed calls from the same three numbers within the space of four hours. One was his girlfriend, Clare; one had a government prefix; and one had a North Georgia area code. Calling any of the three back was going to be the equivalent of sticking an ice pick through his left eye. He tossed the phone on the end table and fished a prescription pill bottle out of the duffel, a special cocktail of ten-milligram hydrocodone tablets and twenty-milligram diazepam. He shook out the pills and washed them down with tap water from the sink. His hands were still a little shaky. He'd done his best to keep them still during his meeting with the sheriff, but today was a long time coming, and to be honest, he was surprised he'd handled it so coolly. Holly was pretty sure he'd sold the right play to the sheriff, even if he'd had to consume a year's worth of fat and carbs at that ridiculous pool-hall diner to do it.

How do these people eat that shit every day? he thought. He needed a gym, and a shower, but he settled for three fingers of bourbon from a plastic traveler's bottle to give the pills a swift kick in the ass. The burn of the whiskey felt good. He sank down into a chair next to the bed and let the chemicals work their magic. It was the only thing making this next part bearable. It was time to roll up his sleeves and start calling people back.

He grabbed the cell phone and punched in a number. A pocket-sized faux-leather King James Bible with gold trim sat on the desk. Holly toyed with it while the phone rang. When the person on the other end picked up, he reached out and slid the Bible into the trash.

2.

"Jessup," the voice on the line said.

"Henry, it's Simon."

"Simon, where the hell are you? You dropped off the grid, and you got people around here crabby. I don't like these people when they're crabby. You know that."

"I'm in Georgia."

"And why in God's name are you in Georgia?"

"I'm working a case."

"You're supposed to be working a case in Jacksonville, Florida."

"Same case."

The silence on the line told Holly that his partner, Henry Jessup, was trying to connect the dots before asking a stupid question. He asked anyway.

"When am I going to be briefed on how what you're doing in the Peach State connects to Wilcombe? What do I tell Jennings?"

The pills were doing their job. Holly felt the tension ease in his neck and shoulders.

"Tell him anything you want, Henry. I'm the AIC on this, and the last time I checked, the ATF was a federal agency, meaning I can follow a lead anywhere in the continental United States. I'm tracking down a major supplier of dope in the Georgia Mountains that ties directly to the guns in Florida, and the money—and Wilcombe."

"You *are* the AIC on this, but you work in conjunction with me and the federal government. There are rules here you have to follow. This isn't some Podunk local operation in southern Alabama. This Wilcombe thing you're so hot about is the only reason Jennings vouched to get you in here, and already you're pulling this cowboy shit. This is the kind of thing he's waiting on to fry your ass and take the case for himself."

"Fuck him. He's a suit. He has no idea how it works out here."

"He's your boss. And he doesn't trust you. You move too far outside the lines on this and he's going to bust you back down to a beat cop. Me, too, probably."

"What can I tell you, Henry? I'm just doing my job."

"Well, then do it by the book. Jennings and them are going to want to be briefed on this, Simon. Stop the radio silence and the free-lancer shit. You shouldn't be up there alone. I should be there."

"Henry, you worry too much."

"You don't worry enough."

"Just give me a couple of days. Let me see where this takes me and I'll let you know the play when I have it figured out."

"Have you called Clare?"

"Not yet."

"She's called me worried about you. She said you're not answering her calls, either. She thinks you're in Florida."

"Jesus, Henry, what are you, my mom? I'll call her when I get a chance."

"I don't like lying for you, Simon. It's getting to be a habit."

"Look, Henry. I am following a lead, you'll just have to trust me on it."

"Whatever you say, partner. Just don't leave me with my dick in my hands. As soon as you know something, I know something, okay?"

"Okay. Thank you."

"All right, man. Be careful around those rednecks and call your woman."

"Right."

"Seriously, Simon. Be careful."

Holly hung up. He poured another glass of bourbon and hit redial on the missed local call. A male voice picked up on the first ring.

"Goddamn, Holly, I'm freaking out here."

"I told you not to call me on this phone."

"Don't worry, chief, I'm on a burner. I was just calling to tell you I got a team ready for this thing. We're—"

"Stop," Holly said. "Stop right there. I told you not to call me on this phone, and you did. That means you can't follow simple directions. If you can't follow orders, then I can't use you. If I can't use you, then I'll have to dispose of you. Do you hear what I'm saying?"

"Yeah, I hear you, but—"

"No, just stop talking. Be where I told you to be, and do what I tell you to do. If that doesn't work for you, then the deal is off."

"Roger that, boss. I get it."

"Do you? Are you sure? Because if you don't, I'll find someone else that does, and you—you they find with your hands tied, your arms broken, floating ass-up in the river. Are we clear on this?"

"Crystal."

"Good."

Holly slapped the phone closed and hammered back the bourbon. What was it the sheriff had said earlier about finding good help?

"The pickin's are slim."

Indeed.

Two calls down and a good buzz. He contemplated calling Clare back but decided against it. He tossed the phone back on the table and picked up his wallet. Behind the two neatly creased twenties and Uncle Sam's credit card was a small photograph of a brown-haired woman barely into her twenties, sitting in the grass with a small boy—a toddler. Holly held the picture, careful of the worn edges, and laid it where the Bible had been. There wasn't a day that went by that Holly didn't take a minute to stare at the woman and the boy in that photograph.

The woman who wasn't Clare.

COOPER BURROUGHS

1950

1.

"Tie those last few off and load them on the truck." Cooper wiped the sweat from his forehead. "Take a few minutes if you need to, but I ain't looking to be out here all day." Cutting and baling marijuana could be exhausting work and the process took up most of the sticky, humid summer months, but Cooper knew he paid well, and his men knew they weren't going to do anything the man himself wouldn't do. Still, the heat of a Georgia summer could wilt a man's back and cook his brains. Delray and Ernest had been humping it since sunup and it looked like they hadn't made a dent in the day's workload.

"Damn, Cooper, we ain't never gonna get all this done. It's hot as the devil's balls out here, and I done sweat out every bit of water in me. We could use a break."

"The only thing you're sweating out is last night's liquor, Delray. So that makes your problem your own. If you're still looking to get paid, then you need to get the rest of those buds baled and packed before I lose it to the sun."

"I don't mind working, Coop, but goddamn, man, take it easy."

Cooper dropped the tightly cinched bundle of tacky green plants to the ground and wiped his brow again. "How much money did you make last year taking it easy?"

"Last year I was running the stills over on the southern side."

"I didn't ask what you did, Delray. I asked how much you made."

"I reckon you and Rye always done me pretty good."

Cooper pulled a thin stem of cannabis out of the bunch at his feet and popped it in his mouth. The casual mention of his dead brother didn't go unnoticed. He shook it off. "Well, I reckon you made about half all year of what I paid you the last three months."

Delray shifted his lips over to one side of his face as he thought on that.

"Well, don't go trying to do the math," Cooper said. "I don't want your brain fryin' any more than it has to before we get this truck loaded. Just get yourself some water and stop all your bitchin' before I get a couple of womenfolk out here to show you up." Cooper looked up toward the truck and called for his son. "Gareth?"

Cooper's boy looked down from where he was positioned in the truck bed, straightening the bales as they were tossed in. "Yes, Deddy?"

"Get up there to the main house and bring these sissies a pitcher of tea. Plenty of ice."

"Yessir." Gareth hopped off the truck and made his way into the house.

Delray pulled down tight on the twine in his hands. Ernest tied it off, picked up the bale, and tossed it toward Cooper a little harder than he should have. Cooper caught it and slung it into the bed of the truck. "If you got something to say, Ernest, spit it out."

It looked like Ernest had a lot to say but wouldn't get a chance to right then. He squinted at something in the distance over Cooper's shoulder, and Cooper turned to look as well. One rider. Horseback. Nobody rode horses wild-west-style on the mountain anymore but a fella named Horace Williams, one of the old-timers that lived out by Johnson's Gap. All three men watched the rider approach in the heat.

"What are you doing out here, Horace?" Cooper helped the old man off the horse.

"We might have us a problem out by the Gap."

"What problem?"

"Well, me and my boy Melvin was out riding through there a few days ago and we saw one of the old stills running."

"Which one?"

"The big one way off the pass. The one Rye used for the peach he'd run into Tennessee."

Cooper took off his hat and used it to rub the sweat off his forehead. "I shut that one down."

"Yes, sir. We knew that. That's why I come to tell you."

"And do I even need to ask who was running it?" Cooper asked the question as if he already knew the answer. Delray and Ernest were all ears.

Horace hung a toothless smile on his face. "It was Valentine. That colored fella Rye was so fond of. Him and a few of his kin. It looked like they were casing up a load to reopen Rye's old route." It made a little more sense to Cooper now why this old-timer would want to ride way out here in the heat to give up a neighbor. Rye's Negro friends were never that popular up here in the first place, and without him around to say any different, old-timers like Horace were itching to see them get run off.

"Didn't you already tell him he couldn't do that?" Horace said.

Cooper had. Rye's sudden disappearance had solved the timber issue but opened up a lot of new problems regarding how to transition out of shine and into weed. Rye was always the go-between for the family and the people living on the mountain. He knew how to talk to people. Cooper would rather not talk to anyone about anything, but he was running things now, so that wasn't an option. Albert Valentine was one of those problems. Rye had promised him a piece of the shine business once the timber deal was in place. Cooper wasn't having it. "I told that old bastard that I wasn't having no Negro run my deddy's Georgia Peach off this mountain. Even if it was a Negro my brother fancied."

"Well, Coop," Horace said, clearly happy to be the messenger, "I reckon he thinks he can do whatever he wants, 'cause he sure is crating up a ton."

Cooper worked at an itch in his beard and took the chewed-up stem from his mouth. After a moment he pointed it at Delray and Ernest. "You two go down to the Gap with Horace and bring Valentine to me." Delray dropped the twine and sheathed his knife. Ernest finished tying off his bale and threw it at Cooper hard like the last one. This time Cooper knocked it to the ground. He took off his hat again and put his face inches from Ernest's. Ernest was a big man with nearly a hundred pounds on Cooper, but he shrank back all the same. "You got a problem, Ernest? Here's your chance to vent, but I'm not taking any more of your fuckin' attitude."

Ernest met Cooper's stare. "Why don't you just give it to him?"

"Give what to who?"

"Give Old Man Val the still. The route. All of it."

"Why the hell should I do that?"

"It's the way Rye wanted it."

Cooper felt the twinge of something mean run up his back, and the left side of his face tightened up. "Rye's dead," he said with a low rumble.

"And don't we all know it."

Cooper backed away from Ernest and turned toward the truck. He could feel the heat rising under his skin and took a deep breath through his nose. Delray fumbled for the right thing to say to lighten the moment but fell short and just stood slack-jawed.

"Rye showed his people respect. He didn't work us like dogs in the heat, and he didn't call us women for wanting to take a minute's rest."

"Shut the hell up, Ernest," Delray said. Cooper said nothing. He just stood with his back to the men, staring at the main house.

"Or what, Delray? Am I suppose to be scared of him just 'cause he's the boss? Nobody was scared of Rye."

"And look what that got him," Delray said, and regretted it immediately. It just slipped out. Cooper turned around.

"What do you mean, Delray?" he said.

"Hell, Coop, I didn't mean nothing."

Cooper took a few steps toward the two men. Delray took a step back and Ernest moved to the side.

"I'm not sure what you're implying there." Cooper stared at Delray hard enough to knock him down.

"I ain't implying anything, Coop, I mean, come on, we all know what happened."

Ernest stepped farther away from Delray. He was going to get them both killed. Standing up to the boss about fair treatment was one thing, but accusing him of killing his brother was something else altogether. Rye was killed in a hunting accident. That was the official story, and whether anyone chose to believe it or not, you didn't question it. Not to the man's face, anyway. Cooper and his son had tried their best to save Rye's life that day. They grieved his death for months. Cooper depended on that truth to be the only truth.

Gareth came out of the house with the glass pitcher of tea and a stack of paper cups and held them both up for his father to take. Cooper took the pitcher and held it in his hand like a hammer. Delray tried to get off a last word, right before Cooper bashed the glass pitcher into his head. The glass shattered and spun Delray down to his knees. A large sliver of glass was wedged into Delray's skull, and smaller chunks, all shiny and reflective in the sun's light, stuck out of his cheeks and bottom lip. It looked like his jaw was broken as well, because it just hung there open and loose, disconnected from the rest of his face. Cooper shoved a booted foot into Delray's back, forcing him down flat in the dirt, then pulled a nickel-plated Colt Python from the waistband of his trousers. He didn't thumb the hammer or point it at anyone. He just held it, letting it be known.

"And that . . . is that," Cooper said. "Ernest, you and Horace get this sack of shit off my mountain, and don't let me see no more of him."

Ernest didn't try to keep Cooper's stare this time. He was too scared to even look at him. He grabbed Delray by the shoulders, careful of his ruined jaw, and dragged him toward his truck parked by the tree line, leaving a trail of red mud, iced tea, blood, and broken glass. Gareth helped without having to be asked. Before they reached the trees they heard Cooper call out, "Ernest."

Ernest turned and looked back at the truck, where Cooper was already working on the next bale.

"Yeah, boss?"

"After you get Valentine up here, take the rest of the day off. But tomorrow, bring a friend. We're going to need to catch up."

"Yessir."

2.

Gareth came into the main house dirty and tired, his hands caked with dry blood and glass dust. Cooper ran him a tub of water to wash up in and went back outside to tarp down the load on the truck. It was getting dark and Gareth's mama would have supper ready soon. Roasted venison, butter beans, and fresh-cut collards were a welcome diversion from the day's events, but thoughts of supper vanished like steam from a kettle with the sound of trucks coming in from the Western Ridge. Cooper pulled the canvas tarp down tight over the bales of marijuana buds and tied it off. Gareth appeared on the porch, toweling off his hands, hoping he wouldn't have to get them dirty again.

"That's far enough," Cooper said, and held up a hickory ax handle he kept under the seat of his truck. The first vehicle stopped and Ernest got out with Horace, Albert Valentine, and a few other men Cooper had working the crops. A second truck following swiftly behind the first carried Valentine's wife, Mammie, and his young son, Albert Junior. Gareth and Albert Junior were almost the same age and spent most of their summers together swimming and fishing in Bear Creek, or picking wild blackberries or scrounging for pecans for Albert Senior to bake into pies. The old man made the best pies. Cooper loved the old man's pies.

"Val!" Gareth yelled from the porch, happy to see the younger boy and oblivious of the trouble his father was in. Albert Junior ran to the porch. Mammie followed after him but kept her eyes on Cooper. Cooper watched the boys briefly before turning his attention to the old man.

"What did I tell you, Albert?" Cooper said.

Valentine held his hat to his chest with both hands. "I know what you told me, Mister Cooper, sir . . . but, well, it just ain't right is all."

"What ain't right? You making and selling shine off this mountain with my family's stills against my wishes? Is that what ain't right?"

Ernest, Horace, and the boys settled in around Cooper and Valentine like a murder of blackbirds.

"It's like I told you already," Valentine said. "Rye done gave me the still. He done gave me the route, too. Ask anybody. Ask the owners of the pool halls down 'round Tennessee, who's been buyin'. They were expectin' me. Rye told them to."

Cooper arched an eyebrow in surprise. "You already been selling?"

"Yessir, and this here is for you." He motioned to the only other black man in the crowd, who produced a brown paper bag from his pants pocket and handed it to Cooper. Cooper knew the feel of a stack of cash, so he didn't bother to open it.

"What is this?"

"Twenty percent of the first run," Valentine said. "I think that's fair."

"You do?" Cooper said softly.

"Yessir."

"You think it's fair to steal from me and my family and come here and throw a little money in my face like that's gonna settle things? You *did* spend a lot of time with my brother."

"But, sir, Rye . . ."

"Rye's dead, and you setting up shop on our mountain after I done told you no is disrespectful to his memory and a goddamn slap in my face."

Valentine squeezed at his hat and looked down at it. "Yessir."

"Now, the way I see it, I got two choices. I can kill you right here and be done with it, or because you were my brother's friend"— Cooper stopped and looked at the length of hickory in his hands— "you could tote an ass-whuppin' and go on home. Either way, you're out of the liquor business."

"Please, Mr. Burroughs, please don't hurt him," Mammie said from the porch. Gareth and Albert Junior sat wide-eyed behind her. Gareth knew his father wouldn't hurt Val's dad. He was just mad is all. Cooper didn't answer.

"You hush your mouth, woman," Valentine said, and stood a little taller. His broad shoulders were nearly twice the size of Cooper's. "You do your worse, sir. I know I can't stop you. But I know what Rye give me, and I know what's right is right." That was all Albert Valentine had to say. Cooper didn't hesitate. He swung the ax handle and hit Valentine in the jaw. The crowd roared with surprise and Mammie screamed. The old man spun almost completely around before falling to the ground. He lifted his hands to cover his face, but Cooper swung again and again, snapping the bones in Valentine's hands and fingers like campfire kindling. The sticky night air was filled with whooping and laughter from most of the men in the crowd as Cooper beat Valentine with the hard wood. Mammie never stopped screaming, and tried grabbing Cooper's arm. He flung her away without much notice and the crowd kept her from trying again. Valentine's son threw himself on top of his father to stop the beating, but Cooper grabbed the boy and tossed him to the side like a bale of weed. He lifted the ax handle high for a final blow. Valentine's eyes were already swollen shut behind shiny purple knots.

"Deddy, stop!" Gareth said, getting in between his father and the beaten old man. Cooper gripped the wood gone slick with blood.

"Move yourself, boy."

"No, Deddy, don't kill him. He's a nice man. He won't do wrong no more. He won't."

Cooper stood holding the hickory up high, twirling it in a slow circle like a ballplayer. He looked around at the faces surrounding him, which ranged from thrilled to terrified. Gareth's hands were shaking as he held them up to block his father from hitting the old man again.

"Please, Deddy, please stop."

Cooper lowered the length of wood. "Get him out of here," he said. Mammie and Albert Junior scrambled to help the old man. Cooper looked at his son with a confused expression, partly impressed and partly disgusted. "Pick up that bag and get in the truck."

Gareth looked around on the ground and found the paper bag full of cash. He tucked it under his arm and slid into the front seat of his father's truck. Albert Junior waited for Gareth to look at him, and when he finally did, he nodded. Gareth nodded back.

"Ernest," Cooper said, wiping the ax handle clean on the canvas tarp hanging off the truck. "I want you to follow these people back to their house and collect the rest of the take from that run and bring it with you to work tomorrow."

"Yessir," Ernest said, and gave Mammie a hand lifting Valentine to his feet.

GARETH BURROUGHS

1958

Gareth sat in the passenger side of his father's old Ford, holding Annette Henson on his lap by her hips. The night outside was starless and pitch black. He tried counting the fireflies blinking on and off outside the truck's window to keep his eighteen-year-old libido in check, but it was the bird that did the trick. "Do you hear that?" he whispered in Annette's ear.

"Hear what?" she said.

"That bird. What is it?"

Annette stopped dry-humping his lap for a moment and looked at him funny. "I don't hear any birds, Gareth."

"Just a second ago. I've never heard any bird like that before."

Annette grabbed one of his hands and put it on her breast. "You need to be paying attention to me and not some bird."

"I'm serious, 'Nett. I don't think that was a bird."

Annette tilted her head, more than slightly irritated that he wasn't giving her his full attention. "You're being paranoid, Gareth."

Of course he was being paranoid. He was Cooper Burroughs's son. He was raised to be paranoid. To be observant. To be aware. The bird outside the truck didn't sound right. He spent most of his nights listening to the night birds sing to him outside his window, and the chirping he'd just heard was foreign. It didn't belong. With both hands, he gently pushed Annette's face back from his and wiped the fog off the window glass.

"Seriously, Gareth, what is it?" she said in a husky whisper, her eyes barely open.

"Shhh," he said, but she made an attempt to bite at his raw lip anyway. This time he pushed her back with a little more force and held a finger to her lips. She almost protested. She wasn't happy about being postponed. The Ruby Bliss lipstick she'd borrowed from her sister just for tonight was supposed to be unpostponable. Out of instinct she scanned the truck's bench seat for her handbag to apply some more.

"There it is again. Did you hear that?" Gareth whispered, and tried to concentrate on the blackness outside the window.

"All I hear is your heart beating, sugar."

Gareth was no longer in the mood for the teenage dream. He slid his hands down her curvy frame and lifted her off his lap. The look of disappointment on Annette's moon-shaped face was one Gareth would remember and talk about for years to come. He slid her over behind the steering wheel. "Keep your head down, and don't get out of this truck, no matter what happens."

"Gareth, I . . ."

"I'm serious. Don't get out of the truck. I'll be right back." He quietly clicked open the glove box and pulled out his father's .44-caliber pistol.

"Jesus, Gareth. What are you going to do with that?"

He didn't answer her. He reached up above his head and switched the overhead lamp to the off position, and slowly opened the door. He waited a few seconds between movements and carefully slipped out the door to the ground. Immediately he thought he caught shadows moving in his peripheral vision. His arms and legs suddenly felt heavy, like he was submerged in a pool of molasses. No matter how fast he tried to creep toward his father's house, he was moving in slow motion. His hands were sweating so bad, every few steps he had to wipe his palms on his jeans and switch the massive wheel gun from hand to hand in fear of dropping it. The path from the truck to the wraparound porch wasn't lit, but he could maneuver the yard with his eyes closed, if he needed to. He must have made better time than he thought, because by the time he approached a small thicket off the back porch, the shadows he saw by the truck had become two full-fledged figures decked out in camo taking the steps behind his house. The figures took each step with a ten count, feeling out each footfall, careful to avoid a creaky board. Gareth's heart was pounding in his chest. The blood rushing in his ears was so loud, he wondered how the two men at his father's back door couldn't hear it. He watched the smaller of the two men pull something out of his coat—a small fixed-blade knife. He crouched down in front of the back door and oh-so-quietly began to jimmy the handle. The bigger man covered him with what looked like some type of military assault rifle. Gareth had seen them only in magazines and on TV. He closed his eyes, but for only a moment, and breathed in through his nose like his deddy taught him. He raised the gun, exhaled, and fired at the bigger man holding the rifle. He hit the would-be assassin dead center, and the big man bounced off the house and hit the porch like a side of beef cut off the chain. The smaller man at the door flinched from the noise but didn't try to stand up. He didn't even turn around. His body just went slack and he dropped his chin to his chest. "Please," he said, "let me explain."

"You should have learned your birds," Gareth said, right before he put three rounds in the man's back and two more in the oak door.

If the men attempting to break into Gareth's house had any more undisclosed members in their hit squad, they had hauled ass after their point man's and his partner's bodies hit the porch. Floodlights filled the pastures. Cooper appeared on the porch completely naked, leading with the business end of a 12-gauge. He saw the two dead men on his porch and his only son holding his gun. The sudden illumination of the porch made Gareth aware of all the blood, and he immediately got sick in the bushes, over the handrail. Cooper had known ever since he was a boy that being around death and being the dealer of it were entirely different things. It was a lesson he'd waited a long time for his son to learn. The older Burroughs barely glanced at the dead bodies on the porch. It didn't matter who they were. He regarded them as a problem solved—a problem *his boy* had solved. He stepped over them and the pools of blood seeping through the cracks between the boards and grabbed his son back from the handrail. He leaned the shotgun against a wooden post and hugged Gareth tightly to his chest. It was the first time Gareth had killed anyone, to Cooper's knowledge. It was also the first time Gareth had ever seen his father cry. They cried together, as father and son, cradled in gun smoke, blood, and vomit.

Annette Henson almost cried, too. She had opted not to listen to the instructions Gareth gave her before he took to killing those two men. Almost immediately after Gareth left her in the truck, she followed him out the same door and watched the whole thing play out from the bushes only a few feet from where Gareth stood. Her panties were soaked through. She decided right there and then she was destined to become Mrs. Gareth Burroughs.

CHAPTER

9

ANNETTE HENSON BURROUGHS

1961

1.

"That's where my boy killed those sons-a-bitches dead," Cooper yelled at the preacher. The crowd of wedding guests cheered and laughed. Gareth smiled at that. Annette did, too, but it came forced. She glanced down through the white veil at the bloodstain on the porch more out of reflex than pride. She'd seen the ugly thing a hundred times before. One of the men Gareth killed that night was Cody McCullin, the son of Delray McCullin, seeking revenge for something Cooper had done to his father. It was the night she fell in love with Gareth. Three summers later, here they were getting married on the same steps. The preacher looked to Cooper for permission to continue and the old man lifted his flask. "Go on," he said. "Get on with it."

2.

Halford Jefferson Burroughs was born the following spring of '62. Annette had heard from other mothers on the mountain how wonderful and blessed the experience of having a little one grow inside her would be, but nothing about it was wonderful at all. She was tired all the time. Her tiny, pretty figure that made all the other women of Bull Mountain envious began to warp and contort into something she couldn't bear to look at in the mirror. And her hair, her hair went from being as slick and shiny as a black diamond to looking like shit-covered straw at the bottom of a horse trailer. When the baby kicked, it wasn't a warm, comforting event. It didn't create a bond between mother and child. It hurt, was all. It just hurt. Sometimes it was painful enough to keep her hunched over in the bed for days. On days she felt well enough to leave the house, she couldn't go nowhere, not even out to the market, without some group of old biddies wanting to feel her up and put their hands on *the blessing*. Most days she just wanted to scream, and scream she did. Childbirth was pain Annette wasn't prepared for. She thought about a picture book she had checked out once from the library down in Waymore. It was full of photographs of Alaska. Picture after picture of sprawling snowcapped mountains and swirling colored lights in the sky that looked better to her than any fireworks she'd ever seen. While Halford was busy tearing a hole in her belly, Annette soared over those mountains in her mind. Sometimes she wondered if she'd ever come back.

The entirety of the Burroughs clan and nearly every other family living on Bull Mountain surrounded Annette, waiting on a chance to see the newborn, while Gareth glad-handed and got drunk. Most of the people there came only to be seen by Cooper. To show respect, they called it. To kiss his ass was more like it, Annette thought. Her own family was no different.

"That's a fine-looking boy," Annette's father said, stroking the baby's cheek with the side of a curled finger. Her mother, Jeanine, held the baby like it was made of fine china.

"Thank you," Annette said out loud. *Fuck you,* she said in her mind.

"And where is the proud grandfather?" Jeanine asked.

Like you care, Annette thought. *You only want the old man to see you holding his grandson so maybe someday if you need some of his money, or a favor done, he'll be more prone to give it.* She wondered when she'd gotten so bitter. She should be happy. If not now, when?

Annette looked at Gareth, who looked around the crowded room. "I'll see if I can find him," he said. He moved through the house, shaking hands and looking over shoulders, until he spotted Cooper through the kitchen window. He was pacing the pastures outside.

"Pop," Gareth yelled, but Cooper didn't respond. He was talking to someone, but Gareth didn't see anyone else out there. He made his way outside, walked up to his father, and took his arm. "Deddy?"

"Goddamn it, boy!" Cooper said, and snatched his arm away.

"What are you doing out here, Deddy? Come see Annette. Come see the baby."

"I don't care about all that nonsense. We need to settle this business right here."

"What business? What are you talking about?"

Cooper took a hard pull from the copper flask in his hand. "Tell him," he said, motioning with the flask toward the woods. "Tell this stubborn son of a bitch."

Gareth looked out into the darkness. "Tell what to who?"

"To Rye," Cooper said. "Tell your stubborn-ass uncle Rye. Tell him we had to do it. Tell him I'm tired of listening to his whinin'."

Gareth considered his old man for a moment and looked back out into the darkness, this time knowing there wasn't anything there. He put his hand on the old man's shoulder. Cooper tried to shake it off again, but Gareth held on. "There's no one out here, Deddy. Just us."

"Tell him we had to do it. Tell him." Cooper shook his flask at the woods, spilling whiskey on the ground. "He just talks and talks and talks with nothing to say. I can't shut him up, boy. We need to shut him up."

"There's no one out here, Deddy. Uncle Rye's dead. You're just confused, is all. Come on inside." This wasn't the first time Gareth had witnessed his father talking to himself, not making any sense, but this was the first time he'd given his hallucination a name. Uncle Rye died out there in the woods when Gareth was nine years old. He tried to contain it, but Cooper never really recovered from losing his brother in that accident. The older he got, the more it seeped through the cracks in his armor. Gareth barely remembered the man. "Just come inside, Deddy. We can sort this out later."

Cooper sipped at the flask and let his son lead him into the house. Annette smelled the whiskey on them both as she handed her newborn baby over to its daddy and granddaddy. If she could've got up and run off right then, she just might've. She closed her eyes and saw Alaska.

3.

Annette had always heard that blood was spilt by the bucketful on Bull Mountain. Hell, she'd even witnessed some of it, but she also knew from experience that sometimes it happened one drop at a time. She didn't leave Gareth the first time he hit her. She was drunk in love with him ever since that bloody night at his father's house, and the slap came more as a shock than an assault. She didn't even remember what set him off. It didn't matter. She would come to find out that it was impossible to gauge what would set him off once he put a drunk on. He carried the burden of leadership on his shoulders and sometimes he lost his head. She understood that. He wouldn't do it again. But he did. The second time he hit her was in front of their two sons, Halford and Buckley. She was eight months pregnant with their third. He was drunk on corn whiskey, but that was no different from most every other night. When they were younger, the whiskey on his breath turned her on. It always led to dark, violent sex. She used to crave it, and shiver at the thought of it. Now the stink of liquor was only a precursor to a different kind of darkness. A violence she prayed would pass over her like a thundercloud. Sometimes it did. Sometimes it didn't. He never hit the children, but she could see it brewing right behind his eyes. If her sons had been born daughters they wouldn't have been shown the same mercies. She tried to convince herself Gareth would always see her the way he did back when she wore the Ruby Bliss lipstick and barely weighed a hundred pounds, but she was fooling herself. She became more of a burden to him as each son was born, as if a part of the love and respect he had for her was transferred into each new boy until one day there would be nothing left for her. The thought of it woke her at night, slick with sweat, her heart beating like a hammer in her chest.

The night Gareth backhanded her at the dinner table in front of her children, Halford let a small laugh escape before he covered his mouth with both hands to stifle it. She thought she might get sick. She wiped a single drop of blood from her nose with a cloth napkin and watched it soak in. It spread across the fabric like a cancer. She saw the sum of her entire life in that growing crimson stain, and in a perfect moment of clarity she knew that when the baby growing in her belly was born, she would have served her purpose. She'd be used up. The days of passionate lovemaking and planning the future with her dangerous new husband and stable of loyal sons were a distant and fading memory. Her life as the partner and confidante to an exciting, powerful man was over. She'd be regarded as no more than a burdensome housekeeper to this family of men. He'd teach her sons to view her that way. The boys would be raised in his image. There was no stopping it. She'd spend the rest of her life living in fear, watching her sons be poisoned, until the one night she stepped too far to the left or right of what was expected of her. Then Gareth would kill her. She was sure of it.

4.

Clayton Arthur Burroughs was born on December 22, 1972. He was named after Annette's father. A small indulgence Gareth allowed her. The family enjoyed one of the biggest Christmas celebrations in the mountain's history.

When Annette recovered from the trauma of childbirth she would leave, without a word or a note. She would vanish into the night as if she had never been there at all. It would have been her fate regardless, but this way it was on her terms. Maybe she could go to Alaska. She would never be looked for. She was sure of that. She would just be referred to as "that no-good bitch that run out on a good man and her three adoring children."

"How could she?" was the question everyone would ask.

"How could she not?" would be her answer.

CHAPTER

10

GARETH BURROUGHS

1973

1.

Gareth pulled the business card from the center pocket of his overalls and tossed it on the table. "Tell them what you told me," he said.

Jimbo Cartwright picked up the card and sat back in his chair. He looked around the table at Ernest Pruitt, Albert Valentine Jr.—Big Val to his friends—and the old man. Cooper didn't add much to these meetings anymore, but Gareth insisted that he be present, out of respect. "We got us a problem, fellas," Jimbo said. "And this guy?" He held up the card between two fingers. "This guy is the solution. A situation like yesterday can't be allowed to happen again. We got lucky and y'all know it. It won't happen like that again. We can't afford to lose any footing here. If Milkbone Arnie or the Hall boys figure out we don't have the firepower to protect these crops, they're going to push harder than they did yesterday and we're gonna lose."

"So what do we do?" Ernest said.

"We acquire sufficient firepower from this guy." Jimbo tossed the card back on the table. Ernest reached for it, but Val picked it up first.

"Wilcombe Exports?" he said, reading aloud.

"We need guns," Jimbo said. "This guy Wilcombe has guns."

"How do you know him?" Ernest asked. Val handed him the card.

"Last year when me and Jenny were having our troubles, I spent some time riding in Florida. Before I came home and threw in with Gareth."

"Riding?" Ernest asked.

"Yeah, riding."

"Riding what?"

"Harleys. What the fuck else would I be riding?"

"Take it easy," Ernest said. "I didn't know you were into that kinda stuff."

"I am. I mean, I was. I had me a brand-spanking-new Electra Glide Classic. Traditional colors. Jenny made me sell it."

Val smirked. "Did you ask Jenny for permission to be here?"

"Kiss my white ass, Val."

"Get to the point, Jimbo," Gareth said.

"Right. Anyway, I fell in with an outfit out of Jacksonville making a little side money working for a fella named Bracken Leek. The guy's solid. Good people. He's a big boy, too, Val. About your size."

Val shrugged.

"Anyway. We made some money, a lot of money, and I trust him. Him and this guy Wilcombe are joined at the hip, and guns are his thing—big guns."

"Where does he get them?" Val asked. "Gareth has gone to great lengths to keep us off any federal radars. We can't put that in jeopardy."

"We won't," Jimbo said.

"It might," Val said. "If, say, a massive shipment of traceable weapons stolen from the military led the United States government straight up our ass."

"They're not stolen."

"So where do they come from?" Ernest said.

"That was my first concern, too," Gareth said. "Tell them, Jimbo."

"They build them," Jimbo said. "Wilcombe Exports has factories throughout the Panhandle, Central Florida, and Alabama. Mostly, they build custom motorcycle parts for shops and motorheads all over the world, but some of their larger facilities are capable of building *other* things."

"Other things," Val repeated.

"Yes, other things."

"And how do you know all this?" Ernest asked.

"Because I've seen it. Bracken showed me. I'm telling you. These guys are stand-up. This solves our problem. I'm not talking about buying some secondhand guns with the serial numbers filed off from some colored street hustlers in Atlanta—no offense, Val."

Val blew Jimbo a kiss and flicked him a bird.

"I'm talking about fifty to a hundred untraceable semiautomatic assault rifles to arm every man we've got working the crops, with access to another hundred more anytime we want. Ammo, too."

"Is this what you want, Gareth?" Ernest asked.

Gareth rubbed at his whiskers and looked at his father. "What do you think, Pop?"

Everyone turned to Cooper.

"Heh?" the old man said, shuffling his weight in the seat.

"What do you think about the guns?"

"You already know what I think, boy."

"Well, why don't you tell us anyway?"

The old man pulled the thin, clear tubing that supplied his supplemental oxygen off his nose and let it hang around his neck. He tapped a thin finger on the table, clicking his fingernail against the hard wood. "I'll tell you, but I already know it ain't gonna matter nohow. You're just going to do what you want."

"Pop, I'm trying to—"

"This family doesn't need anything from anybody."

"Cooper," Ernest said. "This time it's different."

Cooper stared at Ernest hard and long. His look was cold with genuine confusion. "Who the hell are you?" he finally said. "And why are you in my house?"

Gareth and Val both narrowed their eyes at the old man, then at each other. "That's Ernest," Gareth said. "And this is *my* house, Pop. Not yours."

Cooper glared at his son. "You got all the answers, don't you, Rye? No tellin' you nothing. I don't know why you even ask." He tried to replace the tubing in his nose but couldn't. His hands had taken to shaking too bad. They did that when he got upset. Which meant they did that all the time.

"Jimbo, help him with that and do me a favor. Bring him home."

"Sure, Gareth," Jimbo said, and got up to reattach Cooper's oxygen. "Where are we with all this?"

Gareth looked at Val first, and the big man nodded. Ernest did, too.

Gareth slid back in his chair and seated a fresh plug of chew in his cheek. "Everybody give me a minute."

2.

After the room cleared, Gareth picked up the card and turned it over and over in his fingers, running his thumb over the embossed lettering. His father was sick—and dangerous—but he was right about keeping the family safe from outsiders. It felt wrong, but something had to be done. He sat folding, unfolding, and refolding the small cream-colored card between his calloused fingers. Plain block letters printed across it read WILCOMBE EXPORTS, with a phone number underneath with a 904 area code. He noticed the thing barely held a crease. *Some kind of goddamn crazy space paper,* he thought. He wondered how much something like that cost. He wondered what kind of asshole would pay for something like that.

The same kind of asshole that could supply him with what he needed.

The same kind of asshole Cooper had traded his sanity to keep his family safe from.

He slipped the card back into his pocket, walked over to the phone, and dialed. It rang twice before a husky female voice answered. Not at all what he expected an asshole to sound like. More like a vampy late-night deejay spinning those terrible disco records.

"Wilcombe Exports. How can I help you?" The woman's voice dripped with enough honey, Gareth almost asked for a meeting with her instead of her boss. He centered himself and spit a string of tobacco juice into a coffee-can spittoon. "I need to speak with Mr. Wilcombe."

"May I ask who's calling?"

"Go ahead."

There was a long pause on the line before the woman's voice finally said, "Sir?"

Gareth spit again. "Look, honey, my name's Gareth Burroughs. I got this card from a fella named James Cartwright. You might know him as Jimbo or you might not. Why don't you go ahead and put your boss on the phone."

"Please hold the line, Mr. Burroughs," the woman said without losing a bit of her late-night sizzle. Gareth listened to a few seconds of David Bowie crooning "Starman" on the line and looked at the phone like it had just mutated into a dead fish. He guessed that's what folks like Wilcombe were passing off for music in the sunny state of Florida. He held the phone a few inches from his ear until the line picked back up.

"Mr. Burroughs?"

"Yep."

"Oscar Wilcombe here." His voice was nasally and monotone. This was the voice Gareth expected. Weak. Fancy. Entitled. He already missed talking to the female. "Mr. Cartwright said you might be calling."

"He did, did he?"

"How can I help you, Mr. Burroughs?"

Gareth also took the man's voice as foreign, but clearly he'd been stateside long enough to make his accent barely noticeable. *Probably Cubano,* he thought. *Florida is full of them Cubanos.*

"I wanted to let you know I'll be down your way in a few days. Was hoping to bend your ear on some business."

"Yes. Yes, of course." There was the sound of the phone being muffled, and Gareth thought he could make out another voice besides Wilcombe's—a man's voice. Although Jimbo had already taken him from the room, he felt his father's stare across the table from him, and the faint clicking of his fingernail on the wood.

"This family doesn't need anything from anybody."

He shook it off. It was the only idea on the table, and he wasn't his father.

"You still there, Wilcombe?"

"Yes, yes, Mr. Burroughs. Three days' time works well for me. I can assume you'll be bringing something along to make the trip worthwhile for everyone involved?"

"If that means the quote I got from Cartwright, then I reckon it would be a good assumption."

"Outstanding. When you arrive in Jacksonville, call this number and Julie will make all the arrangements."

"Julie, right."

Wilcombe might have said something else, but Gareth hung up.

3.

Three days later, Gareth, Val, and Jimbo checked in to a roadside motel off the interstate in Jacksonville. Gareth called the number on the card from the room phone and got the address for the meet from Julie. Jimbo tucked a camo duffel bag containing thirty grand under one of the room's twin-size beds and sat down.

"Jimbo, you stay," Gareth said. "Don't leave that money alone for a second, and put a hole through anybody that tries to get through but us. Even if you know them."

Jimbo tapped the hand cannon under his shirt. "I got this, brother."

One hour later Val and Gareth pulled the truck up in front of a bar with three dressed-down Harleys parked in front. The bikes were all black—no ornate silver-trimmed saddlebags or flashy paint jobs— just three squat beasts hitched like horses to a post outside a saloon. The building itself was a one-story concrete block with nothing to even signify it was a bar except a flickering MILLER TIME neon hanging in one of the rectangular fixed windows lining the top of the storefront. A sun-faded OPEN sign hung from a suction cup stuck to the plate-glass door. Gareth had expected more. He had expected the place to look like a scene from Sturgis or *Easy Rider*, but aside from the hogs outside, it looked more like a tax attorney's office. Considering Wilcombe's fancy accent, MC errand boys, and hot-shit-sounding secretary, this place was nothing short of a dank shithole.

After exchanging an underwhelmed look, Gareth and Val got out of the truck and walked to the door. Gareth put his hand on the glass but paused before pushing it open.

"I gotta tell you, Val, I'm not sold on this idea. I'm out of my element here."

"That makes two of us."

"If this goes south . . ." Gareth said.

"It won't. You're Gareth Burroughs. You're fucking invincible." Both men smiled, but only briefly. Gareth took a breath and pushed open the door.

4.

They both let their eyes adjust to the sickly blue electric light and took a quick inventory of the patrons and the layout. To their left, two bikers were playing pool under a hanging Pabst Blue Ribbon lamp, and a thin bartender with a huge Wyatt Earp–style mustache stood behind the bar. His facial hair gave him tusks like a walrus. All three of them were sporting JACKSONVILLE JACKALS patches on their cuts. One of the men playing pool looked able to handle himself—tall, with lots of bulky muscle crammed into a denim jacket. His buddy, on the other hand, looked like he hadn't skipped a meal in all of his fiftysomething years. He was soft and pudgy, with a long, stringy gray ponytail. The size-up was reassuring. Three men in an open room matched the three bikes parked outside. That didn't count what could be out back, or in the bathroom to the right, or on the other side of the door behind the bar. Gareth guessed it led to a kitchen or a storage room. It could serve as an ambush point or an escape route, but if shit went sideways, Gareth knew right away his chance of getting out of this box, as it stood, was a fifty-fifty shot. He breathed a little easier, but not much. He'd faced worse odds back home.

They stood in the doorway while every eyeball in the place locked on them.

It was understandable. Gareth may not have looked like much under his straw cowboy hat and canvas jacket—a pale-skinned redhead, weighing in at one-sixty on a good day—but Val was a different story. Val was a solid-muscled farm boy, every bit of three hundred pounds. He was also black as night, no stars. He looked like a mountain of Kentucky coal in a flannel shirt.

They slowly crossed the room, and Gareth took a seat at the bar. Val stood behind him with his arms crossed, trading stink-eye stares with Moe and Curly at the pool table. From the bulges under their jackets, Val counted at least one gun per man.

"Can I help you boys with something?" the walrus said to Gareth.

"Nope, but we'll take two beers. Don't matter which."

"You planning on drinking both of them?"

Gareth just stared blankly at the man. "Do you have a problem?"

"Not with you. I believe we're expecting you. But your boy there might have to wait outside."

"My *boy*? Oh, you mean Val." Gareth motioned with a thumb over his shoulder. "That guy's name is Albert Valentine. Named after his deddy. Some people call him Albert, but not many. Most folks call him Val. You know, short for Valentine."

"I don't give a rat's ass what the boy's name is."

"Apparently. Because if you did, you'd know that it's pretty damn rude to call him *boy*. Nobody calls him *boy*, and you just did it twice. My advice is to not let it happen a third time."

"Tuesday's Gone" played on the jukebox, filling the gap of silence while the bartender sized Gareth up.

"Well, when this train ends, I'll try again, / But I'm leaving my woman at home . . ."

Gareth scanned the door behind the bartender for movement or shadows. He saw nothing. Two minutes in and they were already on the wrong foot with these guys. His palms were sweaty. He needed to keep his talking big enough to back them down but not too big to fit his foot in his mouth. "So are you gonna pour a couple beers or do I need to do it myself?" he said.

The bartender narrowed his eyes and leaned down on the bar with his elbows. "Like I said, if you're the fella I got a call about, then I been expecting you. I'd be happy to pour you a brew, but this here is my place, and I reserve the right to serve, or not serve, whoever the hell I please. So, friend of the boss or not, I'm gonna have to ask you to have your pet gorilla there wait outside, or head back to whatever Mississippi swamp y'all come from."

"We're from Georgia."

"Seriously, mister, I don't give a fuck where you're from. Those are the rules."

Val, who'd been silent up to this point, as if the conversation behind him wasn't about him, finally turned around and sat down on the stool next to Gareth. Without saying a word, he reached into the shirt pocket of his flannel and pulled out a roll of cash the size of a fist. He peeled off a hundred-dollar bill and laid it on the bar. He let the weasel barkeep eyeball it, and Val watched his expression change from angry bigot to curious bigot.

"Mister," Val said, tucking the rest of the bankroll back in his pocket, "I understand this is your place, and you have the right to run it however you see fit."

"That's right," the bartender said, not taking his eyes off the prize on the bar.

"It's also clear to me that you don't like black people that much, and that, too, is your right, but I got to tell you, that remark about me being a gorilla was just downright mean. I'm not a gorilla, I'm a human being. And to be completely honest, that hurt my feelings a little bit."

The barkeep said nothing but did shift his eyes from the cash to keep Val's stare.

"I'll get over it," Val said, "I'm a big boy. No harm, no foul. But the thing is, my friend here is supposed to meet someone you apparently work for, and this is the place they chose to meet. So we're kind of stuck."

"Not my problem."

"No, sir, no, it's not. But all my friend here is asking for is one beer each to enjoy while we wait. We ain't looking for no trouble. Just one beer each. That's it."

The bartender looked at Gareth, then back down at the hundred-dollar bill.

"I can't break that this early in the day."

"You can keep the change," Val said.

The bartender breathed a heavy sigh under his massive mustache. "All right, then. One beer each, and if Oscar ain't here by then, you're waiting in the car."

"That's a deal," Val said.

The bartender swept the cash up from the bar and stuck the bill in his own shirt pocket. He pulled two frosted mugs from the cooler and looked at them for a moment like he was considering something. He put one of them back and reached under the bar. He pulled out a red plastic cup from a sleeve, looked at Val with a contented smirk, and filled them both with draft beer. He set them on the bar, giving the glass to Gareth and the plastic cup to Val. "No sense in dirtying up a clean glass," he said with a grin. Val stared at the cup and felt the tension increase in his jaw. Gareth felt it, too, because he put a hand on Val's shoulder to calm him.

"Thank you," Gareth said. The bartender just smiled and moved down the bar. Gareth picked up his beer, took a sip, and wiped foam from his beard. Val hesitated but sipped his, too. One of the bikers from the pool table, the meathead, approached the end of the bar.

"Everything all right over here, Pinky?"

"We're all good, Rodd."

"That him?" Rodd asked, tilting his head in Gareth's direction.

"Yeah," Pinky said. "That's him."

Rodd drummed his fingers on the bar and walked back to the table.

"Pinky?" Gareth whispered to Val. Val shrugged and both men picked up their beers. Gareth sipped his, but Val turned his up and finished it off in two large gulps. Gareth dropped his chin to his chest and sighed.

Pinky picked up the cup and tossed it in the trash. "Well, I guess you best be on your way, then," he said. Val just stared at where the cup had been—the skin on his face tight.

Gareth wiped more suds from his beard and fished out a napkin from a plastic caddy. "Sure thing, Pinky," he said, putting a hand up to take the bartender's attention away from Val. "But can I ask you something first?"

"As long as he's going."

"You gotta tell me, what in God's name is that infernal racket you got us listening to in here?"

Pinky looked jarred at that. "What, the music?"

"Is *that* what that is?" Gareth said.

Pinky listened again as if to confirm his answer. Ronnie Van Zant was pleading for just three steps toward the door.

"That's Lynyrd Skynyrd," Pinky said indignantly. "That's the pride of Jacksonville. The greatest southern rock band in the world."

Gareth scoffed and elbowed Val, who was still glaring down at the bar. "That ain't no southern music I ever heard. Where's the banjo, or the fiddle? It sounds more like a bunch of retards tryin' to fuck a doorknob."

"Maybe it ain't for you, Gareth," Val said, still not looking up. "Maybe it's only for pig-fuckin' faggots named Pinky."

"What the hell?" Pinky said, and his face reddened like he'd just gotten slapped. "What did you say, boy?"

"And . . . that makes three," Gareth said.

Pinky reached under the bar and came back with a wooden baseball bat, but for a big man, Val moved as fast as a cobra. He grabbed the bat with Pinky still attached and effortlessly yanked him into a head butt. The sound of Pinky's nose breaking made Gareth wince. Pinky let go of the Louisville Slugger and stumbled backward into a row of liquor bottles. A few fell and crashed to the floor. Gareth spun around in his seat, his gun already out and trained on the two bikers, but they already stood holding their own weapons out.

"Well, shit," Gareth said.

Pinky held his bleeding nose and swayed behind the bar, trying to regain focus. He tried to speak, but all that came out was a wet grunt.

"You don't like niggers?" Val asked. "How you like getting your nose broke by one? Now you got a good reason not to like us." Val spun around and looked at the other two bikers aiming guns at him and Gareth. He was still holding the bat.

"Put your gun down," the bigger one named Rodd said.

"Not gonna happen," Gareth said. "Your buddy had that coming. You put your guns down so we can talk about it."

"Sorry, man," Val said softly to Gareth. Gareth shot him a terse look but didn't answer.

"We got you two to one," Rodd said. "Drop your gun or I'm gonna blow your fuckin' head off."

"Nah," Gareth said. "I bet I take at least one of you. I do this shit all the time, boys. You sure you can hit me from there? You don't look too sure of yourself. I know I can."

"He won't have to," Pinky said, and racked a shotgun behind them. Val took a deep breath and Gareth had no choice but to give up the ghost and lower his gun. That's when the front door opened and two more men joined the party.

"What the hell is going on?" Oscar Wilcombe said.

5.

Wilcombe was a small man. Thin and squatty, with thinning sand-colored hair. He wore a dark suit and wire-rimmed glasses. He also carried a metal-reinforced briefcase. The man walking behind him couldn't have been any more the polar opposite. He was an oak tree, well over six feet tall, shiny bald, with gray-blue eyes. He wore faded blue jeans and a denim jacket with the sleeves torn off. His arms were ripped and vascular, both covered from shoulder to wrist with intricate tattoo work, the kind that takes a lifetime of commitment to finish. His jacket also carried the Jackals' rocker on the back, along with a patch above the breast pocket that read PRESIDENT.

"Jackals, lower your guns now," Wilcombe said.

Pinky wiped some of the blood from his enormous mustache onto his shoulder but kept the shotgun in place. "Oscar, these sons of—"

"I said put it down, Pinkerton."

Pinky was hesitant but lowered the gun. The other two bikers looked to the bigger man behind Wilcombe. He nodded and they lowered their guns as well. Gareth took notice of that. The bald guy had to be the top dog in Wilcombe's kennel. The order came from Wilcombe, but the men needed the big boy's approval to obey. That was good to know.

"Mr. Burroughs, I presume," Wilcombe said.

"That's right," Gareth said.

Wilcombe took a few steps into the middle of the room. "Can we all put our weapons away?" he said.

Gareth looked down at the Colt in his hand. "Of course," he said, and slid it back into his pants. Val tossed the bat to the floor as he and the big man with Wilcombe sized each other up. They looked evenly matched. That only made Gareth more uncomfortable. He'd brought Val for intimidation. The President evened that out.

"I thought we agreed to meet at nine o'clock?" Wilcombe said.

"We did. We were early," Gareth said. Wilcombe set the briefcase down by one of the tables and introduced himself, first holding his hand out to Gareth and then to Val. They both shook the man's hand, but Val's eyes never left the President.

"I'm Oscar Wilcombe, and this is my associate, Bracken Leek." The bald man didn't bother to shake any hands, he just turned and clicked the lock on the door.

"It's a pleasure," Gareth said.

"What happened, Pinky?" Bracken said.

Val answered that. "Your man was rude."

"Fuck you, coon," Pinky barked through a blood-soaked bar rag he held up to his face.

Val looked at Bracken. "See?"

"And you had to straighten him out? Is that what happened?" Bracken moved down the bar to survey the damage. "You always come into a man's house and beat him bloody like that?"

"If he's a piece-of-shit racist, I do," Val said.

"Maybe you should try that dance with me." Bracken took a step toward Val, but Gareth put a hand between them. "Enough," he said, and turned to Wilcombe. "Is this going to be a problem?"

"Mr. Burroughs, I'm going to need you to explain to my associate what took place here, so we can move past it."

"Fair enough," Gareth said. "Your man there, Pinky, wasn't none too happy with my friend being in his bar. Called him a gorilla. Called him his boy. Three times, if I remember correctly. Val don't like that shit. Neither do I. I gave him a chance to make nice, but he thought he would get all Ty Cobb and try to swing that bat over there at my friend's head." Gareth pointed to the Louisville Slugger on the floor. "My friend took offense."

Bracken and Val stood close enough to kiss.

"Well, then, no, Mr. Burroughs, we don't have a problem. Rodd, will you and Jeremy assist Pinkerton with resetting his nose? Clean him up and take care of the mess behind the bar." Again they waited for Bracken to approve. He backed out of Val's face and picked up the bat, then tossed it to Pinky, and the three bikers disappeared through the back door. Bracken poured himself a whiskey.

"My apologies, Mr. Burroughs. If I'd known you'd have a colored gentleman with you, I would have given some warning."

"But seeing that we're from Georgia, you just assumed we all run around with white hoods on, right?"

Wilcombe smiled slightly and held his hands up in a shrug, then motioned to the booth behind him. "Shall we?"

"Right," Gareth said. Val retook his seat at the bar.

The little man sat down and pushed his glasses up on his nose. "Now, what is it I can do for you?"

6.

"I need to be able to protect my family's interests. I understand you can help me with that."

"And by 'interests,' you mean the marijuana business your family has cultivated for itself?" Wilcombe talked matter-of-factly, like he was discussing the weather. Gareth studied the little man's face. "I guess Jimbo has been talking out of school," he said.

"Mr. Cartwright has kept me apprised of your family's business dealings, yes."

"If by 'business' you mean three thousand acres of the finest bud in the Southeast, then yeah, you have a good grasp on what we're doing up there."

"We have access to product here in Florida, if we so desired," Wilcombe said. His voice was flat—uninterested and unimpressed.

"I'm not here selling," Gareth said. "But if I was, no one around here could compete. Not for the price, and not with so little hassle. I bet the Cubanos down here are always shuffling to hide product and transport from the feds. Am I right? Ask me how we've been steady growing for more than two decades without a single federal intrusion."

"Okay, I'll bite. How *are* you keeping it from the feds? That's a lot of land to hide from DEA helicopters."

"Geography," Gareth said, and smiled wide.

"Geography," Wilcombe repeated.

"Yup. You see, my father built our entire family fortune on his ability to hide things in the woods. Back in the day, the stills had to run twenty-four-seven if they were going to generate enough shine to get us into the big leagues. We couldn't afford to have any of them found. Not one. And we didn't. Knowing the lay of the land was essential to that fact. He got extremely good at it. Good enough to outsell those cousin-fuckers up in Virginia without taking any of the heat."

"But three thousand acres is a little more difficult to conceal than an average whiskey distiller, correct?"

"Yes, it is, but my father, the crafty sum' bitch that he was, figured out that our mountain has some unique geographical positioning along the northern face. He cleared the forestry out in strips in a way that creates blind spots from the air. We can work those fields all day every day and wave at the federals flying overhead. Dumb bastards are none the wiser."

Wilcombe looked genuinely impressed. "That is indeed something to be proud of. How did you explain what you were doing to the contractors? How did you get the permits?"

Gareth scratched at his beard and sat back in the booth. "Contractors? We didn't have no contractors. We had six men, myself included. And hell, I was just a boy. We cleared, primed, and planted that land, working from plans my deddy drew out with a pencil and a slide rule."

"That's impressive, Mr. Burroughs."

"I know."

"And the processing of said product?"

"Is done completely in-house by men I've known my whole life. We grow it, cure it, dry it, bale it, and package it out all ourselves. No outside help."

"Yet here you are, looking for outside help."

"That's right. Here I am."

Wilcombe pushed his glasses up on his nose again. "Well, I'm not sure how much our mutual friend told you, but if you're looking for distribution into Florida, I hate that you came all this way just for me to tell you that isn't something I can do."

Gareth scratched at his beard again. "I'd hate that, too. Luckily for me, it's like I told you. I ain't here selling. I'm buying. We want guns."

Wilcombe smiled. "I think that might be something I can help you with." He reached down beside him and laid the briefcase on the table. He spun in the combination on the small dials with his thumbs and popped the locks. He opened the lid and turned it toward Gareth so he could inspect the contents. Gareth reached into the form-fitted case and removed the collapsible pieces of an AR-15 assault rifle. He turned them over in his hands and clicked the stock into place. "Well, if you can rustle up a few more of these, I reckon you *can* help me."

"As many as you can afford, my friend. But they are not cheap."

Gareth smiled.

"Bracken, bring Mr. Burroughs and me two fingers of Jameson."

The big man looked unhappy but fished the bottle of Irish whiskey from the shelf. He poured the whiskey, picked up the glasses, and brought them to the table.

The top dog is still just a dog, Gareth thought, and pushed the glass away.

"Make mine Evan Williams, Mr. President, and don't forget to include my partner in the round."

Bracken looked to Wilcombe, who nodded approval, then walked back to the bar. He returned and set a glass and a bottle of Evan on the table.

"Pour it yourself."

"Thanks, *Brack-en*," Gareth said, exaggerating the sound of the man's name. He poured the bourbon three fingers deep and drained it. Val, who'd sat silent until now, looked back at his friend and made a sound in his throat loud enough for them all to hear.

"I'm good, Val," Gareth said. Wilcombe and Bracken exchanged a swift curious look as Gareth refilled and downed another whiskey like it was apple juice. He filled the glass a third time and let it sit. Bracken took a seat next to Wilcombe.

"*Brack-en*," Gareth said again. "What the hell kind of name is that anyway?" The big man didn't answer. Gareth put the gun on the case without bothering to break it down and slid it back across the table to Wilcombe. "So you built that?" he said, motioning to the gun.

"I suppose our mutual friend *has* been—how did you say?— talking out of school," the little man said. "It's sufficient that I have them."

"Well, I like my people to keep me *apprised*, and all that, too. So . . . you build these?"

"I do," Wilcombe said.

"You don't steal them?"

"They're not stolen." Wilcombe looked insulted. He quickly slid the case over to Bracken, who picked up the gun, disassembled it, and returned it to the foam-rubber inlay. He clicked the case shut and set it at his feet.

"Motorcycle parts, right?" Gareth said, mulling it over. "That how you hooked up with the Hells Angels?"

Bracken twisted his weight in the booth and began to say something, but Wilcombe put a hand on his forearm to remind him whose conversation this was. "Mr. Burroughs, I'm quite sure you understand better than most the concept of respect, as was demonstrated by your friend at the bar earlier on Mr. Pinkerton. I backed your move there, because I believed you and your associate were righteous in your action, but now you are bordering on disrespecting me and the people I consider to be my family. Family is important to you?"

Gareth didn't speak, but Wilcombe didn't wait for an answer, either. "My father, God rest his soul, and Mr. Leek here started this club in 1965, and since then the Jacksonville Jackals have been an integral part of creating and sustaining the very business that has brought you to our door. They are men of honor and deserve to be treated as such. Are we on the same page here?"

Gareth finished the bourbon in his glass, swishing it around in his mouth before swallowing it. "Fair enough," he said. "I want two hundred to start."

"I can do that. I'll need twenty-five thousand up front and another twenty-five on delivery."

"I can do that."

"I can assume you brought the money with you?"

Gareth smiled. "It's close. I'll have it when I need it."

Bracken reached into his jacket. Val took notice, tensed and readied himself. "Relax," Bracken said, and slowly removed his hand, bringing out a crumpled pack of Lucky Strikes. He shook one out and laid the pack on the table. Gareth took one and waited for Bracken to light it. He didn't.

"There's a warehouse off the highway I use for these kinds of transactions. Mr. Cartwright knows where it is. You did bring Mr. Cartwright with you?"

"He's around," Gareth said.

"Meet Mr. Leek there tomorrow morning with the money, and your problems at home are as good as solved."

Bracken stood up and Wilcombe slid from the booth. He nodded to Gareth and then to Val, straightened out the creases in his suit, and left, leaving the briefcase on the table.

"Eight-thirty sharp," Bracken said.

"We'll be there."

Gareth motioned to Val and they followed Wilcombe out the door.

11

GARETH BURROUGHS

1973

1.

The motel room was a cold, filthy box. Gareth had stayed in one like this before to handle some business up in Huntsville and it looked exactly the same. He imagined that, aside from bars on the door, there was no difference between a room like this and a prison cell. He stood naked in front of the full-length mirror running up the wall next to the vanity, holding a bottle of whiskey, looking at his reflection in the glass—really looking—taking himself in. He rarely stopped to see the toll his life was taking on him. His body was taut and cut, like a boxer's, cords of sun-reddened farm muscle toned by years of hard work. Work he was proud of. Not the kind of work that resulted in cardboard boxes like this room, it was the kind that resulted in empires. The kind of work his father had taught him how to do. He took a drink from a bottle that was practically empty and stared at the collection of scars from various scraps and foolish ideas. Fights born of both anger and good times. The most foolish idea being the tattoo on his chest that spelled *Annette* in cursive letters above his left nipple—where his heart was supposed to be. He snorted to himself. It was her idea to get it done. Jimbo knew a fella who did it right out of the back of his trailer with a homemade rig made from a car battery and a spool of copper wire. He got it done on their first wedding anniversary. They were supposed to get it done together, hers and his brands meant to prove their love to each other, but Annette chickened out in the chair. Follow-through was never her strong suit. It wasn't the first promise she'd broken—or the last. Probably best she didn't get it anyway. Less explaining she'd have to do to the next poor soul she latched herself on to. He rubbed his thumb over the raised ink in the tattoo and used the rest of his hand to knead the thick muscle in his neck.

He carried his share of scars, but for the most part managed to keep his body whole and in pretty good shape. His face, on the other hand, looked like it belonged to someone else entirely, and maybe it did. It was haggard and weathered like saddle leather. His eyes were disappearing more and more every year behind the crow's-feet branching out from the corners of his narrow sockets, and the skin under his eyes was loose and dry. It was an old man's face.

His old man's face.

He wasn't completely sure why, but he was beginning to hate it. His father used to be the cornerstone of everything. Now he was just a crazy, feeble old coot, more embarrassing than anything else. Gareth wondered how long he had before he would follow the same path.

The young girl sprawled out behind him on the queen-size bed rolled over onto her belly. She was a gift from his new partner. She just showed up at the door with the bottle of whiskey—the same brand he'd drunk at Wilcombe's bar. He wasn't a cheater, but Annette was gone, so it didn't matter. He was drunk and angry, and a go at this one was just what he needed. Now, though, he was ready for her to leave. He hadn't bothered to clean the slick of her off himself. He just crawled off her, laid a couple of twenties on the table, and went back to drinking. He hoped she would take his money and silence as a hint to collect her things and shove off. She didn't. That made Gareth angry, but then again, everything made him angry. Anger was the only constant he had these days. He should be thrilled to have a huge problem taken care of after this deal with Wilcombe and his guns. He should be relaxed after bedding this sweet, young piece of tail, but he wasn't. He was angry, and he felt the slow burn of it right underneath his skin. Every sip of whiskey brought it closer to the surface.

"Oh, Papa, come back to bed," the girl said. "Let me rub some of that tension out of your shoulders. I've been told I'm pretty good at it. Back in Mobile, I took some classes. I thought about doing it full-time, but you know, life and all."

Gareth took another pull from the bottle and rubbed the tattoo. "You mean whorin' and all?"

"Well, you ain't gotta be all mean about it, Papa." She pulled the motel's scratchy wool blanket over her bare ass and patted the bed next to her. "Come sit yourself down right here."

Gareth pictured himself dragging her out of the bed by her hair.

She called herself Angel, but Gareth knew that was her working name. She was more likely to be a Betsy, or a Ruth Ann—something painfully ordinary. He watched in the mirror as she squeezed at one of the pillows, sinking her bleached-blond head into the starched cotton. Gareth sneered and curled his lip in disgust. He wanted her gone. He was done with her. But there she was, frolicking in the sheets like it was Sunday morning and he was going to cook her up some pancakes and bacon. Gareth picked up his smokes from the vanity and lit up. Angel came up behind him and took over rubbing his neck. Her skin was like milk—pale, scarless, and perfect. Nothing stretched out or ruined by childbirth, like Annette's. Her mouth was small and round, and Gareth thought about kissing it just a few minutes earlier. She tasted like hard candy. The kind his grandma kept in little dishes around her house, all sticky and tart. Nothing like Annette, she tasted clean—like rain.

"Hey, baby, you in there?" Angel said, and waved a hand in front of Gareth's blank expression. He looked at her pressed up behind him in the mirror and she smiled crookedly, her lips curling up on the left side. She started to rub the muscles in his shoulders. It was like trying to soften granite. She rubbed her hard raspberry nipples across his back, but he was over her and it did nothing but irritate him further.

"You're bound up tight, sugar. I could have sworn you just had wild sex with a pretty girl. I got you off. I know I did. I normally don't let a man come inside me, but you were so into it. I know I was. That must make you special. Not like all these boys around here."

"Stop talking," Gareth said, and took a swig from the bottle.

"You're starting to hurt my feelings," she said.

"You're starting to irritate me with all the mouth."

Angel moved her hands down his back and scratched her way up, using pink lacquered fingernails to follow the curves of his back. "I know it's none of my business and all," she said, "but you can talk to me, too, you know. That's part of the package."

Gareth took another hard gulp from the bottle, finishing it off, and set it down on the vanity. Angel took notice of the tattoo on Gareth's chest and leaned in over his shoulder to get a better look. "Who's Annette? Your girl back home?"

Gareth shook her hands off him hard enough for her to back off toward the bed. "None of your business," he said. He picked up the bottle, forgetting it was empty, and slammed it back down on the vanity with enough force to break it. The glass cut his hand. He put the bleeding edge of his palm in his mouth and Angel backed away. She quickly wrapped herself with a sheet from the bed.

"I'm sorry, Papa. I didn't mean nothing by it."

Gareth glared at himself in the mirror. Seeing his father. Hearing his wife. Tasting his own blood. The sudden eruption of tears down his flushed cheeks surprised him as much as it did her.

"Oh, Papa. Don't cry. Let me make it better." She came back up behind him. "I can be Annette if you want me to."

Gareth stiffened and went cold. The tears disappeared as quickly as they'd come. He rubbed his thumb over the tattoo again. "You want to be Annette?" he said, and raised the broken bottleneck to his chest. Using the sharpened edge, he sliced into the skin above his nipple and carved through the letters inked into his skin. Blood poured down his chest and Angel jumped back.

"Jesus Christ. You're crazy," she said, and scanned the room for her clothes.

"You want to be Annette?" he said again, turning to face her.

Angel grabbed her dress, panties, and shoes from the floor and held them out in front of her.

"Hold on, mister, I didn't mean nothing by it. I'm just here for a good time. I can go now, okay? I can walk right out."

"Annette's a no-good bitch that thinks she can do better than me. She thinks she can say and do whatever she pleases and up and leave whenever she wants."

"I'm real sorry about that, mister. That sounds really awful, but . . . but I ain't Annette."

Gareth pulled down a hand towel from a silver ring on the wall and wiped the blood from the fresh gash on his chest. "Yeah, but you want to be."

Angel grabbed her purse from the side table and made a dash for the door, but, despite being blind drunk, Gareth was much faster. He reached out and grabbed a handful of white-blond hair. She dropped the purse, and makeup, cigarettes, and several unused condoms spilled out on the carpet.

"Ow. Please, Papa, I didn't—"

"—mean nothing by it. I know. And I'm not your fuckin' papa." Gareth pulled her back and tossed her petite naked frame onto the bed. She kicked and flailed her legs, bunching up the sheets, trying to slide out of the reach of the broken bottle, but once he was on top of her, she couldn't move. He straddled her, putting all of his weight on her chest, crushing the wind out of her, pinning her arms.

Angel screamed. He let go of her hair and slid his hand, slick with his own blood, over her mouth. He leaned in close when he spoke to her. The stink of whiskey and sweat coated her face like a film. She wanted to throw up.

"So, *Annette*, I was thinking about the last time you got lippy with me. You remember?"

Angel just stared back, wide-eyed, unable to answer or breathe through her mouth.

"The last time I had to straighten you out. I hit you right here." Gareth held the edge of the broken bottle to the side of Angel's nose. "Do you remember, *Annette*?"

Angel struggled to push her head down deeper into the pillow and out of the bottle's reach, but Gareth pushed down harder. She squeezed her eyes shut as she felt the glass press into her skin. She screamed through his hand, but no one could hear her. Blood spilled onto the sheets on both sides of her head, forming Rorschach wings on the cotton as he dragged the broken glass across her face.

When he was finished, he got off her and tossed the bottle to the floor. He walked back to the mirror and stared at the blood smeared across his arms and chest. He turned on the faucet and held his hands under the water until it was scalding.

Angel pulled herself to the floor and slowly crossed the carpet toward the door.

"Aw, now where you going?" Gareth said, and she stopped cold. "You don't wanna be my friend no more?" He squatted down and looked at her with the curiosity a hunter would give a wounded animal. "You can't leave until you get paid," he said. "I mean, you *are* a whore after all, right?" He swiped up the two twenties he had laid on the table earlier, crumpled the bills in his hand, and stuffed them into Angel's mouth. She gagged. He stood her up, opened the door, and threw her battered figure into the second-floor guardrail right next to where Val was standing.

"What the hell, Gareth?" he said.

"Get this bitch outta here," Gareth said, and closed the door.

Within minutes he was asleep.

2 .

Val came back out on the breezeway with a bath towel, a wet rag, and a thousand dollars in cash. "Hey, can you hear me?"

Angel shrank back from his voice, lifting her shoes and dress to block her face from this new threat.

"Don't be scared, girl. I'm not gonna hurt you. I want to help you, okay? I want to help." He held out the towel. She hesitated but finally lowered her shoes, snatched the towel from his hands and covered herself the best she could. The left side of her face was on fire and it hurt to breathe. Her ribs felt broken.

"You're . . . his . . . friend," she said between short, stuttered breaths.

"Yes, ma'am."

"He cut me . . . my face."

Val went to touch her cheek, but she winced and pulled away. "It hurts."

"Yes, ma'am. Here, put this on it." He handed her the wet rag. "Keep pressure on it like this." He took her hand in his and pressed the rag down on her wound.

"It hurts so bad."

"Yes, ma'am."

"Can you help me? Can you call the police, or an ambulance or something?"

Val scanned the parking lot below them, then cupped his mouth and sighed into his hands. "No, ma'am. I can help, but I can't do that."

"Can I use your phone, then, or something, please? I can't stay out here like this. Please? You said you wanted to help."

"I do, but you can't use my phone. If you call the police, or if they send an ambulance here, you'll need to explain yourself, and then someone is going to get killed."

"Someone *needs* to get killed." Angel propped herself up against the rail as best she could and dabbed the edge of the towel under her bloody nose. Val held a finger to his lips.

"Keep your voice down and listen to me. I won't call the police, or an ambulance, but I will call you a taxicab. You can get dressed and wait down by the street. I'll tell them where to pick you up."

Angel looked around on the ground until she spotted the twenties she had spit out lying on a steel grate next to her.

"Don't worry about the money," Val said. "I'll take care of it. Just wait for the cab and get yourself to a hospital."

Angel fidgeted under the towel, trying to pull her panties on with her free hand. Val averted his eyes. He reached into his shirt pocket, pulled out a thousand dollars in hundreds, and held it up for her to see. "Can you do that?" he said. "Can you go wait down by the street and then get yourself some help?"

Angel nodded.

"I'm serious, girl. If you send the police or anyone else here looking for the man in that room, things will not end well for you. Things will not end well for me, either. Do you understand?"

She nodded again.

"Say the words."

"I'll go to a hospital and I won't call the police."

"Or anyone else."

"Or anyone else."

"Promise me."

"I promise. Just let me put my clothes on before the rest of the world sees me like this."

"Of course," Val said. He helped the girl to her feet, trying to hold the towel in place to save what little dignity she had left, but it was useless. She gave up on the panties, kicking them off her leg, and tried to slip back into the black dress she'd thought she looked so pretty in a few hours ago. She started to cry again.

"Can you help me?"

"Yes, ma'am." Val helped her slide the dress up and over her shoulders, and it enveloped her like a shadow. She turned and lifted her hair, and Val secured the straps behind her neck. When she turned around to face him, she looked up and took the rag from her face.

"How bad do I look?" she said.

Val wiped the tears from the undamaged side of her face. "You are a beautiful girl," he said, and tucked the fold of cash into the girl's hand. She lowered her eyes and pressed the rag back to her face.

"You're not a very good liar," she said, and still holding her shoes, limped her way toward the stairs. She knew she would never be beautiful again.

12

BRACKEN LEEK

2015

1.

"Can I bum a smoke?"

"Can I bang your wife?"

Moe thought about that and tugged on the soul patch sprouting under his bottom lip. "If I say yes, *then* can I bum a smoke?"

Tilmon reached back into the stash under the steering wheel, grabbed his pack of Camel Lights, and shook one out for his partner. Moe lit up and went back to studying their route on a laminated map. The piece-of-shit GPS never worked this far out in the sticks. Tilmon watched Moe smoke from the corner of his eye. "How long we been doing this?" he said.

Moe looked up from the map and took a drag, tapping his ashes on the floorboard. "Doing what? Riding Highway 27?" He looked at his watch. "About two hours."

"No, I mean, how long we been riding together?"

Moe looked at his watch again, as if he'd set a timer at the beginning of their partnership. "Shit, man. I don't know. Almost two years, I think."

"Almost two years."

"Yeah, about that. Why?"

"I'm just curious."

Moe smoked his cigarette down to the filter and tossed the butt out the window. They burned up another mile of interstate before he bit. "Curious about what? The map? I like looking at the map."

"You can look at the map all you want. That doesn't bother me."

"Then what's up with the cryptic line of questioning?"

"What line? I asked you one thing."

Moe's ears started to burn. "For real, why?"

Tilmon slid his sunglasses up his forehead and pinched the oil off his nose with his thumb and forefinger. "Okay," he said, "I'll tell you. Two years we been riding together and in all that time I can't think of one time you brought enough smokes to make the trip."

Moe stared at him blankly. "Are you being serious right now?"

"Yeah, I'm being serious. Can you think of one time in two years you didn't have to bum off me sometime during the route? Just name one time."

"Go fuck yourself, Tilmon."

"Don't do that. Don't get all shitty about it. I'm just pointing something out. We both patched in about the same time, so I know we make about the same money, but not really, 'cause I got to carry your habit as well as my own. That shit adds up, man. If you think about it, it's kind of a shitty thing to do to a partner of almost two years."

"How much, Tilmon? How much you want?" Moe lifted his ass off the seat and pulled his wallet from his back pocket. "I got seventy . . . seventy-three dollars. Will that cover it?"

"Put your money away, Moe. I'm just trying to make a point. Look . . . we're losing Romeo."

Moe looked out the window at the large sideview mirror and saw the black '66 shovelhead Harley that had been tailing them pull over next to exit 118 to Broadwater Campground. Moe stuffed his wallet back in his pants and grabbed the radio handset.

"Romeo, what's going on back there, bro?"

Static.

"I gotta take a leak. Keep on truckin' and I'll catch up."

"Copy that. Bracken, you hear that?"

The voice of Bracken Leek, riding the Heritage Classic in front of Tilmon and Moe's box truck, came over the radio. *"Yeah, I got it. Do what you gotta do, Romeo, and get your ass back in gear."*

"Nothing to it but to do it," Romeo said.

Tilmon reached for his smokes. "Bro?"

"Huh?"

"A second ago, you called Romeo 'bro.' You can't stand that guy."

"Yeah, well, he don't hold two-year grudges over fuckin' cigarettes."

Tilmon rolled his eyes. "Jesus, I'm sorry I said anything." He held the pack out to his partner.

"Shove those up your ass, Tilmon."

"Keep sharp, boys," Bracken's voice blared over the radio. *"I don't like being a man down. Keep your eyes open."*

The men exchanged a curious look. The big man they were going to see practically owned the state police on this stretch. They'd been making this run uninterrupted for years. Bracken was getting old. Everything made the guy paranoid.

"*Moe, you copy?*"

Moe grabbed the handset. "We copy, boss. We're good back here."

"*Just confirm you heard me, and keep your eyes open.*"

"Copy that." Moe slid the radio back into the cradle. "The fuck is his problem?"

"No idea," Tilmon said.

"You two must've ate a bunch of asshole sandwiches before we left this morning."

Tilmon blew a lungful of smoke at him. "Give it a rest, dude. You know I was just messing with you. *Mi Camel, su Camel.* Here." He held the pack out again. Moe reached out to grab it, but the sudden jerk of the brakes slammed him into the door frame.

"What the hell, Tilmon?"

"Oh, shit. Do you see that?" Tilmon said, and pointed to Bracken's wobbling Heritage right before it dropped to its side and skidded off the two-lane highway in a screaming whirlwind of sparks and dust. Bracken covered his face and rolled across the blacktop into the tall saw grass. Tilmon slowed the box truck, but not enough to avoid the highway spikes someone had painted black and laid out across the asphalt. All four tires blew like shotgun blasts, and the truck fishtailed all over the road, slinging an un-seat-belted Moe all over the cab. He cracked his forehead into the windshield, spiderwebbing the glass, then thrust back down hard into the seat, taking another hard whack to the back of the head against the aluminum wall behind him. The truck finally came to a stop on the embankment, wedged in the dirt and tall grass. Tilmon sat frozen, both hands death-gripped to the wheel. Moe, who ended up mostly on the floorboards, held his battered head with one hand and wiped the blood from his eyes with the other.

2.

One of four men decked out in flannel shirts and clown masks tossed Moe into the saw grass on the side of the road. Another man pried Tilmon out of the driver's seat and forced him onto his knees next to Moe.

"You motherfuckers picked the—" A jolt of hot pain exploded in Moe's jaw as one of the hijackers brought the stock of his rifle down on his face. Moe fell back into the dirt and weeds and ran his tongue over his freshly loosened teeth.

"Until I ask you something, you keep your fuckin' trap shut," the man said, and looked at Tilmon. "You got something you want to say?"

Tilmon did. He had a lot to say, but he liked his teeth so he kept his mouth shut.

"Good boy," the man said.

Two more flannel clowns rounded the truck and tossed a road-battered Bracken Leek by his leathers to the ground in front of his men. His right leg was a mangled mess and he groaned when he hit the grass. Metallic blood-stink came off him, but other than his leg, it was hard to tell where, or if, he was hurt anywhere else because of the head-to-toe leather. It had most likely saved his life. Two of the hijackers patted down Bracken and his crew and took away their guns, stuffing them into their own waistbands. They zip-tied Moe's and Tilmon's hands behind their backs as the man in blue flannel, the one who appeared to be in charge, squatted down in front of Bracken.

Red Flannel stood behind his boss with his rifle trained, while the other two searched the truck.

"You the man here?" Blue Flannel said.

Bracken propped himself up the best he could, nodded, and spit a little blood into the grass.

"I thought so. This is a simple deal right here. Give it to me, and you get to go back to whatever shithole biker bar you came from, a little the worse for wear, but breathing. Or give me a ration of shit, and I let my boy here shoot you all in the face and we take it anyway. You choose."

The man in red flannel waved.

"You know who you're stealing from, son?" Bracken said.

"It looks like I'm stealing from the goddamn Village People."

"Or the gimp," Red Flannel said. Everyone looked at him. "You know, like *Pulp Fiction*. The butt-fuckin' scene with Bruce Willis."

Everyone stopped looking at him.

Blue Flannel shook his head and exhaled heavily through the latex Bozo mask.

"Clowns," Bracken said. "Good choice."

Blue Flannel lifted his rifle from his knee and pressed the barrel against Bracken's forehead. "One more time, old man. Don't make me spend twenty minutes tearing that truck apart in the sun. This mask is hot as balls, and I'm sure everyone here is ready to get out of the heat and head their separate ways."

Bracken spit more blood into the grass and wiped his mouth. "It ain't in the truck," he said. "It's on the bike. The saddlebags."

Blue Flannel whistled for the other two hijackers. They hopped out of the truck and Blue Flannel motioned them toward the wrecked bike. "Check the bike."

"Roger that." After a minute, without taking his eyes off Bracken and the downed bikers, he yelled over, "We good?"

"We good, sir." The two men stripped the bike of the saddlebags and loaded them into their pickup. Blue Flannel stood up and heaved his rifle over his shoulder. "That's some pretty sneaky shit, Grandpa. Driving a box truck as a decoy. That way, idiot hijackers are prone to take out the big target and you ride into the sunset with the prize in tow."

"That's the idea."

"Too bad we ain't idiot hijackers," Red Flannel chimed in.

"That's up for debate," Bracken said.

Red Flannel was about to say something else when shots rang out from the pine trees and pinged off the truck, inches from his head. Red and Blue Flannel returned blind fire into the woods while Bracken and his boys flattened down into the grass and ate dirt.

"Bogies at your six," one of the hijackers at the truck yelled, and fired into the trees. They all bolted toward their pickup, but Blue Flannel took two shots to the back and stumbled onto the asphalt. Purple stains bloomed out across the blue cotton and his rifle slid across the highway. His partner stopped briefly and emptied the rest of his magazine into the pine before jumping into the back of the already moving pickup truck and disappearing into the afternoon heat.

Romeo appeared through the tree line, twin Sig Sauers in hand.

"Holy shit, Bracken. Are you guys all right?" The young Latino biker looked down the deserted stretch of highway before tucking his guns away. He pulled a blade from his boot and cut away the zip ties.

"Where the fuck you been?" Tilmon said, rubbing his wrists.

"I took a piss, man. By the time I caught up, I saw all this shit going on, so I pulled into the woods and hauled ass this way."

"Long fucking piss, bro," Moe said.

"Goddamn. How about a thank-you? If I hadn't stopped back there, there's no telling what these *putas* would have done."

"Enough," Bracken said. "Romeo, call some friendlies and get us the hell out of here."

"Already did it, boss."

"Then somebody go find out who the dead redneck is."

CHAPTER

13

CLAYTON BURROUGHS

2015

1.

Clayton thumped a pencil on his desk and stroked his calico beard for almost an hour before snapping the pencil in half between his fingers and using the eraser end to punch in the number for the GBI headquarters in Decatur. He stared blankly at the blinking line-indicator light and sat through three levels of secretaries and underlings before the right person was finally connected. Clayton heard fumbling on the line, then a deep, scotch-warmed voice:

"Finnegan."

"Charles, it's Clayton Burroughs."

"Well, fuck me running. How's my favorite backwoods lawman?"

"Can't complain. It wouldn't do me no good if I did."

"You got that shit right. What can I do for you, Sheriff?"

"Well, Charles, I had me a federal come in my office this past Sunday wanting to talk about Halford." Clayton heard Finnegan chuckle.

"Again?"

"Yeah, but this fella was different. He had some interesting things to say, and some of it sounded pretty solid. I was hoping to do a little digging on him to see if what he's telling me is legitimate, but I'm hitting a wall. I can't get nothing but name, rank, and serial number from them folks at the Atlanta office and I'm a little short on reliable contacts outside of the state police. Turns out you're the best I got."

"Well, Sheriff, if I'm the best you got, you're in pretty sorry shape."

"I don't believe that for a minute, Charles."

"What's the agent's name?"

"Holly. He's with the ATF."

"Simon Holly?" Charles said.

"Yeah, you know him?" Clayton leaned forward in his chair, took his hat off and laid it on the desk.

"Not personally, but I know *of* him. He was one of the golden boys around here for a while before getting called up to the big leagues. Goddamn super-cop, from what I understand."

"Is that right?"

"Yup." Finnegan cleared his throat and Clayton imagined the hefty GBI agent leaning back in his straining office chair, stretching his legs out under his desk, settling in to pass on some gossip. "The way I heard it, he was some hot-shit beat cop down around Mobile, Alabama. He did some digging outside his job description and ended up doing the local narco detectives' jobs for them. Got himself a big collar. Some local kingpin down there by the name of Fisher. You heard of him?"

"Nope."

"Well, you know how these things get built up into legend around here, but apparently your boy Holly bent a few rules and ignored a few important people, and made Dauphin Street a decent place to take your family to again. You ever been there?"

"Can't say I have."

"Used to be a shithole. Now the place is pretty nice. Like Bourbon Street in New Orleans, but clean and less crappy jazz music."

"Sounds lovely."

"Right. So anyway, Holly's bosses were sitting pretty, taking pictures for the papers and such, but he didn't make any friends with all the local cops he made look incompetent. If he hadn't got the collar, they'd probably have found him in a ditch somewhere. But anyway, he did, so he dipped out on the locals and made the jump to the Alabama Bureau. Pissed off a bunch of folks over there, but was getting it done, so out come the federal headhunters and it was onward and upward to better things, leaving all us state levels in his wake."

"You said he was a golden boy around there. Was Holly GBI, too?"

"Nah, we've done some interagency operations that had him working out of our offices, but as far as I know, he's never been one of ours. Listen, Clayton, if this guy is interested in Halford and what's going on up that mountain of yours, I'd say it was worth listening to, just to see what he has to say. He's a little squirrelly, but he seems like a smart cop."

Clayton scratched at his beard. "Is he good people?" he asked.

"I couldn't tell you if he calls his mother on Sundays, if that's what you mean, but I can tell you he's a good fella to have in a foxhole. The guy gets it done."

"Well, I guess that's what I needed to know. I appreciate your help, Charles."

"No worries, Sheriff. Is there anything my office should know about what you got cooking up there?"

"According to Holly, your office will be one of the first to know if the whole thing goes south."

Finnegan sighed heavily through the phone. "We normally are, but keep me in mind all the same. We could use a win or two around here. Our darling director has us chasing dogfighting rings of the rich and famous."

"Dogfighting?"

"It's a long story. I'm sure you'll hear all about it on the news."

"Of that I have no doubt, Charles."

"When you gonna bring me some of that famous hooch of yours? I was the most popular man in the building when I had a jar of that Georgia Peach in my desk."

Clayton stared down into his empty coffee cup. "I haven't touched a drop in over a year."

"No shit?"

"Kate says it ain't doing our marriage any favors. I tend to agree with her."

"I heard that. A happy wife is a happy life."

"Words to live by."

"All right, then, you call me if you need a few more boots on the ground."

"I'll do that. Be safe out there."

"You, too, Sheriff."

Clayton clicked the phone down in the cradle and looked at his watch. Two o'clock. Not even close to quitting time, or Miller time for that matter. Man, he missed Miller time. By five-fifteen every day like clockwork, he would be warming a seat at Lucky's and warming his throat with happy-hour bourbon. Clayton's mouth started watering right after Finnegan mentioned that jar of peach in his desk. He stood up and filled a Dixie cup with cold water from a plastic cooler by the door. He watched the big bubble break on the surface of the water in the jug and laughed a little when he thought about how alcoholics remember only the good times. It was true he'd enjoyed himself at Lucky's back when he was a five-o'clock regular, but the rest of the scenario wasn't much to be proud of. He'd get home around nine to nine-thirty on a slow night, to a cold supper on the table, covered in plastic wrap, and a colder Kate on the sofa, covered in a blanket. They'd go a couple rounds of the who-can-say-the-most-hateful-shit game, then she'd take the bed and he'd take the couch in the den— sometimes the floor. They would spend the next morning circling each other in silence, her waiting around for him to apologize and him taking his sweet time figuring out that he had to. He wasn't stupid. He knew his drinking made him as mean as a copperhead, but he never hit her or threatened to leave, as if those were flags to be rallied around, and so he always just assumed that the next drink would have a different outcome. He never understood how the buzz that made him happy at the bar turned to piss and vinegar at home, but it did. It always did. The movies always have the drunk turn it around after some kind of traumatic event. That's not always the way it happens in real life. Clayton's drinking wasn't a wildfire turning his life into a blazing inferno, it was a fine layer of rust slowly decaying and dissolving his marriage. She never told him to stop. She didn't have to. He knew Kate would leave before she rusted completely through. Some things are worth fighting for, so he set it down and never looked back. Well, not as often anyway.

Clayton filled the Dixie cup again and gulped it down and tossed the paper cup into a small wicker wastebasket. He walked out into the reception area, where Cricket was sitting at her desk with Darby

Ellis, Waymore Valley's second, and only part-time, deputy. They were chatting with hushed voices. Their conversation stopped completely when Clayton entered the room, like high school kids straightening up for the teacher. Cricket had her elbows on her desk and her fingers interlaced, cradling her chin. She looked upset, as if she had been crying. Darby sat on the edge of her desk with his cowboy hat balanced on his knee. Cricket sat up straight and awkwardly shuffled papers around on her desk. Darby stood up and held his hat to his chest. "Good afternoon, Sheriff," he said.

"Darby," Clayton said, and stood in front of Cricket's desk. He gently lifted her chin until her eyes, red and puffy, met his. "Are you okay?" he said.

"I'm fine, Sheriff."

"Is there anything I can do?"

"No, sir. I'm fine, really."

Clayton looked at Darby, who shrugged. He either didn't know or wasn't telling, and that was fine by Clayton. He wasn't in the mood for office drama. "Where's Choctaw?"

"That's a good question," Cricket said almost too sharply, as if Clayton had hit a nerve. "He hasn't been here all morning."

"Did you try his cell phone?"

"I did. I left several messages. Should I try him again?"

"Nah. Just tell him to call me when he gets in."

"Yessir."

"Um, Sheriff," Darby said, cutting in between Clayton and the front door, still holding his hat at his chest, fingering the rim. "An officer from Cobb County come and picked up our prisoner early this morning."

"I know that, Darby. I was here."

"Right. Um. I'm just saying that I don't have anything going on right now, if you need me to help you with anything. Um, since Deputy Frasier ain't here and all."

Darby Ellis was a good kid. Clayton had taken him on as a volunteer right outta high school just because he admired the kid's enthusiasm for the job. He created a part-time position last year because he figured if Darby was going to spend every waking hour at the station, he might as well be getting paid a little something for it. He aced the deputy exam and shot pretty good at the range, but he wasn't quite what Clayton liked to think of as quick-thinking. Of course, Choctaw wasn't that far ahead of him. Clayton chewed at his bottom lip and scratched his beard.

"All right, then, Darby. C'mon."

Darby smiled a big farm-boy smile. "Where we headed, boss?"

"To see my brother."

Darby lost the spring in his step and stopped cold.

Clayton pulled the Colt Python from his holster, spun the cylinder to ensure it was full, and with a flick of his wrist locked it back in place. "So, are you coming?"

Darby double-checked his hip for his own service weapon, relieved to see he had it, and put on his hat. "Yessir."

2.

The tree limbs slapping against the roof and windows of Clayton's Bronco brought him back to a different time. Although Waymore Valley was considered a small mountain community, this place beyond the civilized was a different world altogether. His and Kate's house was at the base of the mountain, a stone's throw from paved roads and streetlights, but up here Halford had taken up residence in the house they'd lived in as boys—their father's house. Clayton hadn't been this far up the mountain in years. Even after Buckley died or what had happened to his father, Clayton never passed over the invisible line Halford had drawn in the clay. The Bronco's tires dug into the twin trenches of red dirt while Clayton navigated through his childhood stomping grounds. He spun the steering wheel with the inside of his forearm, making turns without thinking, anticipating dips and drop-offs he'd ridden through a hundred times over with his brothers. This place was his home, no matter how unkind it had been to him. Clayton knew he would always be welcome, but the badge had no business here at all. If a thing existed up here, it was because it belonged here. And if it didn't belong, the people who lived here made damn sure it didn't stay. Clayton had struggled with which side of that fence he was on ever since he could remember. The sadness this place brought him was almost equal to the pride it filled him with. He thought sometimes there was nothing he wouldn't do to sit in a beat-up johnboat out by Burnt Hickory Pond and watch his brothers pretend to fish while they drink warm beers with their shirts unbuttoned and their chests poking out. They acted like it was a chore to have him tag along, but they would always bring a few bottles of Sun Drop or Peach Nehi just for him. He took notice of that kind of thing. He doubted Halford would be up for going fishing today.

Clayton shifted into low gear and swerved the truck off the service road onto a trail cut between two gorgeous red maples. The sun was high above the ridge, lighting up the leaves, coloring everything around them shades of orange and purple. He was always surprised at how beautiful it was up here, but he wasn't at all surprised to see the two men standing in the heavy shadow of the tree line, holding AK-47s. Darby didn't take it well at all. The young man braced himself and unsnapped the thumb break on his holster. Clayton let the clutch out and stopped the truck.

"Button that back up, Deputy. We're going to be fine."

"I don't know, boss. You sure this is a good idea?"

"No, I'm not, but you'll be fine. I promise." Clayton clicked on the blue light bar, but turned it back off after seeing the faces of the men in the road.

"Maybe we should just head back," Darby said.

"Just be quiet. I wouldn't have brought you here if I thought you'd be in danger. I grew up with these people. If anything, I'm the one in trouble."

"What do you mean, 'trouble'?"

"Just stop worrying."

"That's hard to do, sir, seeing as two big burly jokers with assault rifles are walking toward us." Darby squinted his eyes to get a better look at the approaching welcome party. "Oh my God, boss. The one to the left looks all burned up or something." Darby dropped his hand to his gun again. Clayton took his eyes off the two men and put them directly on Darby.

"Listen to me, Deputy."

"Yessir?"

"You listening?"

"Yessir."

"These men are not going to hurt you. I promise you that. You are a sworn deputy of Waymore Valley, and these men are not looking to be cop killers. That kind of thing will rain a metric shit-ton of trouble down on this place, and they do not want that. Do you understand what I'm saying?"

Darby nodded, fast and sharp, and awkwardly straightened out his hat.

"So just relax. If for a second I think something is squirrelly, I will handle it and I will get us both out of here pronto. Okay?"

"Okay, boss. I trust you."

"Good. Now, be quiet."

The sheriff rolled down his window and turned off the rumbling AC as the two men approached the truck. One of the men stayed back by the tree line, while the one Darby thought looked burned rested his arms on the driver's-side window ledge and leaned in a little to inventory the truck's occupants. When Scabby Mike and Clayton finally locked eyes, Mike smiled wide and motioned for the other man to lower his rifle.

Scabby Mike had managed to become an old man over that past year, since the time Clayton saw him last, but there was no mistaking who he was. Mike had had a severe case of measles as a child, which left horrible scarring over eighty percent of his face and body. It happened that way up here sometimes because of the mountain's lack of proper doctoring. The disease left his skin a muddled pinkish color with the texture of pitted asphalt, and his beard grew in patchy and only on the right side of his face.

"Sometimes, that's just how shit is," he'd told Clayton once when they were kids. *"I just thank the Lord I never got it on my pecker."* The memory always made Clayton smile.

This made eye contact tough to maintain for strangers like Darby, but Clayton wasn't a stranger, and Mike's face was a welcomed one. Clayton considered him a friend. Maybe the only one he had left on the mountain.

"When they told me we had company comin' up the mountain, I was hopin' it was you. I wasn't really in the mood for killin' any real cops."

"Well, I reckon I should feel lucky, then."

"Lucky you got me standin' here tellin' you to turn around. 'Cause you keep drivin' up this here road, your luck is gonna change."

"I need to talk to my brother."

"Hal don't talk to cops. You know that." Mike shot an intentional glare at Darby, who looked away immediately.

"I thought you just said I wasn't a real cop."

"He don't talk to fake cops, neither."

"Look, Mike, I'm not here in an official capacity anyway. I'm here as his brother."

Scabby Mike leaned down on the Bronco's window frame and shuffled his hat back out of his eyes to look inside the truck. "So what's Deputy Dawg here for?"

"He's here as a witness. That's all."

"We don't like witnesses up here, neither," Mike said, and spat tobacco juice in the dirt. Darby continued to study the floorboards with great intensity.

"Just tell your boys in the woods to come on out, and let the man know we're coming up."

Mike smiled wide, showing off a mouth full of straight but yellowed teeth. "Your brother knew you were coming twenty minutes back." He spat again, then stood up and whistled—two sharp chirps. At least a dozen men, armed with everything from assault rifles to shotguns, shuffled out of the trees like ants from a mound that just got stepped on. Darby sank deeper and lower into his seat and gripped the armrest hard enough to push the blood from his knuckles.

Mike laughed a deep belly laugh. "Tell your fearless deputy there not to be so jumpy. If Hal wanted him dead, we'd have done did it by now."

"He'll be fine," Clayton said.

"You sure you wanna do this, Clayton? He ain't real fond of you, these days."

"He ain't never been real fond of me."

"Well, it's a little worse now, since the funeral and all."

"Hal needs to realize that I lost a brother, too."

"It was the uniform, I think, that set him off."

Clayton shook his head. "Hal's drinking and acting like an ass was a lot more disrespectful than my dress uniform."

"He don't see it that way."

"I don't give a shit how he sees it."

"All the more reason for me askin', Clayton. You sure you want to go up there?"

"I'll be fine, Mike."

Mike narrowed his eyes at Clayton like he was trying to read something written on the sheriff's forehead, then pushed himself back off the truck. "Let them through," he yelled to the posse of gunmen up the road. They cleared a path for Clayton, and he put the Bronco back in gear. He looked out at Mike again and tipped his hat.

"Good to see you, Mike."

"Yup. Yup."

As the sheriff and his deputy rolled past the gathering of hard stares, dirty faces, and loaded weapons, Darby closed his eyes and got reacquainted with the Lord.

3.

"Jeez-us, Sheriff. This is bad. I just know it. You're family to these people, but they could care less about me. Your brother will kill me just for being dressed like this." He pulled at the deputy's star pinned to his chest.

"Nobody is getting killed, Darby. He's not as crazy as everyone says. It's just what he wants people to think. It's how he keeps people doing what he wants them to do. My deddy was the same way. Besides, he'll be too busy with me to worry about you. Just stay in the car, and you'll be fine."

"Whatever you say, Sheriff, but I'm still not feeling good about it."

The road opened up into a vast expanse of red dirt and pea gravel. Clayton counted at least ten more armed men watching as they approached, but with their guns pointed down. A few others too twitchy and haggard to be employees wandered about the yard and hovered around the corner of the house near the rain barrel. Clayton assumed they were local tweekers looking to score. There was a time when Halford would never have allowed scrounge like them anywhere near his home. He was getting either soft or sloppy. Either one was a good sign he might be open to a conversation like the one Clayton was there to bring him.

The man closest to the mouth of the drive was talking into a two-way radio connected to his gun strap with a length of paracord. Clayton had no doubt who was listening on the other end, and hoped it also explained why all the guns were lowered. Halford was being cordial—another good sign. Clayton wheeled the Bronco through the entourage and parked next to a variety of jacked-up, camouflaged pickup trucks, some brand-new and some as old as he was. He thought he recognized his deddy's old Ford F-100. At least Halford had managed to keep that alive. A simple cabin made of cedar and pine stood in the middle of the clearing. To Clayton it looked frozen in time. If it was any different from the way he remembered it, he couldn't tell. His old bedroom window faced east, and the same blue curtains he remembered from when he was a boy were still there. Two old men he didn't recognize sat in rockers on the porch. One of them held a guitar in his lap but wasn't playing. Two children about nine or ten sat with their legs dangling off the porch, neither of them wearing shoes. The blackened color of the soles of their feet made Clayton wonder if they ever had. One of the children held a hand-carved wooden train car. The other held a knife and was picking at a loose board on the porch. Neither of them looked up as Clayton got out of the truck and approached the front steps.

"That's far enough, Sheriff," a deep voice bellowed from behind the screen door. It was the man himself. Halford Burroughs stood every bit of six feet, four inches tall and took up the entirety of the doorway. He was as thick as a redwood but angular and solid like stacked cinder blocks. Clayton and Buckley had grown to resemble their father, naturally thin, cut, with ropey muscles, red hair, and fair skin—the kind that burned in the shade—but Halford retained their mother's features. He was olive-skinned; his hair was a thick mound of dark brown ringlets that matched deep brown eyes that curved down at his cheeks. When they were kids, the girls on the mountain called them "sad eyes," but Clayton never saw a hint of sadness in them. His beard was full and lush, streaked with gray and silver. He stood behind the screen door, unarmed, with a paper napkin draped down the front of a dark undershirt.

He pushed open the screen door, stepped out onto the porch, and let the door slam behind him. He squinted his eyes as they adjusted to the sunlight and pulled the napkin from his shirt collar. He wiped away what looked like gravy from the corners of his mouth and beard, then rolled the napkin into a ball between his palms and tossed it on the porch. The kid with the toy train scurried over, picked it up, and disappeared into the house. The screen door slammed again.

"Long time, Hal."

"Not long enough. I don't know what you're thinking coming

here, but it would be in your best interest to go ahead and get your ass gone." Halford took a step forward and the porch creaked under his weight.

"If you really wanted me to leave, you wouldn't have let me up here in the first place. We need to talk."

"I don't talk to cops. Even wannabe cops like you."

"I'm not here as the law, Hal. I'm here as your brother."

Hal laughed. It was cold and humorless. A yard full of ass-kissers joined in and Clayton gave a quick glance around, feeling uneasy. Halford took another step forward into the sunlight. "First of all, you ain't *the law* up here. Hell, you ain't hardly the law down in the Valley, from what I hear. But more important, the only brother I got done got himself killed by some friends of yours a little over a year ago."

"I had nothing to do with that, and you know it."

"It's one big brotherhood, though, right?"

For the first time, Clayton felt the heat of the day. Sweat was running between his shoulder blades and down his lower back. His shirt was sticking to him and his neck was kinking up from having to look up at Halford. All of a sudden he craved iced tea—laced with a fifth of bourbon.

"Hal, I didn't drive out here thinking we had any shot of repairing the damage between us. I'm not fool enough to think that will ever happen, but I got things you need to hear all the same. You don't want to hear them? Fine. I'll be on my way. But ask yourself something. Don't you think if I drove all the way up here, after all this time, and let all these assholes you call family put guns in my face in front of my deddy's house, that what I have to say might just be important?"

Hal chewed on that. He studied Clayton, then shot some stink-eye over at Darby, who was melting in the cab of the Bronco. The floorboard went back to being the most fascinating thing Darby had ever seen.

"Come on, Hal. It's hot out here."

"Fine. Talk, but you can do it from there. No way in hell you're coming into this house. You lost that right a long time ago."

Clayton sighed and took off his hat. He wiped the sweat off his brow with his forearm, and put it back on. He took another glance around the yard at all of Halford's men, each face more eager than the next to hear what Clayton had to say. "I don't think you want all these people hearing what I got to say."

"Why not, Sheriff?" Halford held his arms out. "We're all family here, right?"

Clayton took a step toward the porch and spoke in a hushed voice. "I think I might have . . . a way to help our family."

Hal didn't say a word. He just stared at Clayton like he was a complete stranger. Clayton took another wary step toward his brother and lowered his voice even more. "A way out, and I mean completely out. It's a chance for you to retire from all . . . this . . ." He held out his arms like a scarecrow and motioned toward the gathered crowd. "I have guarantees," he said, almost in a whisper now. "You can keep everything you have. The money. Whatever. Just shut down the dope." Clayton looked at the tweekers by the rain barrel scratching themselves nervously. "No more looking over your shoulder. No more men with guns at your front gate. Just you and God's country."

Hal still said nothing. Clayton needed to give him more. He moved close enough to Hal to almost whisper in his ear, and Hal let him.

"They're on to your boy in Florida—Wilcombe." Clayton waited to see if that put a crack in Hal's stone visage, but there was nothing, not even a blink. "They also know the locations of all sixteen cookhouses. They know your routes and where it's all going. They've got times, dates, names, everything. If you don't listen to me they're going to storm this mountain like you or I have never seen. I can't stop it. And if that happens, a lot of people—a lot of your people—are going to get killed." Clayton thought about what Holly had said back in his office about appealing to Hal's *other* sensibility—about the money being paramount. Clayton didn't believe it, but he put it out there anyway. "Think about the money, Hal. You'll lose it all. Everything you worked for taken from you before you even know what's happening."

Hal spit on the porch, and Clayton thought he caught a slight shift in Hal's expression.

"Nothing makes a U.S. federal law enforcement agency drool more than a huge pile of money," Clayton said, using Agent Holly's words verbatim. "And they are coming for yours. But it doesn't have to be like that, Hal. You can keep it all and put a stop to all this."

Clayton thought he saw Halford weighing the possibility of what he was saying. He also thought he heard a whip-poor-will singing through the dead silence that suddenly blanketed his father's house, but maybe he only wanted to.

"You've got guarantees?" Halford finally said.

"Yes."

"Just me and God's country, huh?"

"That's right."

Hal reached into the pocket of his trousers and pulled out a coin big enough to be a silver dollar. Without looking at him, Hal motioned to the boy still out on the porch, and he scurried over, the wooden train left abandoned on pine slats. He handed the boy the coin and tousled his hair. "Go inside now and clear my food off the table. I done lost my appetite." The boy did as he was told and hustled off through the screen door, taking only a second to stop it from slamming again, but once inside, he turned back to Clayton and shot him a bird before disappearing from view. The two old men in the rockers collected their things and moved off the porch as if they'd just noticed a thunderhead forming and were looking to take shelter. Old men were intuitive like that. Halford thumped down the steps of the porch and stood just inches from Clayton's face. The sheriff stood his ground. Hal spoke in a low, controlled voice. "Do you know what your problem is?"

Clayton smelled the pork sausage and gravy on his brother's breath. "Hal, think about—"

"Do you?"

Clayton let out another sigh. "What, Hal? What's my problem?"

"You never got it. This isn't God's country. It's *my* country. Mine. It always has been and always will be. God don't have nothing to say about it up here. You could have been part of it, but you turned your back on us—on your family—on Deddy. That was your decision."

"Hal, we don't need to rehash all this."

Halford ignored him. "But it ain't like we all didn't see it coming. Ever since you were a kid, you walked around thinking you were better than us, and now look at you, strutting around with that star on your shirt, still trying to prove how much better than us you are. If Deddy were here right now, he'd be disgusted at how you turned out."

Clayton felt a twinge of anger tighten up one side of his face, and he matched his brother's low tone of voice. "You want to talk about Deddy, Hal? Why don't we talk about why he ain't here? Why don't you tell me the truth about the fire?"

"I don't need to tell you shit."

"You're right. You don't. I saw the barn. It didn't look like no kerosene fire to me. It looked like the place exploded. What happened, you guys learn to cook that shit through trial and error, and Deddy paid the price?"

Hal's upper lip curled. "Get off my mountain before I lose my patience and beat you to death where you stand."

"Why was the old man in there, Hal? I talked to the fire chief, and he paints a whole different story than the bullshit you tried to pass off. Don't you think it's sad? He ran this mountain for seventy years without so much as a scratch and didn't make it through one when you started making the decisions."

Both men stood with their heels dug into the dirt, braced, each waiting for the other to swing. "This is your last warning," Hal said. "Turn around, get back in that truck, and go back to your life, or so help me, Clayton, I will throw your body in the fuckin' ravine for the coons."

Clayton didn't hear the threat so much, as he tried to remember the last time Halford had called him by his first name. Not since they were kids. He held Halford's stare and saw nothing in his brother's eyes but an empty rage churning like the storm clouds those old men on the porch must have seen coming. Clayton had hoped age would change his brother for the better, for the wiser, but it hadn't. He had hoped Buckley's senseless death would have dictated some logic, but it didn't. Hal was still the same man who could sit and hum a tune while his enemies burned alive tied to a tree less than twenty feet away. Clayton was almost ready to believe his brother could kill him, too.

Almost.

"Okay, then, Hal." Clayton backed down from his brother, adjusted his hat, and made his way toward the Bronco, where his deputy was only now able to exhale. Darby pressed the button on the armrest to unlock the doors.

"Nice visit, Sheriff," Hal said, and started back up the steps. His hands were shaking. It surprised Clayton. He opened the door to the truck, took off his hat, tossed it onto the driver's seat, and began to unbuckle his gun belt.

"What are you doing, Sheriff?" Darby's eyes widened. "Are you crazy? We just got a pass. Let's get outta here."

Clayton tossed the belt and sidearm onto the seat and slammed the door. "You want to threaten me, Halford? My whole life I've been listening to you talk about what a badass you are, but I've never seen you do a damn thing that didn't involve you telling people what to do. How about we put all that talk to the test, fat man."

Darby sank his face into his hands.

Clayton rolled up his sleeves, then unpinned the small tin star from his duty shirt and set it on the hood of the Bronco. A new expression replaced the anger on Halford's face, one that was rarely seen by his people—he smiled. "Do you know where you are, boy?"

"I know exactly where I am. I'm on the northern edge of McFalls County, which falls under the jurisdiction of the Waymore Valley Sheriff's Department."

Halford laughed hard enough to make his belly shake. "Is that right?"

"Yeah, that's right."

"Nobody up here gives a shit about your jurisdiction, Clayton. You're a joke. An embarrassment."

"Yeah, I get that, and I made my peace with the way you see me, but that don't change the facts."

Several men in the yard trained their guns on the sheriff, but Halford waved them all down. "Not one of you harms this man," he said. "Put your guns down." Slowly the rifles lowered. Hal cracked his knuckles and twisted his head from side to side to pop the bones in his neck. Then he stepped off the porch.

4.

Clayton swung first, but Hal sidestepped it and threw a solid hay-maker into Clayton's ribs. It hit like a railroad hammer and dropped Clayton to his knees.

"Get up," Hal bellowed at him. "Get up, boy. Don't go down with one punch. It's embarrassing." He loomed over Clayton with a smile while the sheriff regained his breath. It didn't take long for Clayton to spring up and go at Hal again. The big man tried to pivot and side-step the hit again, but this time Clayton anticipated it, and the second punch connected square on Hal's jaw. It felt like the knuckles in his hand had exploded. Hal shook it off, grabbed his brother by his tan duty shirt, and pulled him into a head butt. Another explosion of pain followed by bright white light and black spots.

Don't black out. Don't black out. Don't black out, Clayton chanted in his mind. Before his vision cleared, Clayton swung both fists like twin pendulums into the sides of Hal's head. That hurt him. He let go, and Clayton hammered a quick succession of rabbit punches into Hal's kidney. As the big man buckled over, Clayton brought up his knee and rammed it into Hal's face. It caught him in the cheek and sprawled him backward flat onto his back. He sounded like an oak tree falling against the forest floor. Clayton moved in to kick him but noticed all the rifles were back in the air and aimed at him. These men weren't used to seeing their leader in the dirt. Clayton put his hands in the air and backed away.

"I said put the goddamn guns down," Hal said, holding his face. He got to his feet and spit some blood into the dirt and gravel. "The first one to fire on this man dies next." Hal brushed the dirt from the front of his shirt and trousers and fixed his eyes on Clayton. "You sure this is the kind of fight you want to have?"

Clayton lowered his hands, but only enough to form fists and block his face. "Is there any other kind?"

Hal charged across the lot like a wild boar, slamming into Clayton and lifting him completely off the ground. The two men barreled into the side of one of the hunting trucks, with Clayton taking the brunt of it to his head and shoulder. Before Clayton could gain his breath, Halford pummeled him with punches to the face and gut. Clayton tried to counter and block, but Hal slapped his hands away like they were flies buzzing around his head. When Clayton finally went down, Halford straddled him, pinning his arms under his knees. He crouched down on top of Clayton and buried a massive forearm into his throat, crushing his windpipe. The sheriff scratched and clawed at the ground but barely had any strength left to make a difference. Blood from Hal's busted lip dripped down on Clayton's face as it started to take on the color of an eggplant. The more Clayton squirmed, the more Hal crushed down. No tap-outs. No mercy.

A single gunshot rang out. Hal spun his head, still in a feral state, fully expecting to see one of his men had disobeyed him. Instead he saw Deputy Darby Ellis pointing a shaky service revolver at him. He'd managed to sneak past the redneck hordes who were all engrossed in the fight and got himself close enough to actually become a threat. He'd fired the first shot in the air to get Hal's attention, like a bell signifying the end of the round. He hoped that was all he'd have to do. "Let him up," Darby said, then added, "Mr. Burroughs," then added, "Please."

Hal turned to face the deputy but didn't take his arm off Clayton's throat.

"Or what, Deputy? You gonna shoot me?"

"I don't want to . . . sir."

"Look around you, boy. You see all those itchy trigger fingers waiting for me to tell them to blow your head off?"

Darby nervously scanned the line of barrels that were now pointed at his head. "Yessir, I do."

"Then drop that gun on the ground."

"I can't do that, sir." Darby's knees were shaking so bad he could barely stand. "Mr. Burroughs, I can't let you kill him. It wouldn't be right."

Hal didn't say anything else. He didn't have to.

"He said drop the gun," a voice behind the deputy said, and when Scabby Mike pressed the barrel of a pistol into the back of Darby's head, the deputy's gun fell to the dirt.

"I think he's gonna cry, Mike," Hal said.

"Yup, I think he might."

"Please don't kill me," Darby said. "I didn't even want to come up here. I begged him to turn around. I told him this was crazy."

Hal took his arm off Clayton's windpipe and the sheriff rolled over, clutching his throat, gulping at the fresh air. Hal was barely breathing heavy. "Okay, kid. Come get your boss here, and take him back down to Waymore. He, or you, ever comes here again, I promise you it's gonna end different."

"Yessir," Darby said, and rushed over to help Clayton to his feet. "We're gone."

Hal picked up Darby's revolver and stuck it in his waistband. He looked at Darby for an argument. "You got a problem with that, Deputy?"

"No, sir. It's yours."

Scabby Mike walked over to Hal, with Clayton's gun belt over his shoulder. He must have taken it out of the truck when Darby decided to play hero. Hal took the gun, dumped the contents of the cylinder on the ground, and tossed the whole rig next to Clayton. Mike also tried to hand Hal the badge Clayton had left on the hood, but Hal didn't want that, either.

"Nah," Hal said, "he can keep it. I think it might have peppered his grits a little."

Mike walked back and tucked the tin star into Darby's shirt pocket.

"You be sure he gets it, when he feels better," Mike said.

"Yessir, I will."

5.

Clayton's lip was cut down the middle and a dark yellow swell was forming under his left eye, but nothing was broken, and with a little help, he could walk. Darby practically threw him into the truck and slid behind the wheel. Three seconds later the young deputy had their asses in the wind. He watched through the dust cloud in the rearview as the crowd of hillbilly gunmen laughed and waved.

"Well, boss, that didn't go too well."

"No, Darby, I would say it did not." Clayton pulled a bandana out of the glove box and dabbed at his lip. It hurt to talk. His whole body throbbed. He'd toted an ass-whuppin' before, but his ego had never taken one this bad. Every man on this mountain who believed the sheriff was a joke just had his sentiments reinforced. Maybe even including Clayton's own deputy.

"Darby . . ."

"You ain't got to say it, boss. It's in the rearview and we're both breathing. That's good enough for me. I can't believe you went at him like that, sir. I know he's your brother and all, but he could've killed you."

Clayton pulled the door-mounted mirror inward toward him and examined the bruised flesh puffing up under his eye. "Damn," he said. "Take a left at this fork up here."

Darby squeezed his eyebrows together and gave Clayton a concerned look. "Is that the way we came in? Because that don't look like the way we came in."

"We got another stop to make."

"Are you being serious right now? We need to get our butts off this mountain. That's what the man said. That's what I told the man I'd do. We're getting off this mountain, Sheriff."

"We're taking a left up here. *The man* can kiss my ass."

"I ain't got a gun, boss. You know he kept my gun, right?"

"You don't need it."

"Well, I strongly object."

"Noted. Now go left."

Darby felt his guts tighten back up as he turned the wheel in the opposite direction of the way his brain was screaming at him to go, and pointed the truck toward the Western Ridge.

"Why didn't he keep yours?" Darby asked.

"My what?"

"Your gun. He kept mine, but he gave yours back. Why?"

Clayton picked the silver Colt up from the seat between them and ran a finger over his father's initials engraved on the handle. "I don't know, Darby."

GARETH BURROUGHS

1973

1.

Gareth cracked the seal on a jar of North Georgia's finest and sat down on the steps. He'd been back from Florida for only two days with the solution to one problem before everything else fell apart. With Annette gone, the nursemaidin' of these youngsters fell on him alone. He'd known he'd be coming home to a house without her, but the knowing didn't make it sting any less when he crossed through the door. He could hear the baby crying in the house, so he picked up the jar and walked toward the tree line. It didn't matter how far he walked, that sound would follow him to the end of the earth and he knew it. He drained a quarter of the jar and stared up at the stars. The night was clear, but nothing else seemed to be. He knew he'd have to go in and tell those boys their mama wasn't comin' back. They'd be all right. He'd be all right. He had to be. There was too much to lose if he wasn't. He watched his oldest son, Halford, step out on the porch and look around for his father. "Deddy?"

"Over here," Gareth said.

Halford looked out into the darkness toward Gareth. "I can't get Clayton to stop crying."

"I'll be in in a minute. You and your brother get cleaned up for supper."

"Is Mama coming home tonight? She can get Clayton to stop."

Gareth lit a cigarette and noticed the glow of headlights coming up the drive. Halford saw it, too. "Is that her, Deddy? Is that Mama?"

"Git in the house and do what I told you, boy."

Halford opened the screen door and reluctantly faded back into the house.

2.

Jimbo pulled the truck up next to Gareth's and got out. "Gareth, we got a problem."

"With the guns?" Gareth said, and took a drag on his smoke.

"No, man, Val took care of that. Everyone is on point with the guns."

"Then what's the problem?"

Jimbo took out his own cigarettes and lit one up. He was rubbing his knuckles. It was a nervous tic. It meant he had bad news and wasn't looking forward to telling it to the man whose wife had just run out on him and left him with two little boys and a new baby. They smoked in silence for nearly a full minute, and Gareth thought Jimbo might rub the skin on his knuckles clean off. He dropped his cigarette and put it out with his boot. "Just spit it out, Jimbo."

"Cooper done run off again."

"So? He'll show back up. He always does."

"I don't know, man. It's different this time. He's getting worse and worse. Ernest was keeping watch on him while we was gone and he said the old man was spouting off all kinds of crazy shit."

"That ain't nothing new."

"No, but since we been back he's been acting worse than normal. Ernest said yesterday he locked his self in his room for damn near twenty-four hours, banging shit around, not letting anybody in. This morning he come out all bruised up on his arms and face like he whupped his own ass."

"Why didn't anybody call me?"

Jimbo looked back at the house. The baby was still crying. "Hell, man, we know what you're dealing with here, we didn't want to put anything else on your plate."

Gareth took a swig from the jar and passed it to Jimbo. He took it and drank deep. "Goddamn, that's good."

"How long's he been gone?"

"I don't know, boss. Ernest called me an hour ago saying he left the house talking about going to make things right with Rye. Ernest said he took a rifle with him."

"You didn't think to ask him how long ago he left?"

"Sorry, boss, I just rushed out here."

Gareth sighed and capped the jar of shine. He handed it to Jimbo. "I know where he is."

"Well, tell me where and I'll go get him."

"No. He's my problem. I'll go get him. You mind staying here and looking after the boys 'til I get back? I shouldn't be that long."

"You got it, man."

"I haven't told them about their mama yet. They think she's off visiting a friend in Waymore."

"I won't say a word."

"All right, then." Gareth opened the door to his truck.

"Gareth?"

"Yep?"

"There's something else."

"What?"

"When Ernest called me he said Cooper wasn't wearing no clothes. He said he left out of there with nothing on but some tighty-whiteys and a pair of boots."

"Jesus," Gareth said. "Ernest should've called me this morning."

"I reckon so, boss."

"You tell him we'll talk about it when I get back."

3.

Gareth pulled the truck up to the cabin at Johnson's Gap and turned off the engine. The front door was open and he knew he'd find his father inside passed out drunk on the floor. Most likely having pissed himself, and he'd have to clean him up before he could put him in the truck and drive him home. This wouldn't be the first time Gareth had found him here, but it was getting to be a hard road to hoe. Cooper built this family, but this kind of thing was no good to no one. Gareth got out of the truck and climbed the steps. He picked up the lantern from the table on the porch and lit it.

"Come on, old man, let's go home." He shined the light inside, but there was no one there. The cabin was just a wide-open room, so the light from the lantern filled every corner. He put his hand near the wood burner and felt the warmth. The back door was open, too, and Gareth stepped out.

"Deddy!" he hollered into the darkness. "Come on, Cooper, I'm here to take you home."

He turned to go back into the cabin when he heard the shot. It wasn't too far away. "Deddy!" he yelled again, and bolted into the woods. He knew the path. He'd been out here before. He killed his first buck in these woods. "Deddy!" he kept yelling. Still nothing. Then he saw it. Something white on the ground about thirty feet in front of him. He ran and tripped over an exposed root. He hit the ground hard on his knees, scraping up his hands. "Goddamn it," he said, slowly getting back to his feet. He'd dropped the lantern, so he moved cautiously by the moonlight toward the white thing in the distance until it started to take the shape of an old man—his old man. He could see Cooper's body well enough to know it was him but stopped cold before he could see him well enough to see what he'd done to himself. The rifle was on the ground next to him. His pale naked body was luminous in the moonlight, and all the blood looked glossy black. Gareth fell back down to his knees. "Aw, Deddy, what did you do? What did you do?" Gareth knew what Cooper had done. Suddenly he was very aware of all the things his father had done in these woods. He stayed there on his knees, recalling it all. He thought about his uncle that day. He thought about the hole Cooper had made him dig. He didn't cry. He sat down in the cool grass and reached into his pocket for his smokes. He lit up and pictured his uncle lying in the woods only a mile or so from where his father was lying now. He thought about Annette. After a while he got to his feet and looked down on his father's naked, feeble dead body. Cooper used to say there was no dignity in birth or death. You entered the world helpless, naked and alone, and you were more than likely to go out the same way. Gareth didn't necessarily agree with that, but there was no short-age of indignation in these woods.

"Well, old man. I guess that's that."

CHAPTER
15

CLAYTON BURROUGHS

2015

1.

Darby pulled the Bronco up in front of a small cottage. It was a humble place, no more than two, maybe three, rooms inside, with an outhouse and a rusty but still-operational John Deere tractor in the yard. The porch was covered with potted plants, and armies of violets and red Gerber daisies lined the stone walkway. This place looked more like the bed-and-breakfast cabins tourists rented out in Helen, Georgia, or by the vineyards in Dahlonega. It was in direct contrast to the sun-bleached compound they'd just left. The colors were vibrant in the late-afternoon sunlight and for a split second Darby entertained the idea of this being the home of a mistress Clayton was keeping on the side. It sure had the look of a woman's touch. That idea vanished as soon as the seven-foot black man holding a shotgun appeared on the porch.

"Who's that there?" the man said. He looked to be in his late sixties, maybe older. A ring of silver-gray hair dusted the sides of his bald head, and matching tufts of gray sprouted down his chest. His shoulders were broad, but they sagged under his age, and his belly folded over his red boxer shorts. His muscle tone wasn't the same as it used to be, but he was still a hulk of a man.

"Put the gun down, Val. It's me, Clayton." Clayton got out of the truck and put his hands in the air. Darby cut the engine.

"Clayton Burroughs? Boy, what the hell are you doing up here?" Val took a harder look at his company. "And what happened to your face?"

"Well, if you could loan me a stretch of porch and a piece of venison from your icebox, I'd be happy to tell you."

Val lowered the shotgun. "Get on up here, then. I'll go put some pants on."

"Thanks for that," Clayton said.

"And don't be steppin' all over my garden on your way over." Val turned back into the house and Clayton and Darby eased up to the porch. Darby relaxed for the first time since they'd left the station that afternoon. "You reckon he's got anything to drink in there?"

Clayton laughed. "The best on the mountain."

Val came back out wearing a pair of well-worn overalls, holding a thick hunk of backstrap for Clayton's eye and a large ceramic jug. He handed the meat to Clayton and put a big, calloused hand on his shoulder. No hugs or small-talk sentiment, just a hand on a shoulder and a respectful nod made it obvious to anyone watching that these men were family. It wasn't necessary to *catch up*. They were both just thankful to be there now. The old man fished a sleeve of clear plastic cups from a basket between two pine rockers and took a seat. Clayton sat in the other one and laid the ice-cold slab of meat over his throbbing eye. He leaned his head back and closed his eyes.

"Who done that to you, son?"

"Halford."

"Your brother?"

"Yeah, not my finest hour."

"Why you climbing in the ring with that boy? He could have killed you. What was you thinkin'?"

"That's what I said," Darby chimed in from the steps and tipped his hat at Val.

"He wasn't gonna kill me. He's my brother. Besides, I had Darby there to pull me out when it got bad." He leaned his head forward and looked at Darby. "Thanks for what you did back there. I mean it. Thanks."

Darby tipped his hat at Clayton as well. Val set the plastic cups upside down on the cork and slid the jug across the porch, over to the deputy. "Clayton, what are you doing up here fooling with your brother? I thought you kept your sheriffin' confined to the Valley."

"Normally I do."

"Halford come down there steppin' on your toes?"

"No."

"Then what, then? You was on your way to visit with me and thought you'd go get yourself an ass-kicking for good measure?"

Clayton laughed, then groaned. "No."

"Yeah, that can't be right. None of you boys can ever find the time to come visit an old man."

"I came up here to make Hal an offer he couldn't refuse," Clayton said, and stared up at the wooden beams and tin awning that covered the porch. He wondered if Val had ghosts up in his rafters as well.

"Looks like he refused."

"Refused hard and repeatedly," Darby said. He took a swig from his cup and immediately fire raced down his throat and blew through his sinuses. Tears came to his eyes and he smiled wide. "*That's* what I'm talking about."

"That's my deddy's apple pie."

Clayton looked over at the jug. "Pour me some of that."

Darby frowned. "Is that a good idea, sir?"

"You gonna question everything I say today, Deputy?"

"Sorry, sir." Darby poured a second cup and held it out. Val put up a hand.

"If you's off the drink, Clayton, maybe you ought to stay that way."

"Last time I checked, Val, I'm pretty sure I was grown."

Val let his hand hover for a moment longer and thought about how many times he'd heard Gareth tell him the same thing right before going off and doing something terrible that only one of them would regret. But Clayton was right, he *was* grown. "Well, then, by all means, Sheriff." Val put his hand down. "But would you mind tellin' me why you decided to bring all this to my front porch? You could've doctored that eye down in Waymore."

Clayton took the cold venison from his face and laid it back in the waxy paper it came wrapped in. "Honestly, Val? I was hopin' to enlist an ally with this Halford thing."

"That's not gonna happen," Val said without a second's hesitation.

Clayton sat upright in the rocker. "Don't you want to hear what I've got in mind?"

"Nope. Sure don't."

Clayton looked stunned, like a child who was just denied getting his way.

"Val, you don't understand."

"Clayton, now, I said no. You're welcome to take a load off. Drink a lil' bit, and I'd be happy to patch you up, but you keep that craziness off my front porch, you hear? I just want to plant my flowers and get old peacefully. Your brother keeps his distance from me, and me from him. I ain't lookin' to change that."

"I thought you cared about him."

"I cared about your father. And Halford ain't your father."

"You say that like Deddy was a good man."

"No, he wasn't. Gareth wasn't a good man. But for a long time, neither was I. We come up together surrounded by all this." Val lifted his arms out, motioning around him. "We had each other's backs. Nowadays, that kinda thinkin' don't even exist no more, and I want no part of what happens up here."

Darby drained his cup, suffered the burn, and poured another. Val picked up the jug and took a swig directly from it. No reaction, like he was drinking water.

"That shit they're makin' up here ain't just a drug. It's evil, plain and simple. Your deddy was the toughest son of a bitch I've ever known, and as soon as your brothers brought that shit up here, it killed him."

"The drugs didn't kill him, Val."

"The hell they didn't."

"Cricket told me your daddy died in a fire," Darby said.

Clayton scratched at his beard. "That's the story Halford would have everyone believe, but the truth is he blew himself up learning how to cook that shit. You'd think the high-and-mighty king of Bull Mountain wouldn't go out like some lowly city tweeker, but in the end, that's exactly how it went down."

"You should have more respect, little Burroughs. He was your father, and despite his failings, he only did as his deddy did before him. You want to put that anger on somebody, you put it on your grandfather. That's where this family went wrong. Nobody deserves to die like your deddy did. He died screaming. You ever see somebody burn to death?"

Clayton had.

"It was your grandfather let loose the demons on this mountain, and there ain't no putting that genie back in the bottle. Never was. Not then, not now."

"Wilcombe had a little something to do with it." Again Clayton put that name out there to see the reaction he'd get. This time he got one. Val put the jug down.

"How do you know that name?"

"That's what I'm trying to tell you. I know everything about what Hal's got going on in Florida. I know my father partnered with those people and Hal is keeping it going. Feds are ready to march on this mountain and burn it all down, along with all the people on it—people I don't want to see get caught up in the crossfire, if you get my meaning. I'm up here on damage control, hoping to save some lives, and nobody wants to fucking listen."

"You ain't gotta cuss me, boy."

"Sorry, Val. It's just frustrating. I'm not ready to write this place off. Katie keeps telling me it's a lost cause, Hal just wants to kick my ass, and now you don't even want to hear how all this might end peacefully."

Val reached two enormous hands out and grabbed the side of Clayton's rocker, stilling it. "You listen up, boy. You need to go back down to that little lady of yours and listen to what she has to say. Live your life in that valley, policing decent folk. Nothing up here will ever end peacefully. I've come to terms with that, and anybody making a home here has as well. You need to stay away from here and count yourself lucky that what your granddeddy did to your deddy and brothers didn't take on you. That's the peaceful ending you're looking for. You surviving all this mess. You and Kate growing old together and having a baby, the good Lord willin'. That's the best ending I can think of. If it's time for Bull Mountain to pay for its sins by way of these federal agents, then so be it. You just stay clear. It's time, and believe me when I tell you, all us sons-a-bitches that walked this road, we deserve it." Val spoke that last part quietly, remorsefully, and into his lap.

Clayton stared off into the thick expanse of forest that surrounded Val's home. After a minute or so of listening to the trees sway in the warm wind, it was Darby who broke the silence. "If the feds know everything, like locations and key players," he said, "then why don't they just send in some kinda stealth team to take them all out without a big show?"

"Because that's not how things work up here," Clayton said. "You can't sneak up on the man who has spent his life in the woods sneaking up on things. They've tried it before. People died and nothing changed."

"So go home, boy," Val said, as if suddenly validated by Clayton's own words. "Go home and stop this foolishness. Stop thinkin' you can right something that was born wrong."

Clayton rolled the red plastic cup between his palms and snorted out a dry, humorless laugh. He held up the cup in a toast. "To being born wrong," he said, and drank the cup empty without waiting for a response. It stung the split in his lip but went down welcome and easy.

2.

"Drop me at Lucky's."

"But this is *your* vehicle, sir."

Clayton said nothing, and Darby was done arguing. "Lucky's it is."

Lucky's was the kind of place that took on a different tone

depending on where the sun was positioned in relation to the Earth. During the day, a cantankerous old man named Hollis "Lucky" Peterman and his equally disgruntled brother, Harvey, served biscuits and gravy and the best cornmeal flapjacks in the state to the deer hunters and working folk of Waymore Valley. But in the evening, Harvey's daughter, Nicole, poured bourbon cocktails and pitchers of Bud Light from behind the bar. Lucky's had a built-in crowd, mostly because Lucky's was the *only* bar in the Valley. Clayton half-stumbled out of the Bronco under the influence of Val's apple-pie moonshine. He grabbed the frame of the car door, steadied himself, and slammed it shut.

And that's how it happens, he thought. *One drink, on a particularly bad day, and a year's sobriety blown to hell like it never happened.* Clayton was sure, by night's end, he'd be a smoker again, too, but these revelations weren't enough to keep him from walking into the bar. He pushed those thoughts to the back of his clouded mind and made for the front door. The place was jumping. Old-school Hank Williams Jr. belted out from the jukebox: *". . . and I get whiskey bent and hell bound."* It set the tone with an appropriate anthem for the night. Nicole looked as beautiful as ever slinging liquor behind the bar. Most of the women in Waymore wore clothes they cut from patterns or bought from the discount stores that peppered the countryside, but Nicole was a different type. She wore high heels with her blue jeans. She shopped at the outlet malls down in Buford and Commerce. Tonight Nicole wore a shiny black sequined top that sparkled under the bar lights and dark blue jeans tight enough to keep a man Clayton's age looking straight ahead, in fear of feeling like a dirty old man. Clayton spied an open seat at the end of the bar and slipped in, barely aware of the foul mood, or the shame, he was toting in with him. He eased onto the bar stool and took in a deep lungful of secondhand smoke. It smelled bad and good. He took off his hat and laid it on the bar, accidentally nudging the arm of a large gentleman to his left.

"Hey, buddy, watch your —" The look of recognition registered on Big Joe Dooley's face before he finished his sentence. "Sorry, Sheriff, I didn't see you there. My bad." Joe was known to get a little rowdy. Clayton and Choctaw both had locked him up in the drunk tank once or twice to let him sleep it off before sending him home to his wife and kids, but otherwise, the big boy was relatively harmless.

"S'okay, Joe." Clayton hailed Nicole, who immediately stopped what she was doing, smiled a big pearly smile, and poured the sheriff a ginger ale from a squatty green bottle under the bar. Clayton's most recent usual. She slapped a bar napkin down and set the soda in front of the sheriff, then took notice of his swollen eye and split lip. Her pretty smile contorted into a pretty grimace.

"Ouch," she said. "Holy cow, Sheriff. How does the other guy look?"

"Much better than me, I'm afraid."

"You want me to make you an ice pack for that?"

"That's okay, Nicole."

"It's no problem. I got clean rags in the back. I could fix you up."

"Nah, it's just a scratch. I'll be okay. Busy night tonight, huh?"

"It's a busy night every night, sir." Nicole leaned forward on the bar with both elbows, maybe not so unintentionally creating a perfect view of her sun-freckled cleavage. Clayton did his best not to look. She didn't make it easy. Her big green eyes would stop traffic even without all the eye makeup she shrouded them in, but girls her age never believed that. She was a looker, but a good girl. Clayton liked her. Big Joe made no attempt to reel in his slack-jawed stare and shifted his cumbersome weight on the bar stool to lean toward her and Clayton's conversation. "You think I could get a beer, or do I have to be wearin' a silver star on my shirt, too?"

"Just a second, Joe," Nicole said without looking at him.

Joe frowned an exaggerated drunken frown. "I been waiting here almost ten minutes, girlie."

This time she did look at him. "Look around you, Joe. It's a little busy. I'll be right with you."

Joe shot a quick glance at Clayton, then mumbled something shitty into his empty glass. Clayton assumed it would have been a lot louder if he hadn't been sitting there. He ignored him and took a sip of the ginger ale. That wasn't going to do it.

"I'll be back shortly, Sheriff. Are you hungry? Uncle Hollis's got some country fried steak left over from the lunch rush."

"No, thanks, Nicole, but . . ." Clayton paused. Nicole lifted an eyebrow. ". . . you *could* bring me two fingers of Knob Creek. Straight up."

Nicole, caught off guard, narrowed her eyes at the sheriff. "Um . . . okay," she said, and turned to get the bottle down from the mirrored shelf behind her. Big Joe Dooley dug his pudgy elbow into Clayton's recently bruised ribs, causing him to wince with pain, but Joe didn't notice. He pointed to Nicole up on a step stool reaching for the bourbon. The bright colors of the floral tattoo that covered the small of her back teased out from a sliver of skin above the low waist of her jeans.

"Now, that there is an ass. Right, Sheriff?"

Clayton said nothing and again avoided taking in an eyeful of the half-his-age ass in the air.

"I could sit right here and wait on a beer forever," Joe said, "if I could watch her swing that shit-cutter around all night."

That made the nerve above Clayton's eye twitch. "Shut the fuck up, Joe."

Big Joe crumpled his nose like he'd just taken a whiff of fresh dog shit and honestly searched his brain for a reason why another man would take offense to that statement.

Nicole stepped down, oblivious, and poured the whiskey into a clean glass in front of Clayton. He nodded a "thank you" and she winked a "you're welcome." A short narrow man who looked like he was carved completely out of seasoned leather waved a twenty-dollar bill at Nicole from down the bar. She held a finger up to Clayton and sashayed off toward her tip money. Clayton closed his eyes and held the glass to his nose. It smelled of oak, vanilla, and bad decisions. The moment ended abruptly with another shot of pain up his side. Big Joe landed another elbow to Clayton's ribs, spoiling the sheriff's first sip. Bourbon dribbled down his beard and spilled onto the bar. He put the glass down.

"I hate to see her leave," Joe said, leaning across the bar, his eyes glued to Nicole's backside. "But I love to watch her go."

Clayton used his napkin to mop up the spilled drink and felt the heat rise under his skin. "I thought I told you to shut up, Joe. In fact"—Clayton turned all the way around into the big man's face—"why don't you get your fat ass up and find somewhere else to sit as far away from me and that girl as possible." Clayton's voice was louder than he'd intended, but that's what happened when he drank. A few heads turned. A few conversations stopped. Confusion spread over Big Joe's face like a rash.

"Goddamn, Clayton, I was just cuttin' up."

"Move your ass, Joe. Now." Clayton sat up a little straighter and bowed his chest out. There wasn't much to it, but it looked a lot bigger to most with that star pinned to it. Nicole came back and set a fresh beer in front of Joe. She looked as confused as he did. Joe picked up his frosted mug and gave Clayton a drunken half-assed toast, in the process managing to spill beer down the front of his shirt.

"Yessir, Mr. Sheriff, sir." And off he went, sloshing beer on himself and the floor.

"What was that about?" she said.

"Some folks live their whole lives without an ounce of class," Clayton said, and took a long pull of hundred-proof bourbon, letting it sit on his tongue. Nicole wiped up the spilt beer.

"Well, don't worry, Sheriff, he's harmless."

"He's an asshole."

Nicole leaned in close to Clayton's ear. "Hell, Sheriff, show me a drunk who ain't."

3.

Clayton was on his third drink when Special Agent Simon Holly took Big Joe's vacated seat. He just sat there, smiling that shark smile of his, until Clayton came up out of his rocks glass and took notice. He squinted hard at Holly, either to focus his eyes or to make sure he wasn't seeing things. Maybe both.

"Evening, Sheriff."

"What are you doing here, Holly?" Clayton said, turning his attention back to his glass.

"My travel agent said this place was one of the top attractions to take in while visiting the mountain paradise of Waymore Valley, Georgia."

Clayton just stared blankly, his eyes slowly disappearing into his face. He wasn't up for cheery sarcasm.

"Sorry, Sheriff, I can see you're in a mood. I'm staying at the motor inn across the street. I saw your deputy drop you off a little while ago, so I thought I'd come break some bread. Tough night?"

"Why?"

"Your face looks like shit."

"Yeah, well, you can take a little responsibility for that."

Holly put his smile away. "You spoke to your brother?"

"Well, we didn't do much speakin'."

"I take it it didn't go well?"

"That's one way to say it. Brother shit. I don't think he's going to listen to reason."

"I have no doubt you will find a way." Holly motioned for Nicole, who smiled even bigger than normal when she saw him.

"Well, hello there," she said. "And just who might you be?"

Holly just smiled, leaned back on the stool, and let the sheriff make the introductions.

"Nicole, this is Holly. He's a federal agent sent here to complicate my life. Bring us both one of these." Clayton tapped his empty glass.

Holly held out a hand. "It's Simon, and you better make his water."

Nicole cupped his hand with both of hers and leaned in close, making sure Simon got an eyeful of the same award-winning cleavage she'd showed off to Clayton earlier. She spoke in a whisper. "I was just about to call his wife to come get him."

"I got him," Holly said, and winked at her.

"Cool," she said, and off she floated to the other side of the bar. Holly leaned forward and watched her move. This time, Clayton did, too.

"Your day go any better than mine?" Clayton said.

"We had an incident off Highway 27 near a place called Broadwater. I was close, so they put me on it."

"An incident?"

"Yeah, looks like a hijacking gone wrong. We got one body."

"Who bought the farm? A hijacker, or hijackee?"

"Hijacker, we're assuming, unless he was jogging along the highway with an assault rifle and a clown mask. The scene was scrubbed clean before the state boys got there, but we impounded an empty moving truck, and we think there might have been bikes involved. We found a broken Harley side mirror, and the skid marks are consistent with someone laying one down."

"Bikes," Clayton said. "Is it related to our thing?"

"I'm not one hundred percent, but I've got ears in Florida that tell me they were moving a bundle of cash this way. It fits with the schedule they keep. But nothing is cement right now. The staties are dragging ass on telling me anything else."

"That's because half the state patrol is in Halford's pocket. That whole area around Broadwater is a dead zone. Did you ID the dead guy?"

"Yup. No ID on him, but we ran his prints through IAFIS . . . Um . . . IAFIS is a national database of—"

Clayton held his hand up. "I know what IAFIS is."

"Right. Anyway, we got a hit. The guy's name is Allen Bankey. Does that name ring any bells?"

Clayton thought about it. "Nope."

Nicole appeared and set two glasses of water down on the bar and a fresh bourbon for Holly. He smiled and nodded politely. Once Nicole bounced away, he kept talking. "He's ex-military," Holly said. "We think he was part of a crew but got left after he went down. Surprisingly, the guy's file is pretty clean except for a bullshit statutory rape charge from a few years back."

"How is a rape charge bullshit?" Clayton said, looking at his water like it was some kind of alien artifact.

"The girl was sixteen, but you'd never know it looking at her. The sex was consensual. The parents let it go, knowing their daughter was no prize, but the state picked it up and the next thing you know, boom—G.I. Joe is a lifelong registered sex offender. It happens all the time."

"And now he's dead."

"As Elvis. You're sure you don't know him?"

"Never heard of an Allen Bankey." Clayton swallowed the water in two gulps. "But bring the file by the office tomorrow and I'll take a look."

"Done," Holly said, and guzzled half his drink.

"Hey, Sweet Tits," roared a voice at the other end of the bar. Clayton looked over and shook his head. Big Joe Dooley was back, looking to fill his glass and blowing kisses at Nicole. Clayton pushed up off his stool and put on his hat. "I'll be right back."

Holly saw Clayton steady himself from the alcohol-induced head rush but made no attempt to help him. He watched curiously as the sheriff crossed the room and grabbed Joe Dooley by the scruff of hair on the back of his thick, sweaty neck. Before the big boy could re-act, Clayton pushed down hard and slammed Joe's forehead into the copper-plated bar. The crack of bone on metal reverberated through the room and knocked over several glasses to both sides of them. People scattered and jumped out of the way, making space for the big boy to fall, but Clayton didn't let go. He held Joe's face there against the bar to anchor himself until he could twist one of Joe's arms up and behind his back. Holly smiled. He was impressed that the sheriff could hold his own as drunk as he was. He used the moment to fish a few Percocet from his pocket and washed them down with the rest of his bourbon.

"I thought I told you to watch your mouth," Clayton said.

Joe answered the best he could from the position he was in. "No, you didn't. You . . . you . . . told me to move . . . I did."

"I told you to stay clear of Nicole." Clayton pushed down hard, smearing the left side of Joe's face flatter against the cold metal. Nicole stood back, wide-eyed, with both hands covering her mouth. Holly almost laughed out loud.

"Well, goddamn, Sheriff," Joe said through the side of his mouth not smashed down against the bar. "How am I supposed to get a drink around here? She's the only one working."

"Not my problem."

"This is bullshit. I ain't done nothing wrong."

"Maybe I just don't like the way you talk to women, Joe."

"Maybe I don't care what you think." Joe was getting over his fear of the badge now, being more in fear of town-wide embarrassment. Clayton could feel him starting to buck. He leaned in. "Say you're sorry."

"Fuck you."

That's when Holly saw the lights go out in Clayton's face. He'd seen that look before on the faces of a lot of men he'd had to put down. The sheriff went full dark. Holly knew he would. Clayton yanked down hard on Big Joe's neck and kicked his legs out from underneath him. Joe hit the floor hard. Falling bar stools collided into the few remaining patrons, who quickly made for the exits. Clayton used a size-eleven cowboy boot to kick Joe over flat on his back, and then used that same boot to step down on his face. "Fuck who?"

Holly sipped his water and stood. He was amazed at how fast it had happened. He'd almost written Clayton off as a sloppy drunk. Nothing like what he'd expected him to be, but he was wrong. He didn't even realize how wrong until he saw Clayton's gun drawn and pointed at Joe's head. He never even saw him draw it.

"Whoa, Sheriff," Holly said, stepping into the fray. "That's enough. Put it away. Let him up."

"Apologize," Clayton said again, not letting the big man move.

"I'm sorry, Sheriff, I'm sorry."

Clayton thumbed back the hammer. "To the girl, fat ass. Apologize to the girl." A dark stain spread over Big Joe's crotch as he pissed himself.

"I'm sorry, Nicole. Jesus, I didn't mean anything by it. I'm sorry. I'm so sorry."

Holly put both his hands up in front of Clayton as a form of surrogate surrender for the man on the floor. "Put it away, Sheriff. Put the gun away and let him up."

Clayton switched his rabid glare from Big Joe to Agent Holly, who kept his hands up and repeated slowly, "Put . . . it . . . away." Clayton finally did. He slid the Colt into his holster and took his foot off Joe's face. The big boy scuffled away across the floor toward the door. When he got outside, a few people in the crowd helped him to his feet. For a moment he looked like he was going to say something, but Holly stopped him with three words. From the door, he pointed one finger at Big Joe and said, "Don't. Just go." Big Joe took the advice.

Holly turned his attention back to Clayton, who hadn't moved. He stood staring at the floor as if Joe were still down there. "I think you're done here, Sheriff." He laid a cautious hand on Clayton's shoulder. "Let me take you home."

Clayton wore a look on his face like he'd just woken from surgery that required a heavy anesthetic. "Okay," he said. Holly looked back to Nicole, who hadn't moved much, either, except to survey the damage done to her daddy's place. He nodded at her, then toted Clayton out to his car.

4.

Kate came out on the porch holding a .30-.30 before Holly could open the door on Clayton's side of the Crown Vic. Holly knew about Kate. He knew from photos that she was beautiful, but her standing there with that rifle, in nothing but an oversized nightshirt, put her on the list of the top ten sexiest women he'd ever seen. The porch light silhouetting her legs through the thin material drove her up to the top five. She could see someone else in the car but couldn't make out who it was. "Who are you and what do you want?"

"Mrs. Burroughs?"

"I know *my* name. I asked who *you* are."

Holly smiled.

"I'm serious. My husband's the sheriff."

"I work with your husband. He's here with me in the car."

"Who the hell are you?"

Holly held his hands up slightly higher than his shoulders. "My name is Simon Holly. I'm a federal agent and, seriously, ma'am, Clayton is here in the car."

Kate took a step forward to see the man in the car a little better in the dark. Holly lowered one hand and opened the passenger-side door. Light flooded the interior of the Crown Vic, and Kate saw her husband. She lowered the rifle a little and took two more steps toward the car before noticing the damage done to his face and steadied the gun back on Simon. She racked the lever. "What happened to him?"

Holly put his hands up a little higher. "Oh, no. You got it wrong. I didn't do that. He was already like that. I'm just giving him a ride home."

"He's a friend, Katie. Put that thing away." Clayton raised a wobbly hand in the air to motion for her to put down the gun, and then tried unsuccessfully to pull himself out of the car. Simon lurched forward and grabbed his elbow to keep him from falling. Kate leaned the rifle against the quarter panel of the car and took Clayton's face in her hands. She smelled the whiskey immediately and pulled back.

"Clayton? Are you . . . ? Have you been . . . ?"

"I'm fine."

"You're not fine. You're drunk and you're beat-up. What the hell is going on here?" She examined his swollen eye, but with a lot less compassion than she would have done if he was sober. She looked to Holly to fill in the blanks. "What happened?"

"I suppose you should ask him, ma'am."

"I'm asking you."

"I'm thinking he might want to tell you himself."

"That's enough," Clayton said, grabbing the rifle and making his way toward the porch. "Holly, bring the file on your dead bandito to my office in the morning. Thanks for the ride." He carefully took the steps and opened the screen door.

"Clayton!" Kate said, surprised—confused—disgusted.

"Just come inside, woman. You ain't got no pants on." Clayton disappeared into the house. Kate's cheeks flushed a bright rosy red, but Holly was sure it was caused by anger and not humility. He studied his shoes and puffed his cheeks out. He kept his hands buried deep in his pockets. "Sorry, ma'am," he said. Kate twisted her head so fast from the front door to Holly, he thought it might snap right off.

"Sorry? What are you sorry for?" She didn't wait on an answer. "Are you sorry Halford didn't kill him? I know that's what happened. I know he went up there with some fool idea that you put in his head. I know that's a year of sobriety down the toilet because of this bullshit."

"Wait a minute, Kate. It's bigger than that."

"Don't use my name familiar. You don't know me. Just get back in your car and drive away. I'd tell you to stay away, but we both know that ain't gonna happen, is it?"

"I can't."

"Get the hell off my property."

"All right, Mrs. Burroughs." Holly moved to the driver's side of the car and put his hand on the door. "You know," he said, "the girl down at Lucky's wanted to call you to come get him. I didn't think you'd want that to play out in public."

"What do you want? A thank-you?"

"Well, yeah," he said. He kind of did.

Kate's hip swiveled out to the side on instinct. It showed off her curves even more, and Holly struggled to keep his attention on her eyes. She grabbed the rifle from where Clayton had propped it against the door and flung her hair back out of her face. "I want you to listen to me, Agent Holly. Can you do that? I mean really listen?"

"Sure."

"Good, because I don't plan on ever having to talk to you again. My husband is a good man—"

"Mrs. Burroughs."

"You just said you could listen."

"Yes, ma'am."

"Now, he's a good man and he's a good sheriff—almost to a fault. He can handle himself and he's capable of making his own decisions, but that doesn't let you off the hook for planting the seed. Don't think for a second that I won't hold you just as accountable if anything like this happens again on your watch."

"My intentions here are to do this peacefully."

"Says the man whose face *didn't* get pummeled today. I don't care what your intentions are. I just want my husband to come home to me every night whole. Tonight is your one pass. But after tonight, if you get him hurt again, if *anything* happens to that man while he's acting on your behalf, I don't care who you are, or what your intentions were, you're going to have to answer to more than just the Lord. Are we clear on that, Special Agent Holly?"

Holly studied her resolve; this woman was a piece of work. She'd just threatened a federal agent and meant every word of it. Holly nodded, more in admiration than agreement. He opened the car door.

"Holly, one more thing."

"What's that, Mrs. Burroughs?"

"Another thing about Clayton. Once he gets his mind set to something, there's no stopping him until it's run its course. Not until it's done. So I'd be extremely careful what exactly you set him on."

"Yes, ma'am."

Kate watched the twin red taillights fade to black before she gave her hands permission to shake.

5.

"I'm sorry, baby. It was a onetime thing. It won't happen again." Clayton was barely conscious, drifting off on their bed as he spoke. Kate covered him with the quilt and stroked his rust-colored hair. There was no point in trying to talk about anything now. Clayton waking up in his boots and dirty clothes with a monster hangover would have to be penance enough. She'd deal with the rest later.

"It's okay, Clayton. Get some rest."

Within seconds he was out, and the snoring began. He snored only when he drank. She stayed there, sitting on the bed, running her fingers through his hair for a few minutes more before getting up to put the rifle back in the gun cabinet. She walked into the kitchen and used her foot to slide a small wooden step stool out of the pantry and position it in front of the refrigerator. She stepped up, moved a few bottles of vitamins out of the way, and opened the high cupboard. She pulled out the bottle of bourbon. The bottle she wasn't supposed to know about. She stepped down, opened another cabinet, and took out a rocks glass. Waterford crystal. Expensive. A wedding gift from some friend she'd drifted out of touch with years ago. She carried the whiskey and the glass to the front door, careful not to let the screen door creak and wake up Clayton. Like that would happen. He'd sleep through a hurricane right now. She sat down on the porch swing and held the bottle up to the moonlight. It was a little over half empty. A full two, maybe three, inches below the thin black pen mark she'd put on the back label. Last time she checked, it was at an inch. She closed her eyes and sat quiet, swinging there, listening to the mountain's nightlife competing for the chance to sing her to sleep. She poured herself a drink and set the bottle down beside her. She held the glass for a long time, staring at it, rolling it between her palms before she finally poured it out on the porch and cried.

CHAPTER 16

1.

Angel rested her forehead against the cool glass of the bus window. The tree line buzzed by in a blur of greens, browns, and reds. Every so often she tried to focus on a single point of interest and moved her head to break the blur, but there was nothing to see she hadn't seen a hundred times before. She'd hitched every inch of this highway over the course of the past five years in an effort to escape her life, but always ended up headed back in this direction. She'd spent the last of the money the big black man from the hotel gave her on the bus ticket. If she had done what he told her and gone to a hospital, she might still have it all, but she didn't. She went to Pepé, her pimp. It's true what they say about young gullible women thinking their tormentors love them. Angel was walking, talking, battered proof. Pepé said he cared about her. Promised to take care of her. Swore to her no other man would put hands on her she didn't want there. He told her hospitals led to uncomfortable questions, and that led to police, which led to jail. He would never let that happen to her. He'd protect her, and his protection was absolute. Except, his protection consisted of taking all her money, putting a needle full of opium in her arm, and getting a bunch of Hispanic yes-men to hold her down and shove her shoulder back in place while she drooled into a dirty sofa cushion. She didn't remember all of it, just flashes of color, sweaty faces, and laughter. One of them, the one Pepé called El Cirujano, stitched up her face where that bastard from Georgia had cut her. She hadn't pulled the gauze off to examine the damage. In fact, she'd avoided her reflection altogether since it all went down. Right now she was fine with never seeing her face again, but she knew something bad was festering under there. Pepé kept her doped up for God knows how long, relegated to the back room of that double-wide, until it dawned on him that nobody would want to fuck a skinny whore in her condition with a face that looked like raw hamburger. That's when the dope stopped coming and the sick started. Almost two months she'd stayed cooped up in that shithole. She knew it would be just a matter of time before he'd kill her and have his boys toss her body in a dumpster somewhere. A far cry from the life she'd come out here for. She'd thought to stash one of the C-notes in the lining of her bra, and the first chance she got, she slid it under a corner of carpet. When the time came to bail, she took that money and the clothes she had on and climbed out the trailer window. She made a beeline to the bus station where Pepé had first scooped her up so many months ago and bought a ticket for the first bus home. Why didn't she just go to the damn hospital? Why was she so stupid? Why was everyone else always right, and she got everything so terribly wrong? She moved her forehead around on the window, using up all the coolness of the glass, and closed her eyes. She knew going home was just the latest in her lifelong series of mistakes.

2 .

The young man sitting next to Angel in the aisle seat fished a bag of peanuts from the rucksack on his lap. "You want some?" he asked, shaking the bag toward Angel. He was chubby in a man-child kind of way, with a full head of tightly curled brown hair. He wore blue jeans and a Florida State sweatshirt that sported the same Indian-head logo also embroidered on the rucksack. He was obviously in his twenties, but the rosy cheeks and chub made him look younger. He seemed nice enough, letting her have the window seat when she got on the bus, and, so far, he hadn't mentioned the bandages on her face or the dirty denim shirt and sweat-stained tube top she was wearing. She could tell he was fighting it, but he'd managed to keep his eyes off her tits this whole time as well, and she was thankful for it. She had caught him stealing glances at her bony white legs for the past few miles. She used to like being ogled. It made her feel pretty, but now it just made her feel ill.

"No, thanks, I'm okay."

Florida State tucked the peanuts back into his bag and secured the flap, taking the time to buckle each strap.

Can't be too careful traveling with whores, she thought, and wished she'd taken the peanuts. She was starving.

"Suit yourself," he said, "but you look pretty hungry."

"I'm really not," she lied. "My stomach's a little knotted up this morning."

"You trying to get clean?" he said without skipping a beat, like he was asking about the weather or a local football score. Angel shifted herself toward the window and slowly angled her arms in an attempt to hide the blackened veins that road-mapped them.

"It's cool," Florida State said. "I'm not judging or anything. I think

it's great you want to do better for yourself. I'm Hattie, by the way."
Hattie stuck out a pudgy hand for Angel to shake. She handled it
like it was carved from dog shit.

"I'm Angel."

"Nice to meet you, Angel. Are you headed home or leaving
home?"

"Going home."

"Cool. Cool. I got a buddy down in Pensacola getting married in
a few days. I'm gonna hang out in the gulf and tan up a little before
I hit the wedding."

Angel wanted to laugh. This guy had about as much of a chance
of getting tanned up as she did getting her virginity back. She really
didn't care what Hattie's plans were. She only wanted to sleep away
the last hours of this trip and wake up in a brand-new but slightly
less shitty situation. Hattie wasn't going to let that happen.

"You mind if I ask what happened to your face?"

"Yes," she said. It came out fast and sharp.

"That's cool. I'm just being friendly. I'll shut up."

Angel felt a twinge of guilt for snapping at the guy. She was all
bandaged up, after all, so why wouldn't he ask? "No. Look, I'm sorry.
I'm not trying to be rude. I got into a . . . situation recently, and now
I'm just trying to get out—way out."

"Jeez, sounds rough."

"It was."

"What brought you to Jacksonville in the first place?"

She laughed. Here she was, beaten, bandaged, badly dressed, covered in bruises and track marks, hadn't showered in more than a
week, and answering that question embarrassed her. Angel considered Hattie for the first time. If she wasn't so foul and down on herself, she might have found him cute in a Peter Pan kind of way. She

had to admit, though, it was nice talking to a decent guy. "It's a dumb reason."

"Can't be that dumb if you're gonna up and move to another state. Tell me."

"I wanted to be a singer."

"A singer?"

"Yeah. I told you it was dumb."

"No, it ain't. That's cool. I can't carry a tune in a bucket. What kind of singing?"

"Rock and roll, I guess. A little country, too."

"Like Linda Ronstadt? I love her."

"A little," Angel said. She was brightening up some. No one ever wanted to talk to her about her music. Mostly people just rolled their eyes. "I like Ronstadt, but I wanted a harder edge. More like Janis Joplin, you know?"

"Like her stuff with Big Brother and the Holding Company?"

"Yeah." Angel was excited now. Not many people she met knew the music she listened to. The smile she wore made the wounds in her face throb. "But my idea was to make it a little more southern, like picture Janis singing for Lynyrd Skynyrd, or something."

"Ah, that's why you came to Jacksonville and you didn't head the other way toward California."

"Yeah, I thought I'd get inspired if I lived in the same town those guys were from. I thought some of what they had might rub off on me."

Hattie unstrapped his rucksack and offered his peanuts again. This time she accepted. She popped an entire handful in her mouth but immediately regretted it. It hurt to chew.

"Still could, you know."

"Still could what?" she said carefully from the side of her full mouth.

"Still could make it big. You got plenty of time to get back out there."

Angel finished chewing before she responded to that. "No," she said. "No, I can't." She was suddenly cold, and hugged herself close around her midriff. She stared back out the window. "Things have . . . changed." She closed her eyes and thought about another one of her stupid decisions. In the three months she'd worked johns for Pepé, she'd at least made them wear a rubber. That, or she was slick enough to get one of those stupid sponges in place first. That bastard—*Gareth*, Pepé had called him—he refused. She was too scared to argue. No, she wasn't scared. She was *into* him, so she gave in to him. She was just stupid, and that was nothing new.

"You okay?" Hattie said.

"I'm fine," she said.

"Well, I sure don't see why you can't make another run at the whole singing thing, Angel. I mean, you sure are pretty enough."

Instantly Angel was hyper-aware of how much of her body was uncovered. She tried not to show it, but shrank up a little in her seat out of instinct. "Thank you," she said, polite but frigid. He'd gotten her talking. It was her fault. Here it comes.

"I mean, a girl with your kinda looks, and your figure, could go all the way, for sure." Hattie lightly rubbed a finger down the smoothness of her thigh. Angel continued to shrink. "You don't even know if I can sing," she said. She wanted to scream.

"I'll just bet you sing like an angel. I bet that's how you got your name."

Angel stared out at the whirl of buzzing trees and highway markers. "That's not my name," she said. "That's just what someone else decided I should be called. My real name's Marion."

"That's a pretty name, too, Marion. A pretty name for a pretty girl." Another pudgy finger down her thigh. He shifted his weight to press closer to her. She thought she might puke. Two months ago she would have screamed in his face and punched him square in the nuts, but now all she could see was the face of that man at the hotel, Gareth Burroughs. He'd almost killed her. He would always be right there to remind her how little she mattered. How helpless she really was. She hugged her belly tighter.

Hattie kept talking, kept groping, but she stopped responding. He said something about getting a drink. Finding a quiet place to "talk" when the bus stopped in Destin. He said he knew just the place. She bet he did. She closed her eyes again and hugged herself tighter, trying to disappear into the cocoon of her thin, damaged arms—to squeeze herself out of existence. She had to believe this time around things would be different. If she could just get back home, things *had* to be different. They just had to. It wasn't just about her anymore. Things were going to be better for her in Mobile.

Better for her and the baby.

3.

Marion stood in front of the Grand Central diner on Dauphin Street, holding a pay phone to her ear and a menthol 100 to her lips. It rang twice.

"Hello."

"Mama?"

"Marion? Is that you?"

"Yes, Mama."

"Oh my God, baby, where are you?"

"I'm home, Mama."

"Oh, thank the Lord. Tell me where you are, and I'll send Roy to pick you up."

Marion switched the phone to the other ear as if the first one were defective and she had heard her mother wrong. "You'll send Roy? Mama . . . ? Is he still . . . ?"

"Is he still what, honey?"

"Mama, Roy's the reason—"

"Marion, honey, please don't start that up. You're home, baby. That's all that matters. We'll work it all out. Where are you?"

Silence.

"Marion, baby? Are you still there?"

"I . . . I got to go, Mama."

"Marion, wait. Your father's changed. He's a good man. It was all a misunderstanding."

"He's not my father."

"Marion, baby, please. Tell me where you are and we can all sit down and work it out. You'll see. He's a wonderful man, and he misses you very much."

"Mama . . ."

"Hold on, baby, he wants to talk to you . . ."

"Mama!"

"Hold on . . ."

"That you, pretty bird? You come to your senses? You wanna come on home now?"

Click.

Marion tossed her cigarette butt to the ground and immediately dug in her purse for the pack to light another. She savagely flicked her Bic until the flame held, and she pulled in as much smoke as her lungs could handle. She dropped another coin in the slot and punched another number. It rang three times.

"Hello?"

"Barbara?"

"Holy shit. Marion?"

"Yeah, girl, it's me."

"Where are you?"

"I'm home. I'm over by Grand Central. Can you come and get me?"

"Hell, yeah, I can. Just let me get the keys from Tim, and I'll be right there."

"Thanks, Barb. And Barb?"

"Yeah, girl?"

"I need some clothes, too."

"Um, okay. I got you. Anything I need to know, Marion? I mean, Tim is cool and all, but is there anything I need to tell him first?"

She looked down and rubbed her flat belly. "Goddamn, Barb. I just need some clothes and a shower, can you help me or not?"

"Of course I can. I'll be there in twenty, okay?"

"Okay."

Click.

4.

Marion caught her reflection in the glass pane of the diner's door, right above the HELP WANTED sign. A week's worth of healing and Barbara's magic makeup skills weren't enough to cover up the ugly done to her in Jacksonville, but it was going to have to do. If Marion didn't show back up at Barb and Tim's place today with a job, she wouldn't have anywhere to go back to. She wasn't going back to Roy's. She'd take her chances on the street before asking that son of a bitch for anything. The baby cooking in her belly was about ten weeks, by her estimation. That was kicking up the timetable, too. If she started to show before she could find work, nobody would hire her. Nobody wanted a scar-faced ex-whore, much less an unwed pregnant one. She straightened out the sleeves of the borrowed blouse and opened the door. She snatched the red-and-white HELP WANTED sign off the inside of the door and took a seat on one of the chrome diner stools at the bar, then took a deep breath in through her nose and out through her mouth. She placed the sign flat in her lap and resisted the urge to light up another smoke.

A nice little Indian fellow named Ishmael Punjab ran the Grand Central diner. He was always there. Today was no exception. "Good morning," he said. "Would you like to see a menu?" Without waiting for an answer, he laid a laminated picture menu in front of her and, almost like sleight of hand, produced a set of silverware rolled in a paper napkin from under the counter. Punjab was short and bald, with a few strands of wiry black hair slicked down to his tan scalp.

"Just coffee," she said, "and maybe a job." Marion placed the HELP WANTED sign on top of the menu and slid it toward the little Indian man. He looked at it, then at her. He clearly had trouble keeping eye contact without focusing on the damage done to her face, but did his best.

"Do you have any server experience?" he asked, and put the silverware roll back where it came from.

"I waited tables at the Red Minnow in Gulf Shores every summer during high school and almost two years after. Mrs. Gentry said she'd give me a great recommendation if you want to call."

"That's good. That's good. My place is a little faster-paced than the Red Minnow. Do you know anything about short-order diners?" He took the menu up but didn't move to get the coffee she'd asked for.

"No, sir, I don't. But I'm a fast learner. I work hard and I'm extremely reliable. I can work any hours you need and any days. Even weekends."

Punjab held a finger to the corner of his mouth and stared at her intensely. "Can I ask you why you didn't just get your old job back from Mrs. Gentry?"

The truth was she had tried, but the Red Minnow was more upscale, and the Gentrys hired only pretty girls to parade around out front. Marion wasn't pretty anymore. She'd never be pretty again. "Their staff is full-up right now, and the truth is, I don't think I'd be a good fit there anymore."

Punjab struggled with the next part of the conversation, so Marion picked up the volley. "I know I look rough, but I promise you it will get better. I'll never be as pretty as I used to be, but I won't always be this hideous. The problem is, the bills don't want to wait for me to get better. They want to be paid right now, and I'm a heartbeat away from being out of options."

"Young lady," Punjab said, his face softened, "I don't find you hideous." He held her eyes that time. She could have cried right there.

"Thank you, sir. You're sweet to say that, but I don't think most people will share your opinion. I know I'm not a prime candidate for a job here, but if you were to take a chance, I promise you, I'll do my very best."

Punjab smiled. It was a genuine and warm smile. He didn't look away once. From the same space below the counter he'd retrieved the silverware a few minutes ago, he pulled out a pad of generic employment applications, tore off the top one, and slid it over to Marion. She really could have just started sobbing all over this man's counter. *A break,* she thought. *Finally a goddamn break.*

"Fill this out, and I'll take a look. Okay?"

"Thank you, Mr. Punjab."

"I'm not making any promises, dear. I will check your references and decide if you are the best qualified for the position."

"Of course, sir."

"But maybe I'll just keep this in my office until I have a chance to look over your application." Punjab picked up the HELP WANTED sign, folded it in half, and tucked it in his apron.

"Thank you," Marion said again.

"You are welcome. Do you need a pen?"

Marion pulled a pen from the pocket of the slightly-too-small skirt she'd borrowed from Barbara. "No, sir. I got it."

"Very well, then."

She hadn't finished writing her full name down on the application before Punjab returned with a mug and a small stainless-steel carafe of steaming chicory root coffee, a Mobile trademark. He filled the mug and left the carafe on the counter. The coffee was thick and hot and smelled like heaven.

"If you need anything else, feel free to ask. I will be just through that door." He pointed at the double swinging doors leading to the kitchen. He looked at his watch. "Sarah, my head waitress, will be here any minute, which works out perfectly. She's really the one that needs the help."

"Sounds good, sir."

Punjab tapped the counter with both hands and disappeared through the swinging doors.

Marion was on her third cup of coffee and the back page of her application when she heard Sarah Watson come through the front door.

"Well, look what the cat dragged in," Sarah said, and her voice soured the air in the room. Marion felt that the day and her luck had just taken a turn. The short, squat redhead flipped up the hinged counter, tucked her purse below the bar, and strolled up to Marion's stool. Marion knew this girl from high school, from another life. She was a big girl then and an even bigger girl now, with a face covered in freckles, but not the good, sun-peppered kind. Sarah's freckles made her look like the victim of a big truck speeding through a nasty mud puddle.

"Hello, Sarah, you look well," Marion lied.

"A mile better than you. That's for sure. How long's it been? Three years? I suppose the rock star thing didn't work out too good." Sarah stared at Marion's face as if she were watching a car wreck. "Jesus," she said, her own pudgy face all twisted up. "What the hell happened to you?"

"I'd rather not talk about it, if that's okay. I'm just here for a job."

"Is that a fact?" Sarah picked up the carafe and poured the remaining coffee down the sink without asking if Marion was finished with it. "Isn't it funny?" she said.

"What, Sarah? What's funny?"

"How life is, you know? How all through high school you and all your perfect little friends never even saw me in the halls, never even gave me a second thought, and now here you are, needing something from me. I just think that's funny, is all."

"Yeah, it's hilarious."

Sarah snatched up the application from the counter. After a minute of cycling through a gamut of disgusted expressions, she tossed it back on the bar. "You're kidding, right? I mean, you know there's no way Punjab is going to hire you with your history."

"What history?" Marion said softly, involuntarily scanning the empty diner.

Sarah mocked her and looked around the diner as well, then

leaned in with her own low tone. "Everybody knows about you, Marion. The whole Gulf Coast knows what happened with you and your father."

"He's not my father."

"Whatever you say, honey," Sarah said. She crossed her arms and peered straight down her mud-splattered piggy nose.

"It's not just what I say. It's the truth. Nothing happened." Anger was seeping in around the edges of Marion's voice.

"Not the way I heard it."

"I don't care what you heard."

"Not the way everyone else heard it, either. Your old man do that to your face? You guys have a lover's spat?"

"Fuck you," Marion blurted out on instinct. Her words dropped on the counter like a cinder block. Sarah's sneer twisted into a smile—a freckled pig smile.

"Listen, Marion, I'm going to do you a favor here, since clearly you are lost and in need of some direction. You know the Time-Out over off I-65?"

Marion could taste acid building in her mouth. She fought the urge to spit it in Sarah's face.

"I can see that you do. That's good. I hear they're always looking for girls like you. I bet they even got a late-night slot where that mangled-up face won't be such a big issue. I mean, let's be honest. Nobody goes there to look in a girl's eyes, right? So why don't you take your scary face, your family business, and your burned-up twat down to where you belong and do what it is you do. This here is a diner. We serve food. We ain't hiring whores."

Marion saw what might happen next in her mind's eye. She grabs two big handfuls of Sarah's tight red ringlets, pulls down and bashes her smug grin into the bar. Her nose busts like a ripe tomato, but

Marion doesn't stop. She keeps bashing Sarah's head down over and over into the black-and-white-tiled counter. Screaming at her, wailing like a banshee about how she was molested and almost raped by her piece-of-shit stepfather, about how *she* was the fucking victim. She keeps bashing and bashing until the fat girl's face is nothing but pulp and her lifeless body goes limp. Marion lets it slide to the floor.

But that's not what happened.

She just stood up, wiped the corners of her eyes on a napkin, and left the diner.

Punjab heard the bell on the door chime as Marion walked out, and came out of the kitchen.

"Where did she go?" he asked.

"You weren't thinking of hiring her, were you?"

"Yes. I was thinking about it. She seemed nice. A little sad, but nice."

"Well, then, Mr. Punjab, I think I deserve a raise, because I just did you a huge favor." Sarah handed the application to her boss and crossed her arms. "Read it," she insisted. Punjab put on his glasses and read the form.

"Marion Holly?" he said, a little taken aback. "As in Roy Holly's girl?"

"That's the one."

CHAPTER

17

MARION HOLLY

SOUTHERN ALABAMA

1981

1.

The lights inside the Time-Out Gentlemen's Club washed its patrons in sickly pale shades of pink and green. Other than the girls onstage, who were painted in thick layers of glitter and pancake makeup, everyone in the place looked like they were made of warped, sweaty plastic—carnival versions of reality. Not that they were anything to look at anyway, even in the daylight. Most of the *gentlemen* that frequented the Time-Out were long-haul truckers on the tail end of marathon crank binges, or obese married men from a county over with baseball caps pulled down low-profile in hopes of not being recognized—losers and degenerates, the lot of them. The place always smelled like a gas station bathroom someone had tried to clean up with a bucket of cheap Avon perfume, and the unwashed bodies of a dozen greasy men, sitting around tables scratching themselves, pawing stacks of single dollar bills, didn't exactly help.

Marion set her drink tray down on top of one of the big PA speakers at the back of the stage, near the restrooms, and scanned around the bar for any empty glasses in need of refilling. Louis would be here any minute to make a long and shitty night a little less long and shitty. When it dawned on her that, for once, no one in the place was gawking at her, she slipped a finger under the neon-green string of her thong and pulled the uncomfortable thing out of her crack. She didn't understand why she had to wear the damn thing. It accomplished nothing. She gave herself a good scratching along the back seam and lit a cigarette. She nearly hot-boxed the entire thing by the time Louis appeared at the bar. The barkeep, Todd, pointed in her direction and Louis made his way over. Marion dropped her smoke on the concrete floor and squashed it out under the toe of the ridiculous six-inch heels they made her wear.

"What's up, girlie?" Louis was one of the few black guys allowed to roam free in the Time-Out. The owner, a guy named Bill Cutter, wasn't big on "darkies," but Louis moved a lot of dope, crank, herb, even heroin, and he always kicked up a piece to Cutter for letting him work the room, so he was given a pass.

"You're late," Marion said.

"But I'm here. I saw your kid outside in the car. That shit ain't cool, girl. He should be at the house or something."

"Ain't got no house to be at. Barb and Tim booted us out again. What do you care? It's none of your business anyway."

"That may be, but Cutter don't play that shit. If he finds out . . ."

"He won't find out if nobody says nothing. The boy's fine out there. He's got his comic books and some leftover pizza from happy hour. At least if he's out there I can go check on him when I can instead of . . ." Marion stopped talking and looked at the slinky man in baggy jeans and a wifebeater leaned up against the wall, and realized she wasn't having *that* conversation with *this* guy. "What are you anyway," she said, "a social worker? Are you here to judge me or hook me up?"

"That depends. You payin' or you wantin' to put it on your already inflated tab?"

"I'll get it to you by Friday."

"Always by Friday. Don't the fellas in this place tip?"

"You know waitresses don't make it like the girls up there do." Marion pointed to the sad brunette baring it all from the pole in the middle of the stage, doing her best to block out the obnoxious 38 Special song blaring over the PA and imagine she was somewhere else.

"Well, you know there are a few ways we could work all that out," Louis said, rubbing a gangly black thumb down the smooth curve of Marion's hip bone. She swatted it away immediately. "I don't trick. Not anymore."

"It don't have to be like that, girl. I can make it real romantic."

"Come on, Louis, can you help me out here or not? I need to get back on the floor. Either it's on or it ain't. Don't play games."

"Damn, Angel, you ain't gotta be like that." Louis reached into the pocket of his filthy black jeans and pulled out a small baggie. "Here," he said, and reached out, took Marion's hand, and pressed a tan-colored lump down hard in her palm. "Don't think I'm gonna forget what you owe me, Angel. I got a keen memory, and someday soon you're gonna have to pay the piper. You get what I'm sayin'?" Louis cupped his crotch to emphasize the play on words, and looked down his flat nose at her. She wasn't impressed.

"You'll get paid."

"I always do."

Marion pushed open the door to the women's room but turned back to look at him. "And don't call me Angel."

2.

Marion shut the door and locked it. She looked at the baggie in her hand and worked the knot carefully so as not to rip the plastic. It was lighter than she'd hoped for, but it would get her through the next eight hours of fondling and groping. And maybe if she was lucky, she'd find someone desperate enough to want a lap dance from her so she could get out of the hole, maybe rent a squat for a few days for her and the kid. She spread open the bag in her palm and dug out a bump with a long press-on pinkie nail. She held it to her nose and sniffed. It burned like a blowtorch every time, but she liked it. Crystal that didn't burn was stepped on too many times and never did its job. Louis's shit was always on time. Her eyes watered immediately, and her damaged left tear duct gushed even more than it did normally. She yanked a paper towel from the dispenser next to the sink and dabbed at it. She always wore her dark chocolate hair down in her face, not to mention a ton of foundation, to hide the damage and scars, but under the bathroom's unforgiving fluorescent light it was all she could see. She dug out another bump of crank and hit it again. More tears. More dabbing. She gave herself a once-over in the mirror. She still had her body, even after childbirth. If anything, having a baby added only more definition to her already killer curves. No stretch marks. No oversized nipples. Just Marion—but better. It didn't matter, though. Once someone got a look at her face, it was all they would ever see. She carefully tied the knot back in the baggie and slid it underneath the skimpy fabric of the barely-there neon bikini top. Then she took a deep breath, tilted her head back, and let the crank drain down the back of her throat. That was her favorite part. She faked a quick smile at herself in the mirror and unlocked the bathroom door.

After locating the server tray she'd set down on the speaker, she scanned the room for the best opportunity to make a few dollars. She began to walk toward a table full of what appeared to be college students, bushy-haired twentysomethings with hats on backward and football teams on their T-shirts. The crank was kicking in hard, and she was feeling the confidence it gave. The dope made it easy to forget that this was her life.

3.

By the time the Thursday-night crowd whittled down to just a handful of regulars, Marion found herself at the server well, chewing on the empty baggie of crank she'd depleted in record time, talking to the barkeep, Todd. Todd was a good kid, handsome and clean-cut. She liked looking at him. Other than the few jailhouse tattoos that peeked out from under his shirtsleeves, he didn't even look like the type that belonged in a place like this. He was fit and cut in all the right places and his teeth were so white they glowed.

"You need a shot?" Todd asked, lining up two shot glasses on the bar between them.

"Always," Marion said, looking up from the thin stack of bills she'd been counting. By the look of what was in her hands, and what was still folded and feathering out from under her thong, she'd be lucky to crack sixty bucks. So much for the steak dinner.

"Jäger, right?"

"You know me too well, Todd."

Todd poured the thick German green death-flavored liquor into the glasses and they hammered them down in unison, slamming the empties down on the bar. It wasn't the kind of burn she liked best, but it was free, and free was good. Todd cleared the glasses and turned to an open foam clamshell of chicken wings sitting on the ice cooler.

He dipped one in some kind of white sauce and shredded every bit of meat from the bone with one bite. Marion looked at the box of food and pouted a very intentional and practiced pout.

"You hungry?" Todd said, using one hand to cover his mouthful of food. "I got a ton of them. No way I can eat them all."

The meth in Marion's system stripped her of any kind of appetite—in fact, the smell made her a little nauseated—but she wasn't thinking about herself.

"Oh, no, no," Marion said. "I'm good. I was just thinking that my kid might be getting a little hungry, and I didn't exactly break the bank tonight."

Todd wiped his mouth with a bar napkin and tossed it in the trash. "No problem," he said. "I'll hook you up. Just remind me before you go."

"You're the best, Todd."

"That's what all the ladies say," Todd said, shining his smile at her like a spotlight.

Marion rolled her eyes, but she was pretty sure that all the ladies did say that. Todd had turned back to the wings when the phone hanging next to the rows of liquor bottles behind him lit up. It wasn't the regular bar phone but the direct line to Cutter, holed up in the back. The boss rarely ever came out on the floor. Todd snatched up the phone and held it in place with his shoulder while he listened and tried to divide the chicken wings into two piles. Marion was still lingering in hopes of getting another free shot before returning to the wild, and she watched Todd until he stopped what he was doing, looked at her, and said something into the phone she couldn't hear. Marion raised her hands in a silent "What's up?" motion, and finally Todd hung up.

"Cutter wants to see you in his office."

"For what?"

"Dunno. He didn't say, but he said now."

Marion swirled the soggy plastic baggie in her mouth and slid off the bar stool as if her bones had suddenly turned to jelly. She folded her money in half and tucked it into her bikini top and made her way toward the back of the club, to Cutter's office.

4.

The back office was nothing more than a converted storage closet. No windows or places to sit other than the folding chair behind Cutter's desk. Besides a stack of filing cabinets against the far wall, a few signed photos of various "Featured Attraction" strippers stuck to the wall with Scotch tape, and an ashtray that should have been dumped five years ago, there was nothing else in the room except the man himself. Cutter looked no different from the bums he catered to out front. His clothes might have been more expensive, but his skin was just as cracked and Marlboro-dried, and his tightly curled black hair looked like it had been freshened up in a truck stop sink. He thought the blue-tinted glasses he always wore made him look European. Marion thought they made him look like the cheap pimp he was.

"You wanted to see me, Cutter?"

He didn't even look up from the newspaper he'd been reading. "Get your shit, Marion, and get out."

"What? Why?" She acted surprised but knew why before he even said it.

Now he looked at her. "What did I tell you about bringing kids here?"

Marion's defensive posture deflated. "C'mon, Cutter . . ."

"Don't 'C'mon, Cutter' me. I told you last time not to be bringing that little shit around here. I got enough problems with the cops and the holy-roller commissioners wanting to shut me down as it is. I don't need them finding out I'm running a preschool in the parking lot."

"I got nowhere else to take him."

"Not my problem, honey."

"Give me a break, here, Cutter . . ." Marion leaned down hard on the desk, hoping this would be a cleavage fix. It wasn't.

Cutter stood up. "Give you a break? Are you kidding me? I gave you a *break* when I hired you. I figured that rocking little body of yours might be worth investing in, but it ain't. You act like nobody has the right to even look at it. News flash—this is a *strip club*. I gave you another *break* last time I caught that little rug rat of yours in the men's room. I'm out of *breaks*. You've been here for almost a year, and what do you have to show for it? Nothing. No regulars. No money. Hell, I'm losing money keeping you here. All you do is consort with the darkies and cram as much of that shit as you can up your nose. Don't think it ain't common knowledge that you're gaked out of your head ninety percent of the time, gritting your teeth and scratching like a damn junkie. The other ten percent is spent at *my* bar begging for *my* liquor. Liquor *I* have to pay for. I'm sick of it. I ain't carrying your ass no more and I want you gone. Now get your shit and get the fuck out before I get Moose in here to *throw* your ass out."

Marion had nothing. The gig was up. She knew it. Cutter sat back down and picked up his paper as if his problem child, Marion, ceased to exist. A few minutes later, wrapped in a black sarong and matching flip-flops, Marion was at the back door. She pushed the silver metal bar across it that said FIRE EXIT ONLY in faded red letters. The alarm hadn't worked in years, and the metal door swung open with ease. She stood in the gravel parking lot out behind the club and lit a ciga-rette. Only four left in the pack. At least she was in a comfortable pair of shoes. That thought made her smile. She knew it was the remain-ing drizzle of speed in her brain making her look at the bright side, but it wasn't going to last. Nothing good lasted.

She tossed the butt onto the gravel, crossed the lot, and looked into the back window of the beat-to-shit Bonneville that Barb and Tim had given her, to see her seven-year-old son curled up and sleeping under a pile of her clothes. He'd ripped open the trash bags of stuff in the backseat to make himself a comfortable place to sleep. Marion thought he looked like an angel—a homeless angel. What was that she'd thought about nothing good lasting? Simon was good. He would last. She watched him like that for a moment more, when a second pair of eyes appeared next to her in the window's reflection.

"Where you going, girlie?" Louis grabbed her shoulder and spun her around hard enough for the bones in her neck to crack, then shoved her up against the back quarter panel of the car.

"Goddamn, Louis. Take it easy."

"I take it however I can get it," he said, and squeezed her shoulder harder. "I know you ain't looking to roll out early without saying good-bye."

"It ain't like that."

"Well, then, tell me what's it like? Because I can tell you what it looks like to me. It looks like you're trying to skate on the two bills you owe me, and I told you I always get paid."

"And I told you I'd pay you on Friday."

"Oh, yeah? How you gonna pay me with no job?"

"That's my business, now get your fucking hands off me."

"Bitch, who you think you're talking to?" Louis delivered a haymaker to Marion's soft belly that folded her in half. Louis stepped aside and she immediately fell to the gravel. While she gasped for air on her knees, he snatched her purse off her shoulder and dumped it out on the ground beside her. He shuffled through the makeup, bits of paper, car keys, and loose change, and found the folded wad of bills wrapped in a pink hair tie. All ones and fives.

"This ain't gonna cut it," he said. He stuffed the money into his pocket and lifted Marion to her feet. She tried to speak but could only cough and wheeze for air. "I guess we gonna have to come to some other kind of arrangement." He spun Marion around backward and shoved her up against the hood of a Dodge pickup. She tried to fight him while still trying to breathe, but Louis twisted her arm back and behind her, pressing her face down on the truck while he went to work on the sarong. Behind them, at the back door of the club, Todd laid the bag of chicken wings he'd promised Marion on the ground and quietly slipped back inside.

"I told you I could make this all romantic-like," Louis said, after he tossed the sarong and the ripped thong to the ground, "but I think this is the way you wanted it, ain't it, girl? You like this rough shit, don't you?"

Marion was only able to grunt out three words in a croaked whisper. "Don't . . . do . . . this . . ." She tried to slide out of his grip, but he pulled up on her arm to the point she thought it might snap.

"Yeah, girl, swing it for me," Louis said, unzipping his fly.

Marion didn't see the beer bottle hit Louis in the back of the head, but she heard the hollow thud of impact and watched it bounce to the ground beside her. "Owwww. Shit!" Louis let go of her arm, and she slid to the ground, landing hard in the gravel.

The boy stood about ten feet away with another empty bottle in his hand. Louis was still seeing stars when the kid slung the second bottle like a Major League pitcher. His aim was a little wide and he missed the man standing over his mama, but he hit the side of the truck, and the bottle shattered like a bomb. Shards of busted brown glass went flying and both Louis and Marion covered their faces. "Get away from my mama," the boy yelled, and balled his tiny fists up and raised them like a boxer.

"Well, look at this little fucker," Louis said, rubbing the growing welt on his shaved head. "Shorty here want to play like a man. Come here, shorty. You can watch what a real man does to a whore that don't pay what she owe." The kid was only sixty pounds if that, and tiny even for a seven-year-old, but he stood his ground and dug in, even when Louis produced a knife that caught every bit of the light from the streetlamp. Marion started to stand and rush him but was barely on her knees when the back door of the club busted open and Big Moose, the club's bouncer, a three-hundred-pound bruiser with jowls like a bullmastiff's, walked out into the lot. Todd followed behind him, and last, Cutter himself, toting a pump-action shotgun.

"What in seven hells is going on out here?" Cutter hollered across the lot. Louis slipped the blade back into his pants and made his hands easy for Cutter to see. "This bitch owes me money, man."

"Well, I don't. So get the fuck off my property."

Louis knew better than to shit where he ate, so he didn't even bother to argue. "Happily, Cutter, happily." He smiled at the little boy, who was still holding his fists high, then sneered at Marion. "Our date night is still on the books, girlie. I'll be seeing you." With that, he slunk in between a row of cars and disappeared. With the threat gone, the boy flew to his mother and almost knocked her over again.

His scrawny legs locked on her, scraping off flecks of gravel and rock that stuck to her bare legs and ass. Cutter yelled something else, something about not showing her ugly face around his joint again, but all she heard was Simon sobbing in her ear.

"I'm sorry, Mommy."

"Don't be sorry, baby. Don't you *ever* be sorry. It's going to be okay. I promise. We're going to be okay."

CHAPTER

18

SIMON HOLLY

2012

Officer Holly stood in front of the hospital's vending machine with his phone pressed to his ear and a torn sheet of notebook paper tucked under his arm. He hadn't slept in more than twenty-four hours and needed some caffeine. As the phone rang, he fished a dollar bill out of his pants pocket and smoothed it out. He inserted the money into the machine and pressed the Diet Coke button. Nothing happened.

The phone stopped ringing and a gruff voice answered. "Montgomery."

Holly switched the phone to his other ear. "Yeah, hi, Agent Montgomery. My name is Simon Holly. I'm a police officer here in Mobile. We met on the Fisher case. The one with—"

"I know who you are, son. That was some fine police work you did down there."

"Thank you, sir. I couldn't have done it without the help I received from your office."

"Glad we could help. What can I do for you, Officer?"

Holly pulled the folded sheet of notebook paper out from under his arm and flipped it open. He also kicked the vending machine that had just taken his money. Nothing happened.

"I was hoping I could give you a name to run by your people over there. I'm working on something and I'm having a little trouble getting what I need."

"Why are you calling me? Don't you have access to the databases at your department?"

"Well, I should, but after that whole Fisher affair, I'm not exactly the most popular person around here, if you get my meaning."

"The big boys don't like you rookies solving their high-profile cases?"

"Exactly, sir."

"Well, fuck 'em, son. If you're on a case, you shouldn't be cut off from resources. Who's in charge down there?"

"That's kinda it, sir. This isn't a case. It's personal."

"I see."

The line was silent for a moment and Holly kicked the vending machine again. Nothing happened. A male nurse who looked more like a security guard in scrubs looked over and tilted his head.

"Well, what have you got?" Montgomery said.

"One name. Pepé Ramirez."

"Spell that for me, son," Montgomery said.

The big nurse approached Holly and surprised him when he put a hand on his shoulder. "Excuse me, sir?"

Holly turned his back to him, ignoring him, and spelled out the name for Montgomery. "He's a low-rent pimp, this Ramirez," he said, "a gangbanger out of Jacksonville, Florida. I just need to take a look at his file. He'd be older. Most likely in his sixties, if he's even still alive. That should help you narrow it down if more than one pops up."

The nurse walked around to face Holly again. "Excuse me, sir," he repeated with a little more urgency. Holly covered the mouthpiece of the phone. "Fuck off, buddy. It's just a Coke machine." The nurse looked at the machine and raised his eyebrows. Holly turned away from him again.

"I'll see what I can do, Holly," Montgomery said. "Give me a good number to call you back at." Holly did.

The nurse walked around to face Holly for a third time. "Mr. Holly," he said.

"What?" Holly said, covering up the phone again.

"It's time," the nurse said.

"Time for what?"

"It's time," the nurse repeated, but softer and more compassionate. "We've been trying to find you. Didn't you hear the page?"

Holly hung up the phone.

Within seconds, he was back in the terminal wing, where his mother was being monitored. He knew before he stepped into the room that he was too late. Doctors and medical staff were crowded around her bed and the beeps and buzzing that had filled his head for the past twenty-four hours from all of the various monitoring equipment was painfully silent. When they noticed him in the doorway, the staff backed away and made room for him to enter. His feet were made of lead, each step heavier than the next. A doctor's hand was on his shoulder. The sympathetic stares were squeezing the air from his lungs.

"She's gone, son," the doctor said.

"I . . . I was using the phone . . ." Holly said, unable to think of anything else to say. The doctor cleared the room and Holly sat on the edge of his mother's bed. He took her hand and held it to his face. The coolness in her fingers pushed the reality of what had just happened straight through his chest and he started to cry. He cried in loud sobs—a boy's sobs. He ran his hand down her face and let his fingers explore the scar that crossed it. She never let him touch it. She always pulled away, ashamed of it. He thought it was beautiful. He thought everything about her was beautiful. Even more so now that the sadness was gone, as if it had evaporated along with her breath. He laid his head on her chest and closed his eyes. He stayed like that for minutes or hours. It could have been either.

Another hand was on his shoulder. "I'm so sorry for your loss," a voice said behind him. Holly lifted his head but didn't look at the hospital's pastor, who was there to console him. He looked at the black-and-white composition notebooks scattered all over the floor and stacked on the chair beside his mother's bed. He'd brought them here from the apartment he'd set her up in, to read while she faded away. Until today, he hadn't even known his mother kept a journal. Until today, he didn't know a lot of things. He didn't know hepatitis C caused liver cancer. Or that it could kill you this fast. He didn't know his mother had been keeping it from him. She must have started writing these journals when she got sick. It read like a Greek tragedy. Every horrible thing she went through, and not one word of regret about having Simon. Even when they had to sleep in abandoned cars, or had no food for days. It all started in Jacksonville, with this Pepé, and the night she was cut. From the top of one of the journals he hadn't read yet, he saw the tip of a photograph being used for a bookmark. He sat up and willed himself to stand.

"If now isn't a good time, Mr. Holly," the pastor said, backing up and giving Holly room to move. "Or if my being here is making you uncomfortable, I can go. Maybe I can come back later."

"Officer," Holly said.

"I'm sorry?" the elderly pastor said, clutching a leather-bound Bible to his chest.

"It's Officer Holly." Holly picked up the picture, sliding it out from between the pages of the notebook.

"Of course," the pastor said.

Holly looked at the photo of his mother and him at the Mobile county fair when he was a boy. He remembered having to sleep in the woods that night, and how she'd held him to her warm chest to keep him from shivering. He couldn't stop the fresh tears from spilling over his raw cheeks. He sat back down on the bed next to his mother.

"If you decide you need someone to talk to about Marion's passing," the pastor said, "I am always available. My office is only four doors down on the left. I'll leave my card for you here on the chair." Holly didn't answer, nor did he turn around. When the pastor had left, he laid the photo on his mother's pillow and slipped a bottle of her painkillers from the side table into his pocket. He did want to talk about Marion's death, but not with this hospital-staff Bible-beater. He pulled the folded sheet of paper from his pocket and looked at the name he'd circled. He wanted to talk to someone else entirely.

19

PEPÉ RAMIREZ
PANAMA CITY, FLORIDA
2014

Headlights punched through the polyester curtains. The sound of crunching gravel outside mixed with loud mariachi music announced that the owner of the trailer was coming home. The man in the mask took several deep breaths and sank deeper into the faux-leather recliner. He stroked the barrel of the Glock 17 in his lap and coaxed his heartbeat into a calm and relaxed rhythm.

The trailer's owner stumbled through the door into the darkened room, a cyclone of noise and marijuana stink, a sweet, earthy smell clinging to everything it touched like melted wax. The mark was a gangster from the old school. His tattoos identified him as one of the Latin Kings. He wore khaki chinos drooped way past his ass cheeks, showing a good six inches of powder-blue boxer shorts, and a wife-beater thin enough to see every cut line of muscle underneath. He also toted a massive black pistol tucked into the front of his pants.

How the weight of it didn't drop his pants to the ground was any-body's guess.

The old gangbanger made his way into the kitchenette and pulled the chain of the wall-mounted lamp that illuminated the entire place. The man in the mask's eyes adjusted to the light, and he watched the O.G. pull the enormous hand cannon from his britches and lay it on the kitchen table.

A fucking .44 Magnum.

This guy thought he was the Mexican Dirty Harry. The man in the mask allowed himself to smile. He didn't have one of those. He let the gangster open and close the small fridge a few times, waiting for something new to appear, before deciding on a half-empty bottle of Montezuma. He poured damn near two inches of the contents down his gullet and steadied himself on the counter. When he turned to make a concerted effort to reach the bedroom he noticed the man in the mask sitting in the living room recliner. He also noticed the Glock 17 in his lap. The man in the mask smiled under his balaclava and watched the older man's face go solemn as every possible escape sce-nario played out across it. *Can I get to my gun on the table first before this intruder can pick his up from his lap? Is my safety on? How many steps to the front door? Can I rush the man in the chair before he has time to shoot? Are my homeboys still outside, toking down?* In the end, he decided to play it cool and maybe talk his way out.

"If you are here to kill me, *ese*, you better just get it done. But pre-pare to be hunted down like a fucking dog in the street. I'm con-nected, homes. I got respect up and down the coast. You ready for that kinda trouble, white boy?"

The man in the mask uncrossed his legs, picked up the gun in his lap, and held it loosely pointed at his mark. "Forgive me, Pepé, if I'm not too impressed by an old spic gangster living in an aluminum trailer in the middle of spring-break land. You gonna call up a bunch of date-raping frat boys to throw their checkbooks at me?"

Pepé heard his name. This wasn't random. He flicked his eyes to the massive gun on the table. Only three feet, but it might as well be the span of the Grand Canyon. The man in the mask waved his gun. "You don't want to do that, Pops. By the time you reach it, pick it up, and click the safety, Pepé Ramirez will be nothing but bad tattoos and strawberry jelly. Besides, don't you want to know who I am? Why I'm here with my own big-ass gun?"

"Fuck you, man."

Agent Holly sighed and took off the mask. "Yeah, I guess you're right. Fuck me. I'm sure you've got a laundry list of people who want to kill you. I could be anybody."

"Why don't you stop talking and just do it already?"

"Why don't you have a seat?" Holly stood up, gun trained on his mark, and motioned to the breakfast nook. Pepé hesitated, but he sat.

"Here, why don't I take that out of the equation so we can focus." Holly picked up Pepé's gun and tossed the heavy chunk of steel onto the recliner. The last bit of hope drained from Pepé's eyes, leaving behind two empty dead sockets as the gun bounced on the mahogany seat. "The truth is, it doesn't matter who I am. I'm not here for me." Holly produced a small photograph from the pocket of his black BDUs and placed it on the table in front of Pepé. "I'm here for her."

Pepé didn't look at it. He just dug his eyes into the man with the gun.

"Do you remember her?"

Pepé dug his stare in deeper. Holly gave it right back and leaned in a little closer. "Look at the picture before I put a bullet in each of your fucking kneecaps."

Pepé looked down at the picture of a woman sitting in the grass with a small boy. He studied it closely before hawking up a big wad of snot and spitting on it. Holly moved like a blur. A white-hot blast of pain exploded in Pepé's face as Holly belted him with the Glock. Pepé was used to pain but hadn't experienced it in a long time. Not since getting out of the game. It leveled him.

"Okay, man. Fuck. What do you fucking want?"

Holly pulled Pepé's head up off the table by his obviously dyed, greasy black hair. He yelped. "Ow! Goddamn it, *ese*. What do you want?"

Holly let go and picked up the picture. "I asked you a question, you disrespectful piece of shit."

"What? What fucking question?"

Holly held the photo within an inch of Pepé's face. "I asked you if you remembered the girl."

Pepé looked again. "She look like every other bitch whore I ever ran."

Holly pressed the barrel of his gun against Pepé's forehead hard enough to leave a mark. He put the photo back down on the table and spoke calmly. "This is your last chance, homes. Show me a little respect and answer my questions, and maybe you come out of this alive."

Pepé swallowed a mouthful of the blood. "Who you fucking kidding, *ese*? It don't make no difference if I answer your questions or not, and you know it. I come in here. I see you sitting in my chair, in my place. Don't even have your gun in your hand. Sitting there without a care in the world. Like we good buddies. You wear that fucking mask like it's suppose to hide something, but it don't hide your eyes. You got a killer's eyes, homes. That's why I knew right away, one of us was going to die. You a fucking killer through and through. Just like me, *ese*."

"You're wrong about that, Pops. I'm nothing like you."

Pepé smiled through blood and broken teeth. "I say we just alike, white boy. So go ahead and do it. Pull the trigger. I ain't scared to die. I'll catch up with your white ass in the next life. You can believe that."

"So it's fair to say you don't want to tell me anything about Angel?"

"Who?"

"The girl in the picture. You named her Angel."

"Right, right, Angel. That's the name I have for my dick. The one I made your mother suck on before I—"

Holly swung the gun at Pepé again. Harder this time. Pepé's neck twisted and he slumped down into the seat. Holly grabbed his hair and yanked him back up. The retired gangbanger drooled blood down his chin and the front of his shirt.

"Errgg . . . just do it . . ." he said through a broken mouth.

"Not yet, Pepé. There's someone I want you to talk to." Holly let go of the gangster's hair and pulled out his cell phone. He tapped in a number and held the phone to his ear. When someone answered, he put the phone on speaker and laid it on the table next to the picture. A child's voice came from the phone in frantic Spanish. All the attitude melted from Pepé's face, replaced by panic. He yelled back at the phone in Spanish. Holly tapped the phone and ended the call. "Carlos is your sister's kid, right? He's the reason you got out of the game and relocated here in Titty City. He's a cute kid. What is he . . . nine?"

Pepé sneered at Holly. "I'll fucking kill you, white boy."

"No, Pepé, you won't. But if you tell me what I want to know, I won't let my friend hold your nephew underwater in a motel bathtub."

Pepé struggled to get up and make a run at Holly. Holly easily knocked him back down.

He had nothing left but to beg. "Please don't hurt that boy," Pepé said. "It would kill my sister. He is all she has."

"Then talk to me. Just a conversation, then I call my friend and everyone goes home happy."

Pepé slumped back down, defeated. He looked at the picture on the table. "I don't know her, man. I ran a lot of girls. It was a long time ago."

"Look real hard. She might have had blond hair then. She got her face cut up real bad."

Pepé leaned down closer to look at the picture again, then looked at Holly. "Yeah, I remember her now. Angel. What about her?"

"You remember the night she got cut?"

"Yeah, some john did it. Motherfucker cut her up real good. I sent her packing. She wasn't any use to me no more. But I didn't do that shit to her, man. I helped her. I got her fixed up after that shit happened."

"Who was the john?"

"I don't know, man, I didn't keep records of that shit."

Holly leaned back on the fridge. "Why didn't you retaliate? Do you normally let johns affect your money like that?"

"Hell, no. I tried, but that dude was protected." Pepé rested his forehead in his hands.

"Protected by who?"

Pepé was clearly done holding back. "The Englishman."

"I need a real name, Pepé."

Pepé just sat there, holding his head. Holly tapped the barrel of his gun on the table. "Think about little Carlos," he said.

Pepé looked up. "His name is Wilcombe. Oscar Wilcombe."

"Who's he?"

"I don't know the motherfucker," Pepé said. "He just a rich white dude that threw me a lot of business. He was always using my girls for parties. Entertaining other rich white dudes. The dude that cut up your girl was a VIP for Wilcombe."

"Wilcombe." Holly let the name roll around on his tongue. "Did Wilcombe make it right?"

"What you mean, man? I told you what happened. Call your boy off my nephew."

"I mean, did he pay you for the damage?"

"I don't remember, homes."

"Yes, you do. Did he pay you or not?"

"Shit, man, yeah. Yeah. He paid me twenty-five bills."

"Twenty-five hundred dollars to write it off? You let the john skate for twenty-five hundred bucks?"

"Yeah, man. It was business. That's all. Now call your boy. Let my nephew go."

"I'll ask you one more time: What was the john's name?"

"I told you, I don't remember."

"No, you didn't. You said you didn't know who he was. Now you're saying you don't remember. There's a difference."

"What the fuck, man. It was a long time ago. Just make the call."

"No. Not yet. Something still doesn't add up. If this Wilcombe only paid you two and a half grand to walk away, then there's more to the story. That kind of money would cover one of your bottom bitches, maybe, but not someone like this." Holly tapped the barrel of the Glock on the photo of his mother. "This one would have cleared that much in a few weeks. She was an earner, fresh off the bus. You hadn't even begun to spin her out when some asshole in a motel cuts into your profits and gets to walk away for under three grand? No way. Why did you let this Englishman off so cheap?"

"You and me got different ideas about cheap, white boy."

Holly jabbed the gun barrel in Pepé's eye, and the Mexican shrieked in pain. "I'm not in the mood for glib, Pepé. Now, again, why so cheap?"

Pepé wiped at the streak of blood coming from his eye.

"Okay," Holly said, "allow me. I'm just spitballing here, so you feel free to jump in and correct me if I'm wrong, but I'm thinking maybe this guy in the motel was a bigger deal than you let on, maybe too big a fish for you to fry, and this English fuck knew it, so he gave you whatever he wanted you to have, and you were happy to get it. Is that what happened?"

Pepé sat silent.

"This is your last chance to tell me everything, Pepé, or I'm going to smash that phone, and little Carlos—"

"Burroughs," Pepé said.

Holly repeated it slowly. "Burroughs?"

"Yeah. Some baller from up in Georgia. I didn't even know they had ballers in Georgia. Backwoods motherfucker. He was too well protected for my boys to get involved, so I walked. Cut my losses."

"And his name was Burroughs?"

"Yeah."

"You're sure?"

"Yeah, I'm fucking sure, and that's all I know."

The two men sat across from each other in the breakfast nook for a long minute as Holly studied the bloodied gangster for any signs that he may have more to share. "I think I believe you, Pops," Holly finally said. Pepé closed his eyes, lowered his head, and appeared to start praying.

Holly shook his head slowly from side to side and picked up the phone. He hit redial and held it to his ear. "Take the boy back to his mother," he said, then ended the call and slid the phone back into his pocket.

"Now do it," Pepé said without opening his eyes. He didn't have to ask again. Holly lifted the Glock and shot him once in the chest, and again in the neck.

CHAPTER

20

OSCAR WILCOMBE

JACKSONVILLE, FLORIDA

2015

1.

The office was small, smaller than Agent Holly expected it to be. Motorcycle-enthusiast magazines and paraphernalia were scattered throughout the room. The furniture was nice but not too nice. The paintings on the wall were cheap lithographs of much pricier real-deals, and the coffee at the self-serve station by the door was no better than that at any quick-stop—worse, maybe. Holly set the coffee on the waiting room table and thumbed through a copy of *Cycle World*, pretending not to stare at the only thing worth looking at in the room, the raven-haired beauty behind the reception desk. He pegged her to be in her mid-thirties, closer to six than four, but not a sign of road wear on her face. Huge lips, painted the color of a shiny candy apple, pouted below a sharp nose and dark, almost navy-blue eyes. He had pictures of this one in the file he was putting together on Wilcombe, but to see her in person was breathtaking.

A bald tree trunk of a man decked out in denim from head to toe walked out of the office behind Bianca Wilcombe and whispered something in her ear. They smiled politely at each other, and the man left the office, giving Holly the stink-eye all the way out the door. Holly winked at him, taking in the details. Committing the man's face to memory.

"Mr. Holly?" Bianca said. "Mr. Wilcombe will see you now."

"Thanks." Holly laid the magazine back down on the table, stood, and walked past Bianca to the office door. He hoped she would give him the same smile she'd given the blue-jean giant a moment ago. She didn't. She didn't even look.

2.

"Agent Holly. I'm sorry to keep you waiting. If I'd known you were coming, I would have cleared my calendar." Oscar Wilcombe was pushing seventy and looked every bit of it. His small frame hunched over as he walked and, at some point over the past few years, he'd lost anything that resembled a neck. His head looked more like it sprouted directly from the middle of his shoulders, like he was a human/turtle hybrid. His gray flannel suit hung off him like it was still on the hanger, and his hair had been reduced to a few gray survivors stretched out over his bald head in a comb-over that even he had to know looked ridiculous. He reached out a delicate, thin hand and Holly shook it, careful not to break it.

"Well, you know us federal-agent types. We like to keep people guessing. If we told you we were coming, you'd have time to prepare."

Wilcombe squinted over his wire-rimmed glasses. "Do I need time to prepare?"

"That remains to be seen."

Wilcombe walked back around his desk and took a seat. He motioned for Holly to do the same in the armchair across from him. "What is this about, Mr. Holly?"

"Agent."

"Huh?" The old man squinted again.

"It's Agent Holly. Not Mister. You need to remember that, because I don't want any confusion about how important this conversation is going to be to you."

"Umm, okay." Wilcombe sat back and steepled his fingers in his lap.

"See, me being a federal agent lends a little more weight to what I'm about to tell you. You know what I mean?"

"I suppose I do."

"I hate that word."

"What word?"

"*Suppose.* You either do or you don't. It's just an unnecessary word people throw in to sound pretentious. Are you trying to sound pretentious, Mr. Wilcombe?"

Wilcombe shifted in his seat and pushed up his glasses. "Agent Holly, I'm afraid I'm going to have to ask you again, what this is about."

"That's good," Holly said, and smiled his shark smile.

Wilcombe was confused. "What's good?"

"That you're afraid. I would be, too, if I were in your position."

"And what position is that?"

Holly took his badge out of the breast pocket of his blazer and set it on Wilcombe's desk. He opened the leather bifold and turned the ID to face the old man.

"Can you read that?"

Wilcombe leaned in and examined the credentials but didn't touch them.

"That says ATF," Holly said, "which stands for Alcohol, Tobacco, and Firearms. So it's understandable for you to be pissing into your Depends having me sitting in your little office here. I mean, seeing that you make your money selling illegal *firearms*." Holly tapped the big letter *F* on his ID.

Wilcombe did his best to look indignant. "I have no idea what you're—"

"Stop, old man. Don't give me the I-have-no-idea-what-you're-talking-about speech. I know everything—ev-ery-thing."

"I really have no idea what you're talking about."

Holly shook his head and took a deep breath. He let it out slowly.

"Okay. Here's the deal. That sentence, the very sentence I told you not to say, is the last lie you get to tell me. From here on out, you and me are going to talk openly, and more important, *honestly*, or I'm going to get up, thank you for your time, go outside, and give my people the go-ahead to rush the factory here in Jacksonville and have them take a good look at the east building. Then I'll call my teams waiting in Tampa at 1121 Maple Springs to have them raid that gun plant, too. The other one in Pensacola isn't active right now, but I bet the storage facilities are packed to the gills with assault rifles in boxes waiting to be shipped out to Atlanta."

Wilcombe's indignation vanished, but Holly kept going. "The seven whorehouses you have scattered throughout this fine state and the shipments of gun parts and raw methylamine you receive at your warehouse at the port of Tampa will have to wait, but I bet my boys with Customs and the FBI are gonna have a fucking field day with them."

Wilcombe's face was pale now, and a light sheen of sweat broke out on the paper-thin skin of his forehead. Holly smiled.

"Clearly this is a misunderstanding," Wilcombe said.

"Ah-ah-ah," Holly said, waving one finger in the air. "What did I just say about lying to me?"

Wilcombe collected himself and thought before he spoke another word. "Why are you here?"

"I thought that we'd established that already. You're an asshole gun dealer. I bust asshole gun dealers. We're a perfect fit."

"Allow me to rephrase. If you know all of this about me—about my business—and the ATF is set up outside all of these places you've mentioned, then again I ask, why are you here? Why isn't this office being flooded with more of your people to take me into custody? What are you waiting for?"

"You are a smart one, ain't you? But I guess you'd have to be, to keep this racket up as long as you have without ever bringing the heat down on you. But that's all over now."

"I assume there's a deal to be made?"

"Look at you. You really are a thinker, aren't you?"

"What do you want, Agent Holly?"

Holly's smile vanished. He pulled his wallet from his pants and opened it. He took out a tattered photograph of a young woman hiding one side of her face and sitting in the grass with a dark-haired little boy. He briefly stared at the picture, then laid it down on the desk next to his badge and ID.

Wilcombe looked at the photograph. "What is that?" he asked.

"It's a picture."

Wilcombe winced. "I can see that. Am I supposed to know who's in the picture?"

"You're supposed to, but I'm sure you don't. People like you take a shit on so many lives, it's probably easier to forget them than to keep track."

Wilcombe's face hardened as if he'd just been slapped. He wasn't used to being the one without leverage. He didn't look at the picture again.

"You asked me what I want," Holly said. "That's what I want." He tapped a finger on the photograph. "But I'll never get to have it back because of you and those fucking animals you work with in the Peach State."

Wilcombe squinted again, then removed his glasses and put them on the desk. He waited for the rest.

"I want to know everything you know about the Burroughs family. I know a lot already, but I want to compare notes. I want to know every detail about your business with them. Times. Dates. Money. All of it. I want to know which brother you have the most direct contact with, Grizzly Adams or the crooked cop. I want you to spill your guts about every little dirty deal you've made with them over the past forty years, and I'm not leaving until I've heard it all."

"Then what do you plan to do with the information?"

"Really, am I supposed to answer *your* questions? You got a set of balls on you."

Wilcombe picked up the photograph and studied it closer. His face softened. "This is personal to you."

"Yes, it is."

"The boy in this photo is you, yes?"

"Ain't I cute?"

"And this woman sitting with you. She is your mother?"

"She was. She's dead now."

"I'm sorry for your loss. I understand the bonds of family, Agent Holly."

"Oh, yeah? Like the bond you got with your daughter out there?" Holly pointed a thumb toward the lobby. Wilcombe looked mildly surprised. "After everything else I told you, you're surprised about me knowing something as common knowledge as that hot piece of ass outside being your daughter?"

"I would ask that you watch how you speak of my daughter, Agent Holly."

"I would ask that you go fuck yourself. You're not in the position to ask me to do anything. Maybe I should go out there and tell your darling Bianca about how her daddy dearest is a gun-peddling scumbag. I bet she'd love to find out how you pimp women to your criminal butt buddies. I wonder what kind of family bond you'd have then. No, wait." Holly paused and scratched his head. "Doesn't she do all your bookkeeping, too? I wonder how she could not know something was fishy after all this time. Right? She must be in on it. I wonder how that fine ass will look in an orange jumpsuit."

"She has nothing to do with any of this. Leave her out of it."

"That's up to you. Do what I tell you from here on out, and she'll be none the wiser. She'll get to go on thinking her daddy is a sweet old man who loves motorcycles, and you can just go die of old age somewhere, holding her hand. Which, for the record, is something my mother didn't get to do."

"I do not know her, your mother."

"Not directly. You gave her as a gift to Gareth Burroughs on the night you met him. You called a lowlife wetback by the name of Pepé Ramirez, who, in turn, fed her to that hillbilly. He then proceeded to rape and beat her before mutilating her face." Holly was standing now, but Wilcombe couldn't meet his eyes. Righteous indignation had that effect.

"I . . . did not know."

Simon felt the sting of that lie burn the entirety of his face but didn't show it. He wasn't ready to play that card yet. He let Wilcombe believe he was a fool. "And that's the reason you're still alive. Which is more than I can say for Pepé."

"You do know that Gareth Burroughs died several years ago?" Wilcombe said.

"And good riddance to him. I wish it could have been my bullet that killed him, but sins of the father run deep. Family bonds, right? I want them all."

"And if I tell you everything you want to know, what happens to me?"

"You get to go home and not to a federal prison. Retire. You're done. You're going to sever all ties to the Burroughs clan. Nothing goes in or out. No guns. No dope. No money. Not even a Christmas card. Then you can go play shuffleboard, for all I care."

"And that's it?" Wilcombe began to get a little color back in his clammy, pale skin.

"Well, there is one more thing."

"And that is?"

"When's your next cash run to Georgia? I need every detail. I'll be running it."

21

HALFORD BURROUGHS

2015

1.

"Boss, Scabby Mike just checked in. Two bikes are coming up the east bend, five minutes out."

"Good," Halford said. He sat in the great room of the main house on the compound, at a huge oak table made from a tree he'd cut down himself. It used to serve as a drying room back when weed was the family's largest cash crop, but the meth industry required much less space. These days, Halford used it more as an armory. The place was fully stocked with loaded gun racks and metal cabinets lining the walls for the assault weapons and long guns. Military-grade footlockers stacked up on the floor were all full of handguns and ammo. A thin yellow blanket was spread out over the table, and shotgun parts sprawled across it. The room smelled rich of gun oil.

"Why don't you come in here for a second?" Halford said to the scruffy messenger lingering outside the door.

"Uh, yessir." The young man snapped to attention and walked in, his rifle slung over his shoulder. The screen door slammed behind him.

"Sit down," Halford said.

The young man did.

"You're Rabbit, right? Holland's boy?"

"Yessir."

"How long you been workin' for me, son?" Halford picked up the blued steel barrel of the 12-gauge, looked down it, then blew through it.

"Going on my first year, I reckon."

"You reckon, or you know?"

The boy was nervous. He was aware of his hands shaking so he kept them out of sight, but he couldn't keep his knee from bouncing spastically under the table. "I know, sir. Next month will be a year."

"And how long you been on the shit?"

The boy said nothing. His throat was suddenly frozen shut.

"Did you hear what I asked you, Rabbit?" Halford took a long hooked piece of wire from the table, attached a bit of oiled cloth to the tip, and fished it down the gun barrel.

"Yessir."

"Then answer me."

"I . . . I . . ."

"You know the rules around here, don'tcha, boy?"

"Yessir . . . I . . ."

"I consider that anyone doing my crank, on my time, is stealing from me. You know how I feel about stealing, right, Rabbit?"

The young man found his voice. "I swear I ain't stealing, Mr. Burroughs, sir. I ain't. A few fellas and me just like to party sometimes, but it's always on our own dimes. I would never take from you, sir. Everybody knows that would be . . ."

Halford looked up from the gun parts. His eyes were almost black in the low light seeping through the canvas-covered windows. "That would be what, exactly?"

The young man choked out the rest. "That would be . . . crazy." The roar of multiple Harleys pulling up outside filled the air. Halford looked to the window, and the scruffy kid caught his breath. Halford swiftly assembled the gun and wiped oil off his hands with a paper towel. "I'm going to have a talk with your deddy, see how he wants to handle it. Holland is Scabby Mike's second cousin. Am I right about that?"

"Yessir."

"That makes you kin. It's also the only reason you're still breathing right now. You get me?"

"Yessir. Thank you, sir."

"Don't thank me yet. Your deddy might still kill you once he gets word."

Rabbit looked down at his bouncing knee.

"But today is the last time you show up anywhere near here with that shit in your system. I find out you even dipped the butt of your smoke in that shit before you come to work and it won't be up to your deddy what gets done. You understand that, Rabbit?"

"Yessir."

"Good. Let your *fellas* know the good word, too."

"Yessir, I will. I promise."

"Now get out."

The young man nearly fell and broke his neck trying to get his ass out of that seat and get outside. He managed to reach the door without having a full-on heart attack. Once Rabbit was out, Halford laughed a little to himself. He rose from the table and stretched his bones before following Rabbit through the screen door with a recently cleaned Mossberg over his shoulder.

2.

"Goddamn, Bracken, what the hell happened to you?" Halford ran his hand over the damage done to Bracken's bike.

"We got jacked right outside Broadwater."

"By who?"

"No idea. I was hoping you could tell me." Bracken took off his helmet, hung it on the handlebar of his battle-scarred Heritage. His passenger, Moe, stepped off the bike, and when Bracken followed, it was clear from his careful manner the big biker was feeling the effects of laying his bike down at forty miles an hour. Romeo and Tilmon got off the second bike and crowded behind Bracken.

"You think it was mountain folk?" Halford asked.

"No, I don't think so. Ex- or current military would be my guess."

"What makes you say that?"

"Something about the way they talked to each other. The lingo. The vibe was professional. They were equipped with pro gear, too, but nothing like our hardware. They had all their bases covered, too. Massive intel, like they didn't have a care in the world that we were on the side of a public highway. They knew we'd be alone out there."

"Where's the truck?"

"We had to wipe it and leave it. Don't worry, it's clean."

Halford looked at the three tarped pallets of pot with no truck to be loaded into. He scratched at his mammoth beard. "What did they get?"

Bracken unzipped his leather cut. "They got it all."

"All what?"

"All the money, Hal. They took it all. Let's go in and talk about it."

The little bit of skin that showed through Halford's mane flushed red. "What the fuck is there to talk about? You lost my money. You need to get out there and find it."

Bracken flicked his eyes to his men and then back at Halford. "We didn't lose shit. We got jacked. What we need to do now is sit down and try to figure all this out. These guys were prepared. They had information. It's a very short list of people who knew we were gonna be out here and knew they could work without the law showing up."

"Not my problem," Halford said. "Your people. Your problem."

Bracken tilted his head and looked at Halford as though he might be someone else. "How long have we known each other, Hal?"

"Not long enough to forgive a two-hundred-thousand-dollar fuckup. Folks get killed for a whole lot less around here, and they been knowing each other since before their nuts dropped. You need to call Wilcombe and make it right."

"I tried that already."

"And what did the old prick have to say?"

"I can't reach him."

That gave Halford pause.

"You can't reach him?"

"I've tried to call him six times since we got hit, but he's not answering."

"He's not answering?"

"That's what I said. He's not answering."

"Has that ever happened before?"

Bracken looked back at Moe, Tilmon, and Romeo. None of them had the answer to that.

"No," Bracken said. "Never. That's why I'm saying we got something to figure out here."

Halford dropped the shotgun down off his shoulder into both hands. Bracken and Romeo both reached for their weapons but froze at the echoing sounds of several cocking weapons flanking them on all sides.

"You're pretty goddamn jumpy, Bracken, for an innocent man."

"Hal." Bracken held his gloved hands in plain sight. "Everyone needs to calm down for a second and think. If I wanted to rob you, would I have done it, stashed the money, and then rode up this mountain a day late right into the lion's den? Seriously, would I walk right up to the man I just ripped off and shit on his front porch? I mean, damn, Hal, if I wanted to rob you, I could have just kept riding. I know what a war with you means, and I certainly wouldn't have come here to your doorstep to fight it. Put the gun down."

Halford glared at Bracken and the bikers. At least ten armed men stood behind them, waiting on the word to mow them down, no different to them than picking off turkeys. Bracken kept his hands up, palms out, showing the shredding on the leather. "Hal, I wouldn't have wrecked my bike on purpose."

"With that much money, you could buy another one."

"We were robbed, Hal."

"Right, by the phantom G.I. Joe crew that disappeared into the wind."

"Not all of them," Moe said.

Halford pointed the shotgun at him. "Keep talking."

"Romeo tagged one of them. Killed that fucker in the street."

"That right?"

Romeo nodded in agreement.

"Where's the body?"

"Most likely with highway patrol," Bracken said, edging back into the conversation. "We left it in the street. I didn't recognize him, and it was everything we could do to get to a friendly place to patch up and get here."

Halford lowered his gun. He nodded, and his men lowered theirs, too. "Come on, let's call your boss."

3.

Halford stomped up the front steps of the compound, passed a shaky young Rabbit, and headed straight to the kitchen area. He yanked open one of the drawers and rummaged through the contents until he found a silver-and-white cell phone. It was a dedicated burner used only as a direct line to Oscar Wilcombe. He rarely used it. He rarely had to contact the man directly anymore, but when he did, it never went unanswered. He fished around in the drawer for the battery, clicked it in, and held the power button down until a series of beeps indicated it was powered up. He paced around the kitchen as he waited for a signal, grumbling and cussing under his breath. Bracken and the other Jacksonville Jackals, as well as Scabby Mike and two more of Halford's lieutenants, Franklin and Ray-Ray, entered the great room and spread out into the armory. Each of them filed in quietly, knowing full well they were standing in a house of cards that could collapse at any second with a simple nod from the man with the phone.

Halford put the phone to his ear. It rang only once.

"Hello, Halford."

"What the fuck is going on, Oscar? I've got Bracken and three more of your boys here and they're light. About two hundred grand light."

Wilcombe was silent at first, but when he answered, his voice was restrained. It was a liar's tone. "That's unfortunate."

Halford tilted his head toward his shoulder and shot a brief but confused glance at Bracken. Bracken lifted an eyebrow in response and Halford turned his attention back to Wilcombe. "Yeah, I reckon it is," he said slowly, as if he'd just joined a game where he was unsure of the rules. "Now tell me what you plan on doing about it."

"I wish I could help you, Halford, but I cannot. I assure you I know absolutely nothing about the trouble you're having up there."

"I don't give a shit about your assurances, Oscar. All I want to know is how you intend to get me my money."

"I don't."

"You don't what?"

"I don't intend on doing anything."

Halford chewed his lip and squeezed the phone. "Start making sense, Oscar."

"Listen to me carefully, Halford. I'm truly sorry for whatever is grieving you up there. I think we both know that my club president and his associates were not responsible for anything that belongs to you going missing. In fact, I have complete faith in your business sense that you will be able to recover goods stolen on your turf. It is a minor setback that I'm sure you can sort out. But while I have you on the phone, I'm afraid that I have more bad news."

Halford went eerily calm and the rest of the room remained silent.

"Are you there, Halford?"

"Keep talking, old man."

"I'm afraid that circumstances beyond either of our control are going to force our business together to come to a close. As of today, there will be no more commerce exchanged between our two enterprises."

"Speak English, you Limey fuck."

"I'm out, Halford. Retired. After this call, we will not speak again."

"Just like that? After more than forty years of partnership with my family, you're just going to up and walk away?" Halford's voice was oddly serene. Scabby Mike and the others knew it was a precursor of terrible things to come, like the quiet sound of distant thunder.

"I would hardly call it a partnership, Halford. Just a business relationship that has come to an end."

"You called my father 'family.'"

"Yes, your father was like family. It's a sentiment I never extended to you and your brothers. This is what is best for us all. And Halford, I must ask that you not act irrationally toward the men currently representing my interests. It will only start a senseless, bloody war with the Jackals that will only end in large amounts of suffering on both sides. Something I'm sure neither of us want to endure."

"You done?" Halford asked.

"Yes, Mr. Burroughs, I'm done."

Halford flipped the phone closed, stared at it for a moment, then threw it across the room. It shattered against the stone fireplace. All the men surrounding him stood firm, but each one of them felt the prick of fear in the backs of their necks when Halford Burroughs let out a roar that shook the house. "That son of a bitch!" He grabbed the edge of the oak table and effortlessly flipped it over, sending gun parts and oil containers flying. "I'm going to fucking kill him!" He turned to a massive gun rack behind the table and pulled down a sawed-off double-barreled shotgun. He broke the rifle in half to ensure that it was loaded, and flipped it closed. "That son of a bitch!" he screamed again. Even Scabby Mike felt the twinge of uncertainty as to whether or not Halford was capable of turning on them. Only Bracken had the balls to speak.

"What's going on, Hal? What did he say?"

Halford slowed his frenzy and looked at Bracken, as if he'd just noticed there were other people in the room. His expression was more wild animal than human. "I'm going to fucking kill him."

"Oscar? Why? What did he say?"

Halford rolled his head from side to side and popped the bones in his neck. "No," he said, "not the Brit. He's just an old man closer to death than he wants to admit. He's got heat and he's rolling over. I was ready to put you in his seat anyway."

Bracken looked confused.

"If I were you," Hal said, "I'd watch my back. That old bastard probably already sold you down the river. You said it yourself that the list of people who knew you were coming was short. Who is at the top of that list? Now get out of my way, I got business to handle." Bracken stepped aside, but before Halford could step through, a figure appeared at the screen door.

"You okay in there, Mr. Burroughs?" Rabbit said.

The blast nearly deafened everyone and cut Rabbit in half.

"Goddamn it, Halford," Scabby Mike said. "What the hell did you just do?"

"Clean that fuckin' tweeker off my porch. I'll be back in a few hours."

Mike followed Halford out the buckshot-peppered hole that used to be a door. Rabbit was a mangled mess partially wrapped in pieces of screen mesh.

"Halford," Mike yelled, confused and angry. "Where the hell are you going?" He squatted at Rabbit's body and closed the dead boy's eyelids.

"I'm going to see my little brother," Halford yelled back.

"Clayton? Why?" Mike stood up. "What does Clayton have to do with this?"

Halford stopped and turned around. "He has everything to do with this. He shows up here out of the blue, talking about how cops knew everything about our thing up here and about how my money would be the first thing to go. He even mentioned Wilcombe's name. And now I'm getting jacked at gunpoint on the highway."

"You think cops jacked Bracken?" Mike said, still confused.

"Cops don't operate like that. Outlaws do. That little prick's got my money or he knows who does."

"Let me come with you, then," Mike said.

"You'll just try to stop me from doing what I have to do."

"He's your brother, Hal."

"You're my brother, Mike. He's a dead man."

22

CLAYTON BURROUGHS

2015

1.

Cricket didn't need to ask her boss what was going on when he dragged ass through the door a full three hours later than usual and didn't take off his sunglasses once he was inside. The news of Sheriff Burroughs's bender and the ass-whuppin' he threw on Big Joe Dooley the night before had her phone ringing off the hook before she even finished turning the key in the front door. Still, she was gentle with him. "Morning, Sheriff." She met him halfway across the lobby with a cup of coffee, black.

"Morning, Cricket," Clayton said, taking the warm foam cup but setting it back down on the counter. "I suppose you've already heard?"

"Yes, sir, I have, but let me tell you, that Joe Dooley has gotten out of line a few times with me before, too, so it's my opinion that every single woman in Waymore owes you a thank-you."

Clayton smiled. "Big Joe is an asshole, but he didn't deserve what I did. I was way out of line . . . but thanks for saying that."

Cricket picked up the coffee and handed it to him again. This time she let her hand linger on his for a moment. "Are you okay, sir? Is there something I can do?"

Clayton looked at her hand on his and wondered if they could be any more different. He felt the warmth of it—the genuine concern. Cricket was good people. That's why he'd hired her. "I'm fine," he said.

Cricket raised a skeptical eyebrow.

"Really, I'm fine. It's just been a heavy few days. Down here in this valley it's easy to forget where I come from. This case I'm working with Agent Holly is a full-on reminder of all that bad blood I left on the mountain, and that reality check knocked me sideways for a minute. But really, I'm fine now."

Cricket let go of his hand and returned to her desk. She picked up a yellow file folder and handed it to Clayton. "Agent Holly came by about an hour ago and dropped this off. He said you asked for it."

Clayton slipped the file under his arm and retreated into the sanctum of his office. He smiled again at the mousy receptionist through the narrowing gap of the door until it clicked shut. He tossed the file on his desk and drew the shades before finally taking off his sunglasses. The hangover was brutal. He felt like an overcooked, thoroughly dried-out Thanksgiving turkey stuffed with cold sweat and cigarette ashes. The worst part was that, even now, he still craved the bourbon. He always would. Just a few fingers to even him out. Clear his head. The only moisture in his body was in his mouth, watering at the thought. He sat down and sipped Cricket's coffee. He needed to work—something to occupy his mind so the demons wouldn't have anyone to play with. He opened Holly's file.

2.

He removed the paper clip holding the two-year-old mug shot photos and laid them on the desk. A typical G.I. drunk-tank shot and profile. Short cropped dark hair, military regulation mustache, and a deer-caught-in-the-headlights expression. Clayton thought something about the guy looked familiar. Maybe he *had* seen this guy before. He thumbed through the paperwork for photos of the crime scene, but there was nothing. Allen Cleveland Bankey was his full name. No bells ringing there at all. Clayton opened his desk drawer and found his aspirin. He shook two out and chewed them dry. He skimmed through the rap sheet, but there wasn't anything else in the file Holly hadn't already told him. Bankey was an army veteran. Two tours in Iraq. Two in Afghanistan. All consecutive. He was a desert rat. His military record was impeccable. If anything, the file made this guy look like a hero except for the glaring statutory-rape charge that followed his time overseas. According to the file, the girl was sixteen. He met her in a bar she wasn't old enough to be in, and the sex was consensual. The girl's parents agreed to drop the charges, but the state of Tennessee picked it up and Bankey served eighteen months. Released for good behavior. Raw deal. Now the poor bastard was on a slab for hijacking bikers with a rifle and a clown mask. What a fall from grace. The world is a broken place sometimes. Clayton wondered when it hadn't been. Still, the guy looked vaguely familiar. Clayton scratched at his beard and tapped on the intercom.

"Cricket, has Deputy Frasier been in this morning?"

Static.

"No, sir. I tried to call him a few hours ago, but he didn't answer."

"Well, try to call him again. If you reach him, tell him I need to see him as soon as possible."

Static.

"Yessir . . . Um, Sheriff. Permission to talk to you in person?"

Clayton sat back and looked at the closed door of his office. "Um . . . of course, Cricket. Come on back."

Cricket tapped at the door lightly, then opened it and came into the room. She looked almost embarrassed—nervous. She stood twisting her hands together like she was trying to remove something sticky from her fingers.

"What is it, Cricket?"

"Is Choctaw caught up in this mess?"

"What mess? This?" Clayton held up the file.

"Yes, sir."

Clayton was confused. "Why would he be?"

Now Cricket looked a little confused herself. "Because of his friend." She pointed at the file. Clayton looked back down at the photo, and then again at Cricket.

"Do you know this man?"

"Sure, I've met him a few times when I was out with . . ." Her face flushed, and Clayton finally understood why.

"Listen, Cricket. I don't care what you and Choctaw do in your free time."

"But it says in the SOPs that county employees are not to fraternize."

Clayton stared at her blankly. "Huh?" he said, even more confused.

"I really need this job, Sheriff. I don't think I could go back to waitressing—"

Clayton shook his head and held his hands up to cut her off. "Cricket, I *really* don't care about any of that, and I promise you no one is going to lose their job, but I need you to tell me right now how you know this man."

"He's James's . . . Choctaw's friend. His army buddy. You've met him, I think. I thought he was a pretty nice guy until that whole wrecking-the-patrol-car thing."

Clayton sank into his chair. He held up the photo again and pictured the man in it with a full beard and longer hair. "Well, I'll be damned," he said. "Chester?"

"His name is Allen, but James calls him Chester because of the sex-offender thing that happened. I wasn't supposed to tell you about any of that. Choctaw didn't want you to disapprove."

Clayton almost laughed. *"Chester the molester,"* he said to himself, as if he were answering a riddle.

"Yeah," Cricket said. "Allen said he hated it, but if he let his buddies know, they would never stop calling him that. That's how all those guys are. Always giving each other a hard time. I can't believe he's dead now. I just saw him two days ago."

"Where was the last time you saw him?"

"Sunday night at James's place. All the guys in his old army unit were coming into town for a get-together next weekend, and James asked me to help him plan it."

"Was that the last time you saw Choctaw, too?"

"Yes, sir, and I haven't seen him since. It's not like him to break plans without telling me. That's why I was so upset yesterday."

"Was anyone else at Choc's place Sunday?"

"Two of the guys from his unit had just come into town."

"So Choc, Chester, and two other guys?"

"Yessir."

"Cricket, listen to me. I need you to find Choctaw as fast as you can and have him call me immediately. Do you understand?"

"Do you think he has something to do with all this?" She looked on the verge of tears.

"I don't know. I hope not. Just find him for me, okay?"

"Okay," she said, and scurried out the door. Clayton sat dazed for a minute, letting the information sink in, and then picked up the phone.

3.

"Holly."

"Simon, it's Clayton."

"Well, how you feeling, Sheriff?"

"Like shit warmed over, but listen. I got information on your dead guy."

"Do tell . . ."

"Allen Bankey is a guy I met once, going by the name of Chester. Turns out Chester was a nickname. That's why I didn't recognize the name you gave me. He's an old army buddy of my deputy's. I think he's been bunking at his house."

"You're shitting me."

"Negative."

"You got eyes on your deputy?"

"No. He's MIA at the moment, but I'm tracking him down right now."

"Do you think he's involved?"

"I don't know. I want to say he's not capable of something like this, but either way, he's my deputy, and my friend, so I want to find him first before you go higher up with anything."

"Of course, Sheriff. Right now we'll call him a person of interest and I'll wait to hear from you before I call in the bloodhounds."

"Simon. He's my friend."

"I understand that. You're point on this. I'll sit on it as long as I can."

"Thank you."

Holly hung up.

Clayton's head was throbbing. Dehydration and information overload were ripping his head to pieces. He chewed two more aspirin and tried to suppress the voice booming in his head telling him to search the cabinets for a forgotten stash of whiskey. He almost listened, too, but Cricket's frantic voice on the intercom drowned it out.

4.

"Sheriff?"

"Yeah?"

"I think we have a problem."

"What now?"

Static.

"Cricket?"

Static.

Raised voices and a loud crash boomed from the lobby, followed by Cricket's scream.

5.

Clayton nearly overturned his desk getting up and out the door. He prayed it wasn't what he thought it was, but he knew what was happening on the other side of that door before he opened it. His brother, Halford, stood in front of the double glass doors leading out to the street, dangling Cricket by her hair like a fresh-caught fish on a line. The computer, phone, and picture frames from her desk were busted and scattered all over the floor from when Halford had pulled her up and over it. She was screaming and crying, scratching at Halford's hand, but he only twisted it tighter in her hair. Clayton was horrified as he took in the scene, focused not on the petite, squirming young woman balancing on her tiptoes but on the double-barreled shotgun Halford had jammed up under her chin. Clayton drew his gun on instinct and trained it with both hands on his older brother.

6.

"Let her go, Hal. Now!"

Halford lifted Cricket higher onto the tips of her toes. She screamed louder. "Tell this bitch to shut up, Clayton, so we can get this done. Tell her before I paint the walls."

"Let her go, Hal, or I swear to God, I'll shoot you down where you stand."

"Tell her, Clayton. Tell her right now."

"You're going to be okay, Cricket. I promise." Cricket looked at Clayton, wide-eyed and terrified. "You're going to be okay. He won't shoot." Her screams dialed down into choked sobs. "Now let her go, Halford. I'm right here. Say what you came here to say, but leave her alone."

Halford laughed. "You think I came here to talk? We're beyond talking. You only get to stay in this valley, pretending to be sheriff, because I let you. You're only still alive because I let you. You think you got power? You think you can fuck with me? You have no idea what you're fucking with, little brother."

"I don't know what you're talking about, Halford, but if you don't put her down, it's not going to matter."

"You think I don't know it was you? You come up on the mountain talking about cops taking my money, talking about Wilcombe like you know him, while you send your own boys in to rob me. You think I'm stupid? I want my money."

"What money?"

"Did you really think I would just lay down and let you take what I earned?"

"I don't know what you're talking about, Halford, but I'm serious. I'm not going to tell you again. Let the girl go, and drop the shotgun, or I will put you down."

Halford didn't laugh this time. His eyes went as cold and dark as Clayton had ever seen them. "You're a fuckin' disappointment, Clayton, through and through. Deddy called a spade a spade with you before you could shave."

"Deddy's dead. His death is on you. Just like yours is going to be on me, if you don't let . . . her . . . go."

Cricket had gone quiet. She wasn't scratching or even struggling. Her eyes were closed and her lips were moving, but there was no sound. Clayton assumed she was praying.

Good girl, he thought. *Stay still.*

"Last warning, Halford. If you want to talk this out, I'll listen. No one needs to die. But if you keep pointing that gun at Cricket, somebody will, and it won't be her." Clayton thumbed the hammer back on his Colt and held it steady.

"I believe you're right about that," Halford said, and swung the shotgun toward Clayton. Thunder filled the small office as Halford fired. Buckshot sprayed the ceiling and walls to Clayton's left, but the sheriff's aim was true and he put three bullets through Halford's chest. His huge body bucked and went limp as he fell backward through the plate-glass window behind him and into the street.

7.

Clayton stood frozen in place, still aiming his gun at where his brother had been standing. There was no keeping his hands from shaking now. He dropped the gun to the floor as if it were suddenly a venomous snake. Cricket was balled up against the wall, pulling and holding her knees to her chest. The clamor of the shots in this tight environment had temporarily stolen her hearing, but otherwise she was okay—at least physically. Halford's body was lying on the sidewalk in a growing pool of sticky red, surrounded by thick broken glass that made everything sparkle in the hot afternoon sun. Clayton fell to his knees. All of his will to stand dissipated like smoke.

8.

"Sheriff?" The voice was right next to him but sounded miles away.

Agent Holly knelt down beside Clayton. People were in the room now, EMTs, state police; Darby was there in uniform, and the deputy coroner was tending to Halford's body. The edges of Clayton's vision were blurred, but he could see his brother's muddy work boots sticking out from underneath the white sheet the medics had laid over him. A stocky female EMT shined a penlight into one of Clayton's eyes, and then the other. "Sheriff? Can you hear me? His pupils are reactive and I don't see any outward trauma. I think he's okay, but he's most likely in shock."

"Talk to me, Clayton," Holly said. He was coming in clearer now.

"I . . ." Clayton tried to speak, but it felt like his mouth was packed with sawdust.

"It's okay, Sheriff. You did good here." Holly shooed the medic away and got right up in Clayton's face. "He came here to kill you, Clayton. You have to understand you had no choice."

"No, he . . ."

"Yes, he did," Holly said. "He would have killed you, and that little girl you got working for you as a bonus. You know in your gut that's the truth. He'd have killed you both, left you to rot, and whistled his way back up that mountain. You saved your life *and* hers." Holly took Clayton by the chin and lifted his head to give him a view of Cricket through the shattered window. She was wrapped up in another one of the medic's sheets, sitting on the bumper of the Mc-Falls County ambulance. Mascara streaked down her face and she shivered regardless of the blazing afternoon sun. She would go home today. And that was good.

Holly stood and reached out a hand. Clayton, feeling his strength returning, took it and let Holly help him to his feet. Once he was up, Clayton leaned down and picked up his hat and gun. He put them both back where they belonged.

9.

Holly stepped over the twisted metal and broken glass and onto the street. Clayton followed. Both men squatted down at Halford's covered body, sprawled lifeless on the sidewalk. Holly gripped the edge of the sheet to pull it back, but waited for the sheriff's approval. Clayton nodded. Halford's eyes were no different in death than they'd been in life. No colder. No blacker. No more absent of a soul than a man who could rest easy while another man burned alive, or a man who could hold a sawed-off scattergun to the head of an innocent girl. Clayton could hear the hornets screaming. He fought back the sudden rush of anxiety that peppered his peripheral vision with sun-spots, and squeezed his eyes shut until the feeling of nausea began to fade. He thumbed his brother's eyelids shut and put his gun hand on the dead man's chest—a few inches above the three holes in his shirt—and offered an unspoken good-bye. Holly said nothing. Instead, he stood, offered his hand, and helped Clayton to his feet for a second time.

Cricket thought she was all out of tears until Clayton and Holly approached the ambulance. The paramedics backed off when they saw the men coming and began to repack unused supplies into their jump bag. The sheriff sat down next to Cricket on the bumper. She grabbed his arm through the sheet she was wrapped in and cried gently on his shoulder. "I'm so sorry, Sheriff. I didn't know what to do. He came in so fast. I didn't think he was . . . he was . . ."

"It's okay, Cricket, you didn't do anything wrong. I'm the one who should be sorry for dragging you into my family drama. It's my fault. I almost got you killed."

Cricket backed her face off his shoulder and caught his eyes. "You saved my life, Sheriff."

"You're damn right he did," Holly chimed in. He had his cell phone to his ear and was holding one finger in the air as a signal to Clayton that he would be right back, and then he stepped off to the side of the ambulance to focus on his call.

"You did," Cricket continued. "I know doing what you did must've been hard for you. Probably the hardest thing ever, but you did it and I'm alive because of it. I owe you my life."

"You don't owe me anything."

Cricket said something else, but Clayton didn't hear it. Instead, he caught a familiar voice through the crowded street and focused on it. It was the voice of the one person he really needed to see.

"Kate," he said, and stood to wave her over. She was standing behind the yellow caution tape, her face ghost-white. A couple of state police were giving her some resistance about entering the scene, but once she caught her husband's eye, she barreled through them like a freight train.

"Let her in, she's my—"

Kate knocked the words and the wind out of him with a crushing hug that pushed him back against the ambulance hard enough to rock it. A paramedic turned and opened his mouth with the intention of saying something but thought better of it once he saw Kate's face. Clayton winced but hugged her back. She let him go and looked him over from head to toe to head again. "Oh my God, Clayton. Are you okay? What happened?"

"I'm fine. Who called you?"

"No one called me. I was on my way here to meet you for my doctor's appointment, and I saw all this. What the hell happened?"

"Halford's dead." He motioned to his brother's enormous corpse. Darby, two paramedics, and the deputy coroner were all trying to help load it into a second ambulance. She looked to the men, then back to her husband, and all the remaining color in her face faded with the realization. "Did . . . you?"

"Yes."

"Oh, baby. Oh, baby, I'm so sorry."

"He saved my life," Cricket said.

"He saved both their lives," Holly said, rounding the ambulance, tucking his phone in his pocket. Kate went from pale and sympathetic to flushed red and angry on a dime.

"This is your fault." She shoved an accusatory index finger into Holly's chest. "You brought all this down on us."

"Yes, ma'am, I know you feel that way."

"Are you happy now? Are you?"

"No, ma'am," Holly said.

"Fuck you, and your 'yes, ma'am/no, ma'am' shit."

"Kate, calm down." Clayton took his wife's arm, but she pulled it free.

"No, I won't calm down. Three days ago we lived in a quiet little valley far removed from all this, and now look around." Kate lifted both her arms and spun back toward Holly. "Dead people and chaos for us mountain folk, and a plane ticket home for this asshole. Right, asshole?"

"Yes, ma'am," Holly said.

Kate drew back to deck him, but Clayton grabbed her arm again, and this time didn't let go. "Simon didn't make Halford come into my office toting a shotgun, Kate, and he certainly didn't make him press it to Cricket's head. That was all Halford. If anything, I'm to blame for provoking him and I'm the one who has to live with what happened here."

"That's not entirely true, Clayton. We both have to live with this. We *all* do," she said, and pushed a strand of Cricket's hair back behind her ear.

Clayton pulled her into his chest. "You're not helping things, woman. Let me talk to the staties over there and give a statement. The sooner I can sort out what needs sorting, the sooner we can go home."

She wanted to scream, but she bottled it down to a single compressed syllable. "Fine."

Clayton tipped his hat to Cricket and then turned to Holly. "I'm guessing this changes your plans."

"I would say so, yeah."

"Despite what my wife might say, this was bound to happen someday. I've always known that. I'm not looking to blame you for anything."

"Good to hear, Sheriff. For what it's worth, I'm sorry it happened this way."

"Me, too. We'll be seeing you, then."

"I hope so."

Clayton put an arm around Kate and the two of them turned to go.

"Sheriff," Holly said, "I almost forgot."

"What's that?"

"That call I took a few minutes ago. I called in the info you gave me. I know you wanted to run it down yourself, but I thought you could use the help. One of my boys with the Georgia Bureau put eyes on your missing deputy."

Clayton stopped, and without looking back, asked, "Where?"

"You've got to be kidding me," Kate said, and tugged on Clayton's arm. He turned and looked at Holly. "Where?" he said again.

"One of the GBI choppers that fly regular over the mountain spotted a blue Camaro registered in his name and another vehicle at a cabin on the Western Ridge of the mountain. You know the place?"

"Yeah, Johnson's Gap. It's a hunting cabin that's been in my family for years. Choctaw goes up there sometimes for the fishing in Bear Creek."

"Yeah, well, I bet he ain't fishing today."

"Don't kill him, Simon."

"Don't intend to, Sheriff, but I can't make any promises. People tend to get squirrelly around that kind of money, and if the intel is right, that's where he's got it stashed. I got a team headed there now."

"You got what?" Clayton flared.

"Well, you were a little busy here, Sheriff. I had to make the call. How it turns out is going to be up to him. I'm just giving you a heads-up."

Cricket came off the bumper of the ambulance. "Sheriff, don't let them kill him. Whatever he's done, I'm sure it's a mix-up. James is a good man. Please, Sheriff, you know he is. Please don't let them kill him." Cricket was back in full sob, crying into Clayton's chest. Kate stood cold as a slab of granite by his side, burning a hard stare into Holly. She was in a state of suspended animation, waiting to hear her husband say the words she knew he'd say. It made him who he was. He didn't have a choice. It was his father's pride. It was the reason she loved him and the one thing she was completely sure would crush her heart into dust. She pulled on Clayton's arm. He shook her off.

"Let me go get him," he said. There it was. Kate felt like she'd been punched in the gut.

"Clayton, you're hurt," Holly said, "not to mention you're probably in shock. Go take care of yourself and yours. Let me handle this."

"No," Clayton said. "You're right. Situations like this cause people to overreact. There are too many guns and too many questions. I don't want anyone else to die today. We don't know if Choctaw was even involved."

"The odds aren't good, Sheriff. What does your gut tell you?"

"It tells me if I want to see my deputy again upright and breathing, I need to be the one to bring him in. Call off your dogs and let me do this."

"Are you sure?" Holly pointed over the sheriff's shoulder. That's when Clayton noticed Kate wasn't holding on to his arm anymore. She was already crossing back under the yellow caution tape. He watched her work her way through the crowd, and a few seconds later she was gone.

Clayton scratched at his beard and spit on the asphalt. "I'll drive."

CHAPTER

23

CLAYTON BURROUGHS

2015

"Are you sure you're up for this, Clayton? I can have my people here within the hour. Full tactical squad—pros. They'll do everything possible to take this idiot kid alive. You have my word."

Clayton responded by mashing the gas pedal down, and hammered the Bronco farther up the dirt mountain road. "You can't promise me that, Simon. I know you got good intentions, but your people won't see Choctaw as an idiot kid caught up in a bad situation. They'll only see a target. I'm not going to let someone else up here die if I can help it. Not today. Give me your phone."

"Huh?"

"Your phone. You carry one, don't you?"

"Yeah, okay." Holly dug into his pants pocket, pulled out a silver flip phone, and handed it to Clayton. "Here," he said. "Hit send after you dial."

Clayton took the phone and smirked at Holly. "The hillbilly sheriff knows how to work a cell phone."

"All right. I'm just saying."

Clayton didn't flip open the phone. Instead, he rolled his window completely down and tossed it out into the blurring trees.

"What the fuck, Clayton?"

"I don't want you calling anyone."

"And you couldn't just trust me?"

Clayton slowed the Bronco down and pulled over to the side of the road. "Get out, Simon."

Holly twisted his face into an expression of surprise. "You're kidding, right?"

"Nope. Get out."

"I'm not gonna do that, Clayton."

The sheriff dropped the shifter into neutral and let his foot off the clutch. He put an arm up on the seat and turned to Agent Holly. "Look, the place we're headed is less than two miles up this road on the left. It's about a fifteen-minute walk. By the time you get there, I'll most likely be sitting on the front porch waiting for you, Choctaw sitting beside me, sipping iced tea."

"I'm not going to let that happen, Sheriff. I can't even begin to tell you how many protocols I'd be breaking if I did what you're asking me to do."

"Something tells me a man like you doesn't give a rat's ass about protocols. Besides, you can tell anybody that asks I forced you at gunpoint."

It was Simon's turn to smirk. "And you think anyone will believe that?"

"Anyone who knows about me drawing down twice in the past two days will."

"And what if there's more than just your deputy waiting up there?"

"Won't be anyone I don't know."

"You know all his ex-military buddies turned hijackers?" Holly saw in the sheriff's face that he hadn't thought of that, but Clayton shook his head dismissively.

"If I get there, and it looks like I just stepped in shit, I'll pull back and wait on you."

Holly still didn't move to open his door. He sat with his arms crossed like a stubborn child.

"Look, Simon, this is the only way I know I've got an honest shot at not getting this kid killed like his buddy Bankey. I can tell him I came alone, and I won't be lying. If he thinks a fed is creeping around, it could spook him into doing something stupid. It's only a fifteen-minute walk. I need you to do this. Goddamn, it's not like I'm asking for your gun. Just get out and meet me there."

Holly unclicked his seat belt and popped open the Bronco's door. Before he was fully out, he turned to Clayton and said, "You know, I've been running marathons my whole adult life. I can cover two miles in a lot less than fifteen minutes."

Clayton tipped his hat. "Well, I best be on my way, then." He dropped the shifter and punched the hammer down as soon as Holly had both feet on the road, letting the vehicle's sudden motion slam the door closed. Holly shielded his face from the kick-up of dust and red dirt. When the Bronco was far enough from sight, he brushed the road spray off his dark blue suit, chewed a couple Percocets, and pulled out his cell phone. Not the burner phone he let Clayton throw out the window, but the one he was issued by the United States government. He chewed the pills into paste, punched in a number, and held the slick black smartphone to his ear. As the phone rang, Holly smiled his shark's smile and began to jog up the road toward Johnson's Gap.

CHAPTER

24

CLAYTON BURROUGHS
WESTERN RIDGE, JOHNSON'S GAP
2015

1.

Clayton pulled the Bronco over and cut the engine just before he reached the clearing where the cabin his great-grandfather had built sat quiet and serene. His deddy had brought him here a few times when he was little, but something about the place never sat right with Gareth. Clayton always got the impression his father was never comfortable here. Choctaw came out here all the time. He swore Bear Creek was the best trout fishing in all North Georgia. Clayton just took his word for it.

The midnight-blue Camaro that Choctaw had thrown most of his extra bones into restoring for the past five or so years was parked out front. No other cars. If someone else had been out here with him before, they were gone now. Clayton could breathe a little easier. The driver's-side door hung wide open and gently rocked in the breeze.

The cabin was covered in the shadows of the heavy canopy of trees and brush surrounding it. Clayton could easily slip in from the back and surprise anyone inside, but he was going to play this completely straight. Even he was aware of just how foolish his next move was, but he wasn't taking any chances at getting anyone else killed on this mountain, except maybe himself. He carefully slid his Colt from his holster and held it up over his head, letting it dangle on one finger. "Choctaw," he yelled, "you in there? It's me, Clayton." He walked up the gravel drive toward the front porch and glanced in the open door of the Camaro as he passed it. Dry blood the color of coffee grounds stained most of the front seat. It looked a few days old, most likely from the hijacking. No fresh blood at all. A 20-gauge shotgun lay across the seat. "Choctaw," he yelled again, and this time the curtain shuffled slightly in the window next to the door.

"It's just me, James. I just want to talk. I'm here to help you with whatever this is."

"You alone, Sheriff?" Choctaw yelled back.

"Yes, I am, James. Are you?"

"Are you sure?" Choctaw asked, still concealed within the cabin.

"Have you ever known me to lie to you, Deputy?"

Thirty or so seconds passed as Choctaw mulled that over. Finally he yelled back.

"No, sir."

"Well, then, how about I come in there and we sort this out. We don't have a whole lot of time before we have company up here, and my arms are getting tired."

Another thirty seconds.

"All right, boss." Deputy Frasier appeared at the door, thin and pale like a scarecrow up for three days on a meth binge. The repeater in his hands looked to weigh more than he did, and he held it pointed at the ground, as if it were a relief to let it drop. "C'mon in," he said, and disappeared back through the door.

Clayton holstered his weapon and followed Choctaw into the cabin.

2.

Clayton hadn't seen the inside of this place since he was a kid. Nothing hung on the walls, and the wood-burning stove was a rusted-out firetrap. There was nothing else in the wide-open space except dust, a few cases of crushed empty beer cans, a fold-out bed against the wall with no sheets, and two black plastic garbage bags stuffed to capacity by the back screen door. One of the bags was torn open at the top, allowing a view of the cash inside. Clayton blew all the air from his lungs and let out a disappointed "Damn."

Choctaw took a seat on the bed and laid his rifle down next to him. Like magic he produced a quart of shine from the foot of the bed and took a long, gulping swig. He wiped his mouth and held the bottle out to Clayton. "I know you're all sober these days, but I ain't tryin' to be rude."

Clayton took a seat next to him on the bed and took the bottle. He held it a good long while before screwing the cap back on and setting it on the floor.

"How did you get pulled into this mess, Choc? Was it your buddy Chester's idea?"

The deputy laughed, which turned into a dry cough, which quickly turned into a sob. Clayton wasn't expecting that. Not once in eleven years of knowing the man had he ever seen Choctaw cry. He didn't think he knew how. He reached across to put an arm around the deputy's shoulders, but Choctaw abruptly stood up, snatched the bottle, and crossed the room. "Chester didn't get me into anything. He was a good friend—a real solid dude. He saved my life over there in that shithole desert more than once. He got dealt a raw deal with that bitch in Tennessee. He couldn't get any real work. He needed this. I told him it was a bad idea, but what else could I do? He was my friend, boss. I owed the guy my life. You don't know how it was over there."

Clayton waited for the rest.

"It was supposed to be a quick payday. Nobody gets hurt and even the guy we were ripping off wouldn't come looking for what we took. Nobody was supposed to get hurt, boss. Chester—Allen—wasn't supposed to get killed. It just ain't right."

Clayton stood up. "So tell me what happened. The only way I can protect you is if you lay it out straight. How did you know about the money in the first place?"

Choctaw wiped his raw, reddened eyes and took another swig from the bottle. "Let's just take the money and get out of here," he said. "Frankie and Lenny already took their cut, so that leaves a little over a hundred and twenty-five grand here." The deputy reached into the open garbage bag and grabbed a wad of crumpled bills. "We could just take a bag apiece and dip out, boss."

"Are you out of your mind, Deputy? There are federal agents on the way here right now to recover this money and haul your ass into custody. I talked them into letting me bring you in, to keep you from getting shot to hell. I need to know how you and Chester knew to rob these guys. Why wouldn't the owner come looking for you? Who's going to just write off a loss that big? Where did you get your information from?"

Choctaw laughed a delirious laugh. Clayton grabbed his shoulders and shook him. "This is no joke, Deputy. I had to do a lot of convincing to get them to let me come out here and bring you in myself. Now, I can't help you if—"

"Who did you convince?" Choctaw suddenly looked hard and angry.

"What?"

"Who exactly did you have to convince?"

"The feds."

Choctaw loosed another laugh; this time it was a deep belly laugh that bordered on maniacal. Clayton grabbed Choctaw by the front of his loose red flannel shirt and pulled him face-to-face. "What the fuck is going on here?"

"It's rigged, boss. The feds are what's going on here."

"What are you talking about?"

"I'm talking about how it doesn't matter what you do to protect me. I'm not walking away from this."

"What are you not telling me, James?" Clayton was close to shouting.

"Chester said it was a fed who set him up with the robbery. He said the guy knew exactly when and where to hit those biker guys. He said no one would come looking for it. He said by the time we rode into the sunset, the dude we were stealing from would be dead."

"That's bullshit. That doesn't make any sense. Why would a dirty fed do that without taking a cut for himself? What does he have to gain by serving it up to you guys? Why not just take it himself?"

"I don't know, boss. I was just doing Chester a favor. Frankie and Lenny were in, I couldn't say no. Chester was convinced the guy was on the level."

"You got a name?"

"No. Chester never told any of us, but I did think it was pretty weird that the day after Chester comes to me with all this, that Holly joker shows up out of the blue, saying he knows all kinds of shit about Halford and you."

"Holly? You think he's Chester's dirty fed? That's crazy. He's the agent assigned to the case."

"I don't know shit, boss. I just know I'm in a lot of trouble and whoever it is isn't going to let me live through it. I didn't know what to do, so I came out here."

Clayton let go of Choctaw's shirt and pushed him back toward the bags of cash. The wheels in his head were spinning to a blur. This didn't make sense.

"Start at the beginning, and tell me everything you know."

"That's it, boss. That's all I know."

"Did you know the money was on its way to my brother?"

"Halford? Oh, Jesus. Now I *know* I'm going to die. What am I going to do?"

"You don't have to worry about that." Clayton took the jar of shine from him and turned it up. Choctaw looked confused but didn't ask, and Clayton didn't explain. Instead, the deputy looked at the bags of cash at his feet. "It's a lot of money, boss. I mean, why can't we just walk away, right now? I can disappear. You can say I wasn't here when you got here and—"

"That's not going to happen. We're going to sit here and wait. If Holly is involved in this shit at all, we'll know in just a few minutes."

"He's coming here?"

"Any minute now."

The deputy snatched his rifle up off the bed and pointed it at Clayton.

Clayton set the jar on the floor. "What are you doing, Deputy?"

"They're going to kill me, boss. I can't be here. You can't keep me here."

"You have lost your mind. Put the rifle down. I won't let anything happen to you."

That's when Choctaw's head exploded.

3.

Clayton watched Choctaw's headless body collapse to the floor, and spun around to face the back door. Holly racked the shotgun and lowered it.

"Are you all right, Sheriff?"

Clayton raised his Colt.

"Hey, slow down, Sheriff."

Clayton held his gun on Holly and wiped blood spatter from his beard. "You just killed that boy in cold blood."

"The hell I did," Holly said. "I saw him holding that rifle on you and thought you were in trouble. A thank-you for saving your ass would be nice."

Clayton thumbed the hammer back. "Bullshit. I had this under control. You killed him to keep him from fingering you."

"Fingering me for what? You're talking crazy."

"Am I? He told me Bankey had a federal agent feeding him information on the robbery. He said it was a fed with intimate knowledge about the players moving the money."

Holly looked at the bags of cash. "And you think that agent is me?"

"I know you just killed the only man capable of helping me make that distinction."

Holly slowly held the shotgun out with both hands, bent over, and slid it across the floor to Clayton. "Well, that's insane, but if you want to play out this little fairy tale, so be it. Here . . ." He removed his sidearm and slid that over to Clayton, too. The sheriff stopped it with his boot and kicked it out the back door. He holstered his Colt and picked up the shotgun. "Now let's take a ride."

"I'm your friend, Clayton. You're making a mistake."

"If I am, I'll apologize, but right now, you and me are going to drive to Waymore and have a chat with the Bureau, and see if I can sort all this out." He motioned the barrel of the gun toward the front door. Holly started to walk.

"What about all your money?" he said.

"It ain't my money."

"So you're just going to leave it there, sitting in your boy's blood?"

"You're going to pay for that boy's murder," Clayton said.

Holly sighed and turned around to face the sheriff. His eyes were different now. That shark smile was back and every sense of urgency had left him. If anything, Clayton thought he looked disappointed.

"Why am I the one going to pay?" Holly said. "You're the one that killed him. You came in here and decided that all the money was better than half the money, so you executed the poor bastard with his own shotgun. That's pretty brutal, man."

"Nobody is going to believe that."

"Of course they will. I mean, come on. When Halford found out it was you that ripped him off, he was so pissed he brought his big ass down the mountain personally to kill you. He hasn't come off the mountain in years. Everyone in that shithole dust farm you live in saw that. They also saw you kill him."

"And that's what you wanted, wasn't it?"

"Either way would have been fine by me. You kill him. He kills you. If it would've worked out the other way, I just would've called the big son of a bitch and told him his money was in here with the dipshit Indian that stole it. One way or another, I'd still be standing here, and one of you bags of shit would be standing there."

"So everything you said about a bloodless takedown was bullshit."

"Nobody bled that didn't need it comin'." Holly glanced down at the headless corpse of Deputy Frasier. "Except maybe him."

"All this for a couple hundred grand?"

Holly laughed. "You really are dumber than you look, Clayton."

Clayton felt a nerve in his eyelid twitch and gripped the shotgun with white knuckles. "It was all bullshit. You never had anything on Halford. No task force. No knowledge of his operations."

"No, some of that was true. There was never any plan to move against your brother, but I do know everything about his empire." Holly smiled wider and his eyes darkened. "You want to know how I found out?"

Clayton mashed his teeth.

"Your brother Buckley told me, before I killed him."

"You're a fucking liar."

"Before I set him up to have my team put several hundred bullets in him, I picked him up for a little one-on-one and convinced him to talk to me. After three days of withdrawal from your family's honey-pot, he told me all kinds of shit about Halford, you, this place, this cabin, times, locations, all of it. That idiot knew it all and gave it up just to keep a steady flow of crank in his veins. It sucks having a junkie in the family. There's no telling what they'll do to stay high. Believe me, I know. I bet that retard would've blown me if I'd wanted him to."

"I ought to kill you where you stand."

"Well, do it, then, *Sheriff* Burroughs." Holly dragged out his words, mocking the title of sheriff. "Stop pretending you're something you're not. You're a piece-of-shit hillbilly gangster like your dead daddy and all your dead brothers, but you know what? You're the worst of them all because you hide behind that star and think it masks who you really are. Buckley gave you up, too. He told me all about his brother the sheriff, who turned a blind eye to everything going on up here. At least the rest of them admitted to being outlaws. You're just another criminal who thinks he can dress up like one of the good guys and that washes the stink off him."

Clayton glared at Holly. "Nothing like you, huh?"

"We're more alike than you think, Clayton." Holly reached around into the small of his back.

Clayton pulled the trigger.

Click.

"You rednecks and your long guns. I knew you'd go for the shotgun over that Colt."

Clayton tossed the empty shotgun at Holly, but he was ready for it and sidestepped it. He pulled his backup nine-millimeter, but Clayton was on him and grabbed his hand. Holly fired, but the first two shots went into the ceiling—the third through the screen door. Clayton shoved Holly hard into the wall and banged his hand over and over into the wood until the gun fell to the floor with a thud. Holly went for Clayton's Colt, but the sheriff hooked him around the throat with his forearm and landed a solid blow to Holly's gut. Holly gasped for air and slid down the wall to his knees. Clayton pulled the Colt and pressed the barrel to the agent's forehead.

"Well, go ahead, Sheriff. You're Gareth Burroughs's son. Do what you do best."

"I should. I should kill you like you did that boy over there, and then I should bury your body in the woods like my deddy would've done." Clayton took two steps back. "But I'm not my deddy. Now get up."

Holly slowly rose to his feet. "You better kill me, Sheriff."

"You have the right to remain silent."

Holly laughed. "Are you fucking kidding me?"

"Anything you say can and will be used against you in a court of law."

"You're a joke, Clayton. You're a perversion of the law."

Clayton spun him around and shoved him toward the front door. "Put your hands on your head."

"This is not how it's gonna end, Clayton."

Clayton shoved him again, this time pressing the gun between Holly's shoulder blades, pushing him out onto the porch. "It's *Sheriff* Burroughs," he said. "Now put your hands on your head, or I can start beating on you. Your choice."

Holly did as he was told, and both men took the steps down to the gravel.

"You have the right to an attorney. If you can't afford one, one will be appointed to you. Do you understand these rights as I've read them to you?"

Holly spit blood into the gravel and kept walking. Clayton limped behind him, nudging him every foot or so with the barrel of the gun. When they reached the middle of the clearing, Holly stopped. "Can I ask you to do something for me, Clayton?"

"Just keep moving."

"Seriously, I just want to know if you'll send our daddy my regards when you get to hell?"

"What?"

"Gun!" Holly yelled, and dropped flat to his belly.

"What are you . . ." The half-dozen pinpoints of red light hovering on Clayton's chest caused the rest of his sentence to lodge in his throat.

He closed his eyes and pictured Kate.

The first shot from a high-powered rifle hit him in the chest. It pushed him backward but not off his feet. Maybe it was the confusion of the moment or Choctaw's whiskey dulling his senses, but Clayton didn't drop his gun. Instead, he swung the Colt a half-turn to the left before the second shot hit him right below the first. It hit like a sledge-hammer, and Clayton buckled. It was over in seconds. He never stood a chance. Dozens of agents in body armor and blue windbreakers emerged from the tree line, just as Clayton's body hit the gravel. Holly took his hands from his face, opened his eyes, and crawled over to Clayton's shaking body. He was still breathing, but blood filled his mouth and streaked down his beard. His eyes were wide.

"You make sure you tell him this mountain belongs to me now, big brother. You tell him it belongs to Marion's boy."

Clayton choked out a cough that could have been a laugh and looked at the sky.

"You tell him, brother." Holly rolled over onto his back. "You tell him . . ."

Clayton struggled for air and bled into the dirt less than a quarter mile from the buried bones of his great-uncle Riley. He could hear Holly talking but could only see Kate lifting yellow caution tape and walking away.

Holly gripped a hand over his breast pocket—the pocket that held the tattered photo of him as a boy sitting in the grass with his mother at a small carnival back in Mobile. He closed his eyes and listened to the sounds of the amusement park rides. The organ music. He smelled the thick aroma of fried dough in the air mixed with his mother's lavender perfume. He didn't remember much more about that day, but he'd committed every detail of the photo to memory. "It's done, Mama," he said to himself. "I got every last one of them."

4.

"Are you all right, Simon?" Agent Jessup asked, and helped Holly to his feet.

"Yeah, I am, now. None of this blood is mine. It belongs to the poor bastard inside. The good sheriff here blew his head off with the shotgun you'll find inside the cabin."

Jessup looked down at the field medics assessing Clayton's wounds. "Nothing worse than a dirty cop," he said.

Holly agreed.

CHAPTER

25

OSCAR WILCOMBE

JACKSONVILLE, FLORIDA

2015

Full black was beginning to give way to pinhole stars and flashes of light from the corners of Oscar Wilcombe's eyes. His head was pounding, a crushing throb in time with his revved-up heart rate. Thick blood and dehydration—it felt like waking up after a night of heavy drinking. He tried to lift his arms to rub the dry sleep from his eyes, but they were made of wet sand. All his efforts resulted in a small shrug of his shoulder. He could hear the chatter of other people around him, but it came in waves crashing over his returning senses. He was trying to think—to remember. He'd been sitting at his desk, going over Bianca's ledger. He remembered her leaving, and then a sharp pain in his neck—a needle, maybe—then nothing. He'd been drugged. That had to be it. His awareness was flooding back and he made another attempt to reach up and probe his neck. He couldn't move. It wasn't just whatever he was injected with, though. His arms were stuck on something—stuck *in* something. Someone had taken him from his office, drugged him, and put him in something.

"Wake up." There was a blurred outline of someone in front of him. A flash of intense heat stung his face, and his sight sharpened. His face didn't burn. It wasn't heat. It was water. Ice water. He shook his head, crushed his eyes shut, and opened them again.

"Bracken? Bracken, is that you? What's the meaning of this? Where am I?"

"Welcome back, Oscar." Bracken stood in front of his captive, holding a lit cigarette in one hand, and a now empty Big Gulp cup in the other. He took a long drag on the butt as Wilcombe took in his surroundings.

"Bracken, what is going on here?" He swiveled his head back and forth, freed from his temporary blindness to see the huge tin-framed facade of Warehouse One. He knew the place well. He had had it built. The warehouse was a place the club used to do the kind of business that needed seclusion. Business Wilcombe never did himself. Primer-gray Harley frames in various degrees of disrepair and stacks of used tires in all shapes and sizes were scattered about the yard. Everything was rusted and choked out by overgrown grass and weeds. It had been a long time since this place had been used. Behind Bracken and the other members of the Jacksonville Jackals' inner circle loomed a massive airbrushed club insignia painted on the side of the building: an eight-foot cartoon jackal wearing crisscross bandoliers, holding twin .45s, under a scrolling banner spelling out the MC's name in Old English.

"We need to have a conversation," Bracken said.

"Whatever this is about, Bracken, I demand you untie me and get me out of whatever this is you have me in."

Bracken crushed his cigarette out on Wilcombe's cheek. The pain shot through him like a blade. He screamed. He was wide awake now.

"You don't make demands, Oscar. Not anymore."

"Jesus, Bracken," the old man shouted, frantically shaking from side to side, struggling to free himself. "Let me out of here this instant," he said.

"We had a couple of the prospects come out here a few years back and bolt together a couple stacks of truck tires for situations like this one. We had to take two of them off of the one you're in, just so I could talk to you face-to-face."

Wilcombe shook about, slightly rocking the steel-belted cocoon back and forth.

"It took Moe nearly an hour to break off the rusted bolts to get it to fit a tiny little man your size." Bracken called back over his shoulder, "What do you say, Moe? About an hour?"

Moe looked up from the concrete picnic table he was sitting on and nodded. "Yup, about that."

"As you can see, we went through a lot of trouble to accommodate you, so I'm hoping to have an open, honest discussion here. Can we do that, Oscar?"

The gravity of the situation crushed down on Wilcombe as hard as the dry-rotted rubber prison, so he played the only card he had available.

"Of course we can, Bracken, we're family. We can talk about anything. Whatever it is, I'm sure we can straighten it out."

"Family," Bracken said, dragging out the word.

"Of course we are. Our fathers—"

"Our fathers are dead," Bracken said, finishing Wilcombe's sentence. "And I would say tonight, I'm glad of it. If they could see what a spineless-rat piece of shit you turned out to be, they both would have died out of sheer disappointment."

"Bracken, listen to me." Sweat formed on Wilcombe's bald scalp, dripping salt into his eyes and the fresh cigarette burn on his face. He let the tears come to reinforce his play at sympathy. "Whatever you think you know has to be a mistake. Someone is telling you lies. I would never turn on you, or this club. My father helped build this club."

"You sold me out to those hillbillies in Georgia, Oscar. You talked to the feds and gave up the route. I guess you thought we'd all be killed or locked up, but it didn't go down that way, and here we are."

Wilcombe scanned the crowd of bikers. "Bracken, you've got it all wrong," he said, doing his best to look surprised. "I lost a lot of money and a lucrative business partner after that hijacking went down."

Bracken hammered a left jab to the old man's jaw. He thought he heard bones break. "The feds shut you down, and you fed them me and my boys plus two hundred thousand in bonus cash to save your own ass."

"No, Bracken, that isn't what happened. I swear to you." Blood covered Wilcombe's teeth and dripped from his split lip. Bracken tapped out another cigarette and lit it with a flick from a silver Zippo. He held the Marlboro up with two fingers. "Maybe you need a matching reminder on the other side of your face not to lie to me."

"No. Wait." Wilcombe paused for dramatic effect. "I thought your man, the Latin one . . ."

"Romeo?" Moe said from the picnic table.

"Yes, that's it. Romeo. I thought he went AWOL once you got home? I thought he was the one working with the police. I can help you find him. I can hire someone to find him."

"You would do that?"

"Of course I would. We are family."

"Wait a minute," Bracken said, and scratched his head. "You mean *this* guy?" The bay door of the warehouse slid open and two more members of the Jackals dragged a broken and bloodied Romeo out into the yard. They dropped the barely conscious biker at Bracken's feet and stood with him.

Bracken rested a leather boot on Romeo's swollen face and pointed down. "This the piece of shit you're talking about?"

They weren't supposed to find him, Wilcombe thought. After he used Romeo to keep Bracken and his men safe during the hijacking, Wilcombe set him up with everything he needed to disappear. A new name, a new ID, money, even a few acres of cattle ranch in South Texas.

"As you can see, Oscar, we already found him." Bracken ground his boot down on Romeo's head, causing more blood to ebb down the sides of his beaten face. "You want to know how we found him?"

Wilcombe said nothing.

"I got a call from a friend of yours. A federal agent named Holly. Turns out he hates your guts. He told me exactly what he did to you and how you gave us up inside of two minutes. Then he told me right where to find this wetback sack of shit, who basically organized the whole thing. So tell me again, just one more time, that I got it wrong. Tell me why you shouldn't die tonight."

Wilcombe spoke softly and without hope. "Because we are family. And family forgives."

"No. *This* is what my family does." He pointed a gloved hand at Moe, who stood up, walked over, produced a small-caliber pistol, and shot Romeo in the side of the head. Then he sat back down and resumed cleaning his fingernails with a pocketknife.

Bracken pointed again, this time to one of the elder statesmen of the club. A man named Pinkerton Sayles. The rail-thin ex-barkeep had come out of retirement just for tonight's festivities. He reached down next to a brick barbecue pit and produced a rusted metal gas can.

"Please, Bracken," Wilcombe said, "don't do this. You've got it wrong. I had Romeo protect you. You were never in any danger. Please!"

"This is how my family protects itself," Bracken said.

Pinky splashed gasoline into Wilcombe's face. The acrid taste of it made him gag and gasp for air.

"Please . . . stop . . . gli."

"You remember me, motherfucker?" Pinky said.

Splash. More gas.

Splash.

"Happy trails, you prick." Pinky set the can down next to the rubber coffin and took a seat next to Moe and Tilmon on the picnic table.

Bracken tapped out another cigarette. "You were like a father to me, Oscar."

"I'm . . . still . . ."

"No, you're not."

Bracken reached into his pocket and pulled out his Zippo. He looked surprised for a minute, as if he'd just remembered something, and pulled out a roll of cash from his other pocket. "Oh, yeah," he said. "This is a gift from your special agent friend. He said twenty-five hundred dollars would do it. He said you can keep it." Bracken tucked the roll of bills down in the barrel, lit his smoke, and tossed the lighter onto the stack of gas-soaked tires. The fire burned for nearly nine hours straight.

CHAPTER
26

SIMON HOLLY
COBB COUNTY, GEORGIA
THREE MONTHS LATER
2015

1.

It was cold in the apartment. Simon kept himself bundled up in the quilts and sheets like a schoolkid not wanting to face the day. He didn't. The day was going to be just like the rest of them. Cold, long, and empty. His blood was thick and his joints hurt. He knew the bottle of oxy he'd left next to the couch would even him out, but the trip from the bed to the next room seemed like an insurmountable journey. He pulled the quilt over his head to block the winter-gray sunlight from cutting slices across his face. He had no idea what time it was. He hadn't known the time since he hit Atlanta. It was either day or night. Cold or hot. His days were filled with absolutes. The details didn't matter. He needed a shower. A gym. That made him laugh. He didn't even want to walk into the next room, for fear of getting spent. A gym was just a pleasant memory of a life he had long since buried.

He wanted coffee—a hot, steaming cup of black office coffee. The kind his secretary used to bring him in the morning as he went over case files. He hadn't craved that bitter mud in months. He didn't think he ever would, but this morning, or whatever time it was, the thought of it was making his mouth water. Well, it made his mouth pasty anyway. There wasn't enough water in his dehydrated husk of a body to produce any real drool. He pulled the quilt back and sat up. The bone ache from lack of hydrocodone in his bloodstream shot up his back and settled in his stiff neck. It wasn't the thought of coffee that had him craving it. It was the smell. He could smell it. It was strong. Did he make some last night? Did he even have a fucking coffeemaker in this flop? The muted sound of footsteps and a thump from the other room answered at least part of that question. Simon reached for his gun. Then he remembered he had left it next to his pills on the sofa. Stupid. His head was pounding, but he forced himself to his feet. He was still dressed in the clothes from the day before—from the week before. A filthy blue cotton oxford and a pair of khakis complete with a belt buckle that spent the entirety of the night digging a grooved impression into his new soft white beer belly. He scratched at the red marks, half tucking his shirt in, and crept slowly to the door, pushing the throb in his joints to the back of his mind. What he saw in the kitchen made him think for a moment he might still be asleep.

A woman.

A tall, shapely woman, standing with her back to him at the kitchen sink. She was drying dishes—dishes she must have just finished washing. Her brown hair obscured most of her face, but for a moment, peering at her through the crack in the door, Simon thought he could see the scars on her cheek. He shook his head slightly and rubbed the thick crust from his eyes. When he looked again, she was still there. She moved from the sink, picked up the coffeepot, and poured the black steaming sludge into two freshly washed mugs on the counter. Simon felt himself shrink down to the size of a nine-year-old who had just woken up in the old house back in Mobile.

"Mama?" he said, barely audible.

Kate turned around and shattered the fantasy. "How pathetic," she said. She picked up her mug, leaving the other to sit, and crossed over to the sofa. She gave it a disgusted once-over but sat anyway, blowing into her mug.

"What do you want, Kate?" Simon said. The nine-year-old boy was gone, replaced by the forty-one-year-old junkie.

"I'm not sure," she said. "I thought I knew what I was coming here for, but now I'm not so sure."

"I know you didn't come here to wash my dishes and make me coffee."

"That's true. I came here to kill you."

Simon looked to find his gun. It was right where he'd left it, but not *as* he'd left it. Kate had obviously disassembled it and placed it on a dirty sofa cushion in several pieces. He also took notice of the bulge on Kate's hip covered up by her sweater. The blood pounding in his head was a tidal wave breaking on rock.

The oxy was missing, too.

"You change your mind?" he said.

"About what?"

"About wanting me dead."

"No, I still want you dead. I'll always want you dead." She paused and sipped her coffee. "But after seeing you, seeing this place, I'm wondering if I need to be the one to do it. I mean, look at you. I'm not sure if you're more worried about me being here or that I took your dope. It's over there, by the way." She pointed over to the counter by the sink. The old faithful orange medicine bottle was sitting next to the other coffee mug. The look of relief on Simon's face was too obvious to cover up, and Kate shook her head like a disapproving parent. "Go ahead. Pop a couple of those. Even out. I know you want to."

Simon debated waiting it out to prove a point but held out for less than thirty seconds before making a beeline to his stash. He flipped the plastic lid off the bottle, poured four oblong white pills into his palm, slammed them to his face, and washed them down his gullet with the piping-hot coffee. It's surprising how the confidence of a drug addict can flood back by simply performing the ritual of doping, even way before the dope itself can take effect. He swung back toward Kate, renewed and inspired, but then deflated when he saw she had set her coffee mug on the floor and produced a Ruger nine-millimeter equipped with a homemade silencer and a grip wrapped in duct tape. Bile mixed with the bitter coffee in the back of Simon's throat.

"I'm at a crossroads here, Agent Holly."

"I'm not an agent anymore."

"Right, you're just Simon now. The Bureau fired your ass. Too many questions that couldn't be answered is the way I heard it."

"Something like that."

"Nobody ever asked me. I could have answered all their questions. I could have spelled out what a murdering piece of shit you are for anyone that wanted to know, but nobody really wanted to know anything. They just wanted you to disappear before you embarrassed them any more. That's what you are now, Simon. An embarrassment. I could have told them how you lied and manipulated everyone you came into contact with so you wouldn't have to pull the trigger on your own blood yourself."

"Well, then why didn't you?"

"Two reasons," Kate said, and stood up. She held the gun loosely but kept it trained on Simon. "One," she said, "I once told you if you pulled Clayton down a rabbit hole he couldn't get out of, I'd kill you myself. I meant it. Michael even gave me this gun." She paused when she saw that the name wasn't striking a bell with Simon. "Scabby Mike," she said. "Michael Cummings is his Christian name. He assured me I could put every one of these fifteen rounds through your miserable black heart and not one of them would lead back to me."

Simon smirked at her. "You can't kill me, Kate. I might be down right now, but I still have friends on the force that—"

"Friends?" Kate said, cutting him off. "Friends like who? Like your ex-partner, Jessup? Like the guy you fucked over and made an accomplice to all this? How do you think we found you, Simon? Your own people gave us a list of addresses. You think any of the people you manipulated into helping you want any of that shitstorm to get out in court? You're circling the drain, and your *friends* aren't looking to go down with you."

"Bullshit," Holly said.

"Look at me, Simon. Do I look like a liar to you? You're a master at it, you should be able to tell."

Simon chewed his lip, and Kate drove it home. "Yeah, Simon. Everyone who has ever met you wishes someone would make you disappear."

"Yet, here I am," he said. "Still standing. The *only one* standing. It's been what? Three months? And nobody has the balls to kill me."

"Is that what you think? That no one has the balls? Here's the news, Simon. No one has shown up here to kill you out of respect for *me*. What you did, you did to me. Not one of the men on that mountain was going to rob me of the chance to settle this my-self. You're not the last one standing . . . I am." She pointed the gun at his face.

"You think I'm supposed to be scared of you, Kate? I took down Bull Mountain. Me. I did what no one else could do for damn near seven decades, and I did it by myself. So if you're gonna do it, then get on with it, but don't think for a second I'm going to be scared of some poor little hillbilly girl with a gun."

Kate laughed.

"What's so goddamn funny?"

"You sound just like him," she said. "Hell, seeing you here, like this, you look just like him. I wish to God I could've seen it before."

"Like who, Kate?" The pills were kicking in, and Simon was be-ginning to feel like his cocky self. He licked his teeth. "Who do I look like? Your drunk of a husband? Is that why you can't kill me?"

The muscles in Kate's face tightened and she aimed the gun di-rectly between his eyes. This time Simon took a step back.

"No, you son of a bitch. You're nothing like Clayton. You look just like your father. For all your wanting to twist Clayton into what you imagined him to be, he's nothing like that psychotic old bastard, but you? You're the protégé he always wanted. You fought so hard to pun-ish him and everyone else for a wrong he did you and your poor mother, and now look at you. You're the one most like him. He's the one you made proud, not Marion."

Simon looked surprised at the mention of his mother's name. Kate noticed and smiled. "Oh, your boy Jessup? He gave me a whole box of poor Marion's journals. They belong to me now. I assume that's what got you started on this vendetta in the first place, right?" She didn't let up and kept going. "You're a joke. I guess that's the one dif-ference between you and the man that sired you. People on that mountain respected your father, God knows why, but they did. They still talk about him. But you? No one will ever respect what you did. No one will talk about you. You're no better than Halford or any of the people you claim did you an injustice. You're exactly the same. And it looks like you'll end up the same as they did without any help from me."

She lowered the gun, but Simon stayed planted against the counter. They stood there in silence for a long time.

"You said there were two reasons you never talked to the feds," Simon finally said.

Kate was tired, it was showing on her face, but she reached down with her free hand and smoothed the front of her baggy sweater over the small bump of her belly. She held the sweater tight for Simon to figure it out. It didn't take him long.

"You're pregnant," he said. It was more a statement than a question. Kate put both hands back on the gun.

"I wanted to tell you myself," she said. "I needed to see your face. For all your plans and years of preparation to end the Burroughs bloodline, it was all for nothing. You failed. Clayton would have found out about his son the day you set him up to die. You took that from him. From me. But you're done taking things, Simon." She raised the gun again. "So that brings me to the crossroads I mentioned. Do I kill you? Right here, right now, and be done with it? Do I infect myself with the same sickness you brought into my home, or can I be content letting you rot away in a federal prison, or watching you kill yourself in a hole like this one, one pill at a time?"

Simon didn't say anything. The oxy was doing its job and he felt his strength returning to his sore muscles. He'd let her talk just a few more minutes.

"I needed to see your face," she said. "I needed to know if you would come after my son. I needed to know if you are that twisted and dead inside that you would come after an innocent child. Or . . . if you could let it end."

Simon glared at her.

"So tell me, Simon. Can you let it end?"

He took his time answering. He looked down at the bottle of pills he was still holding and rolled it around in his palms. He set them on the counter and met Kate's eyes.

"Yes, ma'am," he said.

Maybe it was the glint of sunlight on his teeth, or the slight upturn of the corner of his mouth. Maybe it was the way his left eye blinked just as he spoke. Or maybe it was nothing at all.

"I don't believe you," she said, and shot him in the chest.

2.

Kate was still holding the gun, standing over Simon's body, when Val and Scabby Mike came in the front door. Mike slid his hands over hers and after a time she let go of the gun, and Mike tucked it into his pants at the small of his back. "Mrs. Burroughs," he said in a kind voice. "Are you okay?"

Kate nodded. "I'm fine."

"I think you best be going, Katie," Val said as he dropped a rolled canvas tarp on the kitchen floor next to Simon's body.

"What happens now?" she said.

Mike gently moved her back toward the door. "We clean this up and you go home."

"What are you going to do with him?"

"Doesn't matter, Mrs. Burroughs. We'll take care of this. You need to get going now."

Val put a hand on Mike's shoulder and moved him to the side. It was easy to do; Val was nearly twice Mike's size. "We're going to take him back to the mountain, Katie. Where he belongs."

It made sense. Simon was a Burroughs. But they weren't going to take him to the lush green banks of Burnt Hickory where his father and brothers were buried, or the garden up near Cooper's Field that held his grandfather and great-grandfather. They would take him deep into the backwoods by the Western Ridge, out by Johnson's Gap. Out where the graves went unmarked, unnoticed, and forgotten. She bet they'd already dug the hole. She cupped the side of Val's cheek and stared at the cracks in his face, dug there by decades of events like this one, and something passed between them like static current. They shared a moment of crushing sadness that tightened her chest and suddenly made it hard to breathe. It was the kind of sadness brought on by turning corners that led you to places there was no finding your way home from. They had both looked deep within themselves and found an ugliness that couldn't be stuffed back inside. She'd seen that look on the faces of people before, but now she understood it. Now she owned it.

Mike had already spread the canvas across the linoleum and kicked Simon's body into the center. He was wiping up blood from the floor with a roll of paper towels from the kitchen with no more thought than if he were cleaning up spilled milk. He smiled at her and she recognized the sadness in him, too.

"Katie," Val said, "you need to go. There's no more reason for you to be here."

Kate nodded to Mike, who went back to work on the floor; then she turned and left without another word.

She'd only just pulled the hospital-supplied Dodge Caravan onto I-85 when she heard the first noises from her passenger waking up in the backseat. She turned the volume on the radio from low to off and adjusted her rearview mirror to get a better look.

"Where are we?" Clayton said. His voice was groggy, coarse, and dry from the pain meds, and he wanted to scratch himself all over. An IV bag swung from a special hook above the window and he rubbed at the tubing taped to the top of his left hand.

"We're going home, baby. You just rest."

"I been resting for three months," he said.

"You've been *healing* for three months. Now the resting starts."

"I don't want to rest." He scratched at the stubble on his chin. The doctors at the trauma center had shaved him. He hadn't shaved in more than twenty years. He wasn't happy about that at all. Kate didn't mind it, though. She liked his face.

"Clayton, you got shot. Twice. You should be dead. So if the people who saved your life say I need to take you home and let you rest, then that is exactly what I intend to do. And I'm not listening to any arguments."

Clayton sipped his ice water through the straw of a huge plastic cup and laid back against the mountain of pillows Kate had him propped on. "Well, how about some singing, then?" he said. "Will you listen to some singing?" After three tortured verses of "Up on Cripple Creek," Clayton faded back into the oblivion of a morphine drip. Kate left the radio down so she could listen to him breathe over the hum of the highway. After a while she was convinced it was the sweetest sound she'd ever heard. She knew eventually they would have to talk about the things that had happened out here, about the things that happened on the mountain. She knew there would still be questions about whether or not Clayton was guilty of anything. She was sure there would be more federals at their front door with their notepads and sunglasses and their accusations. And she was sure they would deal with it. But not today. Today her husband was breathing. He was alive. He was going to be a father. The right kind of father. They were getting a late start, but they were going to be a family. She didn't feel one ounce of regret for what she'd done. She'd do it again if it needed doing. Several times she thought about taking a hard left and just going somewhere new. It was a new day. She had a cousin in Augusta, and an uncle she'd never met in Huntsville. They would take them in. They had to. They were family. But she didn't take any hard turns. She kept the van headed toward Bull Mountain. It was her home. It was Clayton's home. It would be her son's home.

And no one was ever going to take that away.

⊷⊐⊙ ACKNOWLEDGMENTS ⊙⊏⊶

I'd like to thank my wife, Neicy, for being my beautiful distraction, and for always keeping me grounded (*"Baby, we got an offer on the book!" "Good, we need a new sofa."*), and for introducing me to life in North Georgia. Without her, there wouldn't be a Bull Mountain. Thanks to my mom for always being supportive regardless of the swearing. Thanks to Zelmer Pulp, my writers group/gang, made up of some of the most talented people on earth, including Ryan Sayles, Chuck Regan, Chris Leek, Isaac Kirkman, and Joe Clifford. Now that there might actually be someone watching, I think we better burn down the clubhouse. Seriously, though, Google their names and buy their books. Tell them I sent you. Thank you to Brian Lindenmuth at *Spinetingler Magazine* for holding me up high enough to be seen by the big dogs. Thank you to Ron Earl Phillips for publishing my first story at shotgunhoney.net. Thank you to Susie Henry for lending me her woman's perspective, and thank you to Dan Adams of the Dan Adams Band (look them up and buy their records) for providing Bull Mountain with a soundtrack. You may be living in Austin, buddy, but you're a Georgia boy through and through. Thank you to my boys at the firehouse for all the stories. Keep it in the house, fellas.

I owe a huge debt of gratitude to my agent, Nat Sobel, for the belief he had in my work and for the pit-bull tenacity he showed in finding this book a home. My life is clearly divided into Before Nat and After Nat. Thank you to my editor, Sara Minnich, and the folks at Putnam for taking a chance on me and the good people of McFalls County. (No plot knots, Sara, I promise.)

And last: Thanks, Dad. For hiding the remote. For the comics. For never once giving up on anything. For the ride home from New York. And for Waylon. But mostly for being the best goddamn father a son could ask for. I miss you every day, old man. I'll see you when I get there.